SIDE EFFECT

A NOVEL BY

Sandra Feder

To Jody
with my best wishes,
Sandra Feder

THORNWOOD PUBLISHING CO. LLC *New York* 2000

This is a work of fiction. Names, characters, places,
and incidents are either the product of the author's
imagination or are used fictitiously, and any
resemblance to actual persons, living or dead,
business establishments, events or locales
is entirely coincidental.

Library of Congress Card Number: 00-190471
ISBN 1-930541-05-8

Manufactured in the United States of America
First Edition

To G.C.
and
my husband, Jack Feder

Prologue:
Westport, Connecticut
Wednesday, October 10

Edith Howell didn't recognize the return address on the ivory-colored envelope she found in her post office box. She was tempted to just throw it out; so much junk mail these days was disguised as personal letters. But it might be something important, a nagging voice said. So she sighed and put it at the bottom of her stack of mail, after the AARP bulletin. She would go through all of it when she got to the park.

She was slightly tired by the time she reached her favorite stone bench overlooking the Saugatuck River, in the small park bordering the Westport Library. But the quarter-mile walk had been worth it, both for the view and her sense of accomplishment.

Putting down the cappuccino and biscotti she had brought, Edith went through her mail while she sat in the sun. The first few envelopes she decided were clearly junk mail, and she put them aside without opening them. The next two were bills, which she quickly checked and then put in the pocket of her windbreaker.

There was a letter from her daughter! Edith felt the thick envelope and smiled. It must contain pictures of her new grandson. She put it next to her on the bench. She would save the letter and the pictures for last.

She took the lid off the cappuccino and tasted it: sweet, just the way she liked it. She nibbled on the biscotti and drank the coffee as she went through the rest of the mail.

When she finally reached the ivory envelope again, she frowned. She opened it and slid out the folded letter. It seemed to be stuck, so she moistened her thumb and forefinger with her tongue and pulled the letter open.

Edith began reading, and halfway down the page realized she didn't know what she had just read. I must not be paying attention, she thought, I'm so eager to see the baby's pictures. Maybe I can afford to fly out to visit them next month. She licked some biscotti crumbs from her fingers and started the letter again. Again she couldn't remember what she had just read. Absently, she noticed that her damp fingertips stuck to the letter and left impressions.

Edith began to feel funny. First she felt a slight pain in her stomach. She assumed it was because of the walk, and she unzipped her windbreaker a little. That didn't help. Then the pain got worse and she became alarmed. She looked around to see if there were anyone else nearby, but she was alone. Suddenly Edith started to choke. She coughed until her eyes watered. When her vision cleared, she saw droplets of bright red blood on her yellow slacks.

"Oh my God!" she whispered, terrified.

As she struggled to stand, she knocked her mail off the bench.

The last thing she did was to bend down to take her daughter's letter from the grass at her feet. Then Edith dropped into blackness, and her body tumbled down the short incline into the river, her hand clutching the pictures of the new grandson she would never see.

———————

Across town Joel Thomas kissed his wife and dropped her off at the train station. Then he went through his usual routine before he drove to work in Greenwich. He parked, got a cup of coffee and a sweet roll, and walked to the Saugatuck Post Office to pick up their mail. As he slid into his BMW, he gulped down half the sweet black coffee and took a big bite of the roll; he always needed a caffeine and sugar kick to get him going. And this morning he had a big presentation.

Joel went through the mail as he sat in his car. He put the catalogs and junk mail aside, to be thrown out; he tucked the bills in his briefcase. He smiled when he saw Highlights magazine; it was his daughter Jenna's first mail as a big girl.

When he got to the ivory envelope, he paused. He didn't recognize the return address. Wondering who had sent it, he tore open the envelope and took out the letter. His fingers were sticky with icing and stuck to the letter, so he licked them as he read. He was puzzled by the letter and turned it over, trying to figure out why the person had sent it. Finally he gave up and put it with the junk mail.

He backed out of his spot and headed toward the turnoff to I-95. Almost at once he got a sharp pain in his stomach. He berated himself for taking caffeine when his doctor had told him to cut back. He dumped the rest of the sweet roll in the bag and put the coffee in the cup holder.

Joel began to choke on something and started coughing. Liquid splattered his steering wheel, and he was horrified to see that the tiny droplets were red. All thoughts of his presentation went out of his head. He had to get to Norwalk Hospital.

He was about to turn the wheel to the left when an excruciating pain in his gut hit him.

Reflexively, he shut his eyes against the pain. His foot slammed the gas pedal to the floor and the car lunged straight ahead. Joel's eyes were still closed when the BMW slammed into one of the concrete supports of I-95, accordioned into it and exploded into flames.

———————

"Hon, can you reach in my pocket for my keys?"

Both of Herb Rickman's arms were full; in one arm he had a week's worth of mail he had just picked up from the neighbor, and in the other arm he had his baby son.

While Cindy unlocked the door, Herb leaned over and nuzzled her neck.

"Herb!" she said, blushing. "The neighbors could be watching."

Herb followed her into the foyer, grinning, and dumped the mail on a nearby table. He took the baby into the living room and started to toss him up in the air over his head

"Honey, put him down," Cindy said. "You've been tossing him too much and he is going to return the favor. He is going to spit up all over you and then you're going to be sorry."

"You're a tough little guy, aren't you, Justin?" Herb said, kissing him. But he sat the baby on the floor. "I'll get the rest of the luggage out of the car."

Cindy went through the mail as she kept an eye on Justin. He was teething and seemed a little out of sorts. The poor little guy's gums must hurt, she thought. She got a big cookie out of her bag and put it in his lap. Justin sat looking at it.

"Here's something for you to chew on, muffin."

The mail included the usual bills, which she put in a pile, and junk mail that she threw out without opening. An ivory envelope caught her attention. It was addressed to her, but she didn't recognize the return address.

She had just torn open the envelope and pulled out the letter, when the phone rang. She picked up the receiver and listened. "What? You had to do what?" She dropped the letter and ran to the window, motioning Herb to hurry in.

Justin had the cookie in his hands and was lifting it to his open mouth. But when he saw the letter flutter to the floor, he dropped the cookie and crawled over to investigate.

Herb came through the door, arms full of luggage, panting. "What is it?"

"They just put mother in the hospital," she said.

"But she was fine when we left."

"Well, something happened. Dad can't tell me all the details, but they called the ambulance."

Justin reached the letter and stretched out his chubby little fingers.

"Where did they take her?" Herb asked.

"City Hospital."

"Not there! That's the worst place. She'll get no care, and they have the highest rate of nosocomial infections in the city."

"You're a doctor," Cindy pleaded. "Get her transferred somewhere good."

While Herb made a call and Cindy watched and listened nervously, Justin tried to pick up the letter. But he didn't have the dexterity. So he got on his tummy and held it down while he chewed off a corner.

Justin was chewing happily and watching his parents when

he started to choke quietly. Herb and Cindy didn't notice.

His choking got louder and Herb finally caught sight of him. He turned with terror in his face and ran toward Justin.

The baby was staring at him and turning blue. As Herb reached him, his eyes began to close. Herb leaned over and grabbed him, snatching him up.

For a moment he lost it. He gave the baby a shake. "Justin, Justin!" Herb said, as if trying to awaken him.

"No!" Cindy screamed. "What are you doing?"

As Herb held the baby, he suddenly threw up all over Herb's front, and started crying.

That snapped Herb out of it. He carefully checked the little boy, his mouth, his eyes, his breathing. Cindy stood beside him, her face white, looking from Justin to Herb. Finally Herb decided the baby was unharmed.

"Oh God, baby," Herb said, tears falling as he clutched the baby to his chest. Out of the corner of his eye Herb saw the chewed letter on the floor; he crumpled it angrily and threw it away.

Late that evening she sat in her living room, bent over a beautiful rare wood coffee table, listening to Connecticut's local station on her television. She was folding letters and stuffing them into ivory envelopes. It was slow work because she was wearing rubber gloves. Even though the gloves were thin, they tended to grab the paper and wrinkle it or even tear it. But she couldn't take a chance of getting what the letters contained on her hands.

She lifted her head when the announcer gave the lead story: two deaths, a woman who had drowned in the Saugatuck River, and a man who had lost control of his car and crashed into the I-95 overpass supports.

"Damn," she said quietly, as she made a check next to Howell and Thomas on her list. Then she put a question mark next to Rickman.

Her mouth became a thin line as she looked at another name on her list. I am so close, she thought. So close. She began circling the name with her pencil.

"We'll take everything from you, and you won't even know why," she whispered, pressing the pencil harder and harder with each narrowing spiral. "Your precious drug will go next, and then..." She pressed the lead into the paper until it obliterated the name: Grant Fraser.

Thursday,
October 23

1

Running down the stairs on his way to work, Dr. Grant Fraser stopped abruptly. Blocking his way to the front door was a beautiful golden retriever, stretched out pancake-flat, looking mournful.

"Bailey, you do that every morning," Grant said in a stern voice. "I'm immune to it." Which was a lie, and Bailey knew it.

In response, Bailey gave his best rendition of an abandoned dog as Grant stepped over him.

Grant suppressed a smile. "OK. I'll come home early and we'll go for a run."

Bailey's head lifted triumphantly at the word run, and Grant saw something under the dog's chin. He retrieved a small terrycloth rabbit. A child's toy.

"You miss him, too," Grant said. "Don't you?"

Grant lifted the rabbit to his nose and inhaled. He could still smell baby lotion, though faintly. Grant put the rabbit on a nearby shelf, next to a photo. In the photo Bailey nuzzled a little boy. Behind Bailey and the little boy, a young woman knelt in the grass, her blonde hair streaming, her mouth open in a laugh: Dena Horcroft, who would have been Dena Fraser.

Something's changing in me, Grant thought.

This morning, for the first time since Dena was killed, he had been awakened by Bailey licking his face, instead of by a nightmare. He had enjoyed the small pleasures of showering and dressing without feeling numb or guilty for being alive. He had even been able to make Dena's side of the bed and pull the bedspread over her pillow, without imagining them pulling a sheet over her face.

For three years Grant had been obsessed with the drug he was creating. But last year after Dena died, he had let his research take over his life. He had practically lived at the labs. Grant shuddered when he remembered how he had looked many times:

unshaven, hair unkempt, in a disheveled lab coat, oblivious to everything but his chemistry. He hadn't been surprised to learn that they called him "Dr. Freezer" at the labs. They could have called him worse.

Well, maybe I'm defrosting, he thought.

Grant was at the front door when the phone rang, startling him. Who would call him this early? he wondered, as he hurried into his office to answer it.

"Dr. Fraser?"

Grant knew the voice. It was his lab assistant, and she had never called him at home. The back of his neck began to prickle. "Angie. What's up?"

There was a pause so he repeated his question.

"There's an envelope here for you," she finally said. "From Payne."

Whitney Payne, director of research at Altimate Pharmaceuticals. Nothing from his boss was ever good news. Grant figured he might as well get it over with. "Open it up."

"It could be personal," she said.

"You want me to know it's there, but you don't want me to know what it says?"

"Still..."

"Angie, it can't be worse than anything he's said in front of the whole lab."

Grant could hear the envelope tearing as he stared at the packed bookshelves surrounding him. He imagined a dozen different and devastating messages before she slid the letter out.

"Be advised that the review of drug D-41 is scheduled for Tuesday, October 28, at 8:30 a.m. in my conference room," she read. "Be prompt."

It was just a standard announcement of what should be a standard drug review, Grant thought. Except it was way too early to have this review. Grant's hands were cold, and his stomach was a knot.

"He's reviewing the white twin," Angie whispered.

The drug Grant had created existed in two mirror image forms, designated L-41 and D-41. But their preliminary effects were so markedly different that Angie had dubbed them the black and white twins. The black twin's performance had been disappointing, and it had been canceled. But the white twin had shown dazzling promise.

"Are you still there, Dr. Fraser?"

"Yes. I was thinking," he said, his gaze on the calendar on his desk. "The twenty-eighth is next Tuesday, only five days away."

"This is the same kind of notice we got when the black twin was reviewed," Angie reminded him.

And this is the same kind of anxiety I had then, Grant thought. "I know," he said.

"It was shut down right after that review," Angie added.

Grant didn't need to be reminded. He made a fist of the hand that wasn't holding the phone.

Grant had spent nearly every minute of the past three years developing a drug that would help the human body fight invaders like bacteria. If his drug turned out to be everything Grant hoped it would be, it would revolutionize the way doctors fought disease. Currently, doctors prescribed antibiotics which often failed when bacteria became resistant to them. But with Grant's drug, doctors could help patients fight disease with their own immune systems.

The white twin had shown "astonishing abilities to help fight infection." Grant winced when he remembered the unusually encouraging language the animal testing unit had used. Grant didn't want to jinx himself.

Expectations at Altimate were running high. Even Grant—normally cautious—had begun to think he might achieve the goal of a lifetime: creating a drug that would save people's lives.

"I didn't expect the black twin to be canceled," Angie said.

I didn't either, Grant thought. Even though I know only one member of a twin pair of drugs is usually effective. But he said, "They told me it hadn't performed in animal testing, that this was a business decision. Period."

"I don't know why you couldn't do the animal testing yourself," Angie said. "After all, it was your drug."

Grant would have been grateful if he could even have seen

the results of animal testing. "You know Altimate's policy," he said. "They say that separating drug discovery from drug testing is necessary to keep its scientific research honest." Grant hadn't realized—until the black twin was canceled—how much the two drugs symbolized to him.

"Dr. Fraser?"

"What, Angie?"

"Is the white twin going to be canceled, too?"

In spite of the stellar preliminary performance of the white twin, Grant was worried. He had put so much of himself into it that its failure would be crushing. Now Grant's insides were ice.

"It's too early," he said. "We haven't even delivered the purified drug to animal testing yet. And later—if it needs to be modified—I've done a lot of work, figuring out how we can change it."

Grant heard Angie sigh.

"I'll be ready when you get here," she said.

Grant promised to be there soon and hung up. His hand stayed, still gripping the receiver.

For better or worse, Grant's work at the labs was his life. And his success in helping to produce useful drugs was his measure of self-worth. Right now he felt as if he were in suspended animation. The black twin had been canceled. And while the white twin was still an ongoing project, its fate hung in the balance, awaiting the review on the twenty-eighth.

Grant stared at nothing for what seemed like a long time. Finally he shook himself. He couldn't let himself get paralyzed by anxiety.

He had to get Payne to reschedule the review. The twenty-eighth was too soon, even for a preliminary review like this one. They needed reliable data, and that took time. Grant *knew* that his drug was good; it deserved the chance to show what it could do.

Grant hefted his briefcase and headed out to the car. He knew that Payne hated him, but this shouldn't be personal. Altimate needed good drugs. What could Payne possibly have against postponing the review?

2

"Damn!"

Garbage cans were knocked over, their lids off and the contents strewn all over Grant's driveway and into the backyard. Raccoons, he thought.

Grant was burning to talk to Payne, but he had to clean this up before the neighborhood dogs got to it. Irritated, he locked the briefcase in the car, took off his jacket and got a pair of work gloves.

Intent on finishing, he was noisily dumping trash back in the garbage cans when he thought he heard a sound and stopped to listen. But it was too indistinct and weak to place, so he kept going.

He was almost finished when he got to a chewed, half-empty package of chocolate chocolate chip cookies. Now he was grateful that he'd done the clean up. Dogs had a sweet tooth—including Bailey—and chocolate could kill a dog. He bent down to pick up the scattered cookies.

And recoiled in disgust from the sight and smell of two raccoons.

Lying face up in the grass among the exposed roots of an enormous maple tree, one of them was already dead and the other one was dying. His small delicate fingers clawed the air, his body contorted in agony, and his mouth made piteous cries as it trickled a thin stream of blood.

Grant suddenly realized this was the sound he hadn't been able to identify or locate. His disgust was replaced by pity. How long had it been in its death throes? How long would it take to die?

He couldn't leave the raccoon like this.

Grant wheeled around and ran to the house. In the office he unlocked his desk and pulled out a revolver. As he loaded it, he had a sobering thought: Would he be able to do it? He hadn't shot anything in years, and never anything living. The gun was a gift.

Racing back to the yard, Grant hoped that the raccoon was already dead. As much as he didn't want to let a helpless animal suffer, he didn't want to pull the trigger.

When Grant reached the animal, it was still. Gently, he prodded it with his shoe. Nothing. Grant sighed in relief.

Grant stared uneasily at the animals, the hand with the gun hanging at his side. There had been nothing poisonous in the garbage. He never used pesticides or even harsh chemicals. Maybe someone at another house put out poison, he thought, and the raccoons ate it there and died here. That made sense, but something told Grant that these animals had ingested something that hadn't taken that long to kill them.

"What killed them?" he asked aloud. "I picked up every single piece of trash with my gloves and nothing looked unusual. Nothing."

He stood upwind of the raccoons, staring around him in the quiet morning as if he might find some clue. The dead animals seemed so out of place in this setting: comfortable, big houses and the lush, green foliage that surrounded them. Even though it was late October, the temperature was still in the high fifties and most of the leaves hadn't even turned, let alone fallen.

With a last troubled glance at the raccoons, Grant went into the house to call the animal control department. He found out their office didn't open until 8:00 a.m., so he called the police. Then he waited in the driveway, glancing uneasily from time to time at the stiff, furry bodies.

A man in a small van arrived, resentful and abrupt. He lurched his van up Grant's driveway and stopped twenty feet short of where Grant stood. Then he sat in the van for a long while, writing something.

Finally he got out. "Where are they?"

Grant led him to the two animals under the tree.

The man sniffed the air and wrinkled his nose. He frowned up at Grant. "*When* did you find them?"

"Just now," Grant said, "when I was cleaning up the garbage. They must have knocked the cans over during the night."

Grant began to tell the man details—anything he thought would help them figure out why the raccoons had died. "I don't use pesticides or poison..."

But the man turned his back in the middle of Grant's sentence and went to his van.

He came back with a sack, gloves and a long-handled kind of pincer. Without even a glance at Grant, the warden returned to the animals. Bunching his sack on the ground, he began to dump the raccoons inside.

It was then that Grant saw something he hadn't noticed earlier. One of the raccoons lay partly over the other one. When the warden lifted off the top animal, Grant saw that something was clutched in the previously hidden paw of the animal underneath.

"What's that in its paw?" Grant asked.

The man ignored him. He lifted up the second animal, its rigid fist held close to its body in a protective gesture.

"Wait," Grant said, moving toward the warden. "Maybe it has something to do with their deaths."

"Step back!" the man yelled. He lifted the second raccoon over the bag, and the animal swayed for a moment in the pincers.

All Grant could do was watch. He had put his gloves away, so he couldn't examine the raccoon himself. And he didn't want to take the time to go to the garage for another pair, because he was sure he wouldn't get back in time. Grant could just make out that the object in the raccoon's paw was ivory-colored and was bunched up. It looked like a piece of paper.

The man dropped the raccoon in the bag and gathered the top.

"Don't you care what it had in its paw?" Grant asked.

The man finished tying the bag before he answered. "No."

Grant was amazed. "What do you mean, 'no'?"

"Look, mister, I don't know what I'm doing here. You're supposed to take care of dead animals by yourself. If this raccoon didn't get in a fight with your dog or bite you, we don't care."

"Are you kidding?" Grant couldn't believe that was policy. "It doesn't make any sense. What if they were poisoned? What if they were diseased? They died on my property. I want to know why."

"Then you should have looked in their paws before you called us."

The man dragged the bag to his van and hefted it into the back. He got in without another word and backed out of Grant's driveway.

Grant stared after the van, frustrated and angry. Normally his compulsive scientific nature would have made him push the man to let him see what the raccoon had in its paw. But with the fate of the white twin uppermost in his mind, he had neither the time nor the heart for it. Grant told himself that he was making too much of the death of the two raccoons. He had to get to Altimate.

3

Daniele walked through the lab into her office at Altimate Pharmaceuticals as if she were picking her way through medical waste. She didn't want her ice blue wool Chanel suit to brush anything. No matter how careful she was, other people in the lab managed to get traces of chemicals everywhere, and she had had several suits ruined by acid.

As she did every morning, she looked with disdain at her office. Then she put her purse and briefcase on her desk and sat down at her computer. She turned it on and reviewed her work from the previous day and her schedule for today. Then she checked her email.

She stepped from her office into the large lab that was connected to it and grimaced. Of all people, she had to share a lab with Grant Fraser.

Daniele shot a glance toward Grant's section. He wasn't there. The little toady is late this morning, she thought. He's usually in here looking busy long before now.

She hated him. Always trying to show her up with how brilliant he was. Making Altimate think that he knew best what direction the company's research should take, and the kinds of drugs they should develop. She knew he planned to ride the white twin to the top of Altimate.

Her gaze swept his experimental equipment in a nearby hood, and she clenched her fists, pressing her polished red nails into her palms. How she would love it if all that delicate glassware were broken into tiny shards.

Daniele lifted her shoulders, shrugging, her blonde hair tightly twisted into a French knot that barely grazed her collar. She pushed her glasses back up the bridge of her nose. It didn't make sense to get upset about him. Grant wasn't worth it. Besides, she had other plans to prevent him from becoming head of Altimate.

That reminded Daniele of the main event of her day, the school referendum, and she checked her watch. The polls would be open from 6:00 a.m. until 8:00 p.m., she thought. Plenty of time for the people in Westport to vote on the single question: Should the school budget be reduced by two percent—which was one million dollars?

She shivered. By 8:00 p.m. it would finally be over. How much work she had put into this referendum! Calling people, cajoling them to sign the petition against the increase, sending out letters. She grimaced, thinking how many envelopes she had been forced to stuff.

She hoped her father appreciated all of her efforts. She had kept him posted every step of the way, knowing that an interest in community affairs was important to him.

She heard the lab door open behind her. She turned to face an older, patrician-looking man. Nathan Horcroft, the president of Altimate Pharmaceuticals.

"Hello, Daddy," she said.

Nathan gave her a broad smile and said, "Hello, darling!" But Daniele was sure she saw him stifle a look of disappointment before the smile appeared. He's probably here looking for his precious Grant, she thought.

She went up to him and kissed his cheek. He returned the kiss, but Daniele was sure that if her sister Dena were here, he would have hugged Dena.

"I'll have to spend this morning working on the referendum," she told him. "I'll be back this afternoon."

He nodded, the smile still on his face. "Whatever you need, dear. You're doing a good thing."

"We're handing out flyers, calling to remind people to vote, and I'm one of the drivers picking up people who don't have a way to get to the polls," she said.

Nathan looked surprised at that.

Daniele was annoyed at his reaction, but she didn't let it change her expression. Why couldn't he believe that she would do something nice for someone? He would never have been surprised if Dena had told him the same thing.

"Well, the polls are already open," she said. "I had better get started.

She had her hand on the doorknob of the lab when she remembered.

She turned to face him. "Dinner is still tomorrow night?"

He nodded yes with the same smile, but she was sure that he wished she wouldn't come.

4

As she drove away from Altimate, it was still eating at Daniele that Nathan had remained in the lab after she left. He was probably going to wait for Grant. Daniele had a bitter taste in her mouth.

Nathan had been withdrawing into himself for the past year. Daniele knew how much Nathan liked and admired Grant. And he seemed to be even closer to Grant than before. She was terrified that Nathan might be planning to hand Grant the reins of power at Altimate.

With a shudder Daniele thought again how close it had been: if her sister Dena hadn't died last year, Grant would have married her and he would have become Daniele's brother-in-law. And if that had happened, he would probably already be sitting in the president's office.

Daniele was so absorbed in that hateful scenario that she didn't see the red light until the last moment and screeched to a stop. Her heart was pounding, and her teeth were clenched. What did Grant Fraser have to do with Altimate? The company was hers by right. All her life she had wanted Altimate.

Someone behind her blew his horn, and Daniele suddenly remembered with annoyance that she was chauffering people today in her beautiful Mercedes. At least she had put a cover on the passenger seat. She checked the first address on her list. Now she was glad that she'd had her technician locate each address on the map; she didn't know most of these neighborhoods.

The first person she was supposed to drive to the polls didn't answer the door. The second one, an elderly man, answered the door in his pajamas and waved her away. The third person on her list was a woman, Mrs. Jean Porter. She lived in a small Cape Cod near the train station.

Daniele had to knock several times before the door opened a little.

"Mrs. Porter? I'm from the Westport Taxpayers Group," Daniele told her. "I'm here to give you a ride to the polls."

Mrs. Porter opened her door wider. Daniele's gaze flicked over her with disapproval. She was indifferently dressed, and her hair was askew. She seemed fuzzy, squinting her eyes as she looked at Daniele. Then she opened them wider and smiled in recognition.

"Dena!" she said. "How glad I am to see you, my dear. You haven't been in the store in ages."

Daniele cringed inside. People were always mistaking her for Dena, even now. She wasn't sure whether she should bother to correct Mrs. Porter; the woman seemed disoriented enough as it was.

"I'm Daniele," she said. "Dena died in a plane crash almost a year ago."

The old woman looked stricken and embarrassed.

"Oh, of course. I'm so sorry. I can't believe I didn't remember."

The old woman swayed slightly on her feet, and for a moment Daniele was afraid that she might faint.

"It's very hard to lose someone who loves you," the old woman said. "I know."

Daniele didn't talk about personal things with anyone, let alone strangers. But she decided it was safe to be honest with Mrs. Porter; the woman probably wouldn't remember in half an hour what she heard now.

"No, Mrs. Porter," she said. "Dena did better than that. Anyone can love you. They can love you because of what you are or in spite of it. They can love you even though you have failings. Love isn't the best thing. Dena *believed* in me. She was the only one who did. And I hated her for that."

Mrs. Porter stared at Daniele with a look that was half-sorrowful, half-confused. Then she asked, "How is Grant?"

"In the prime of his life," Daniele said. "At the top of his form. With all of his life ahead of him. He has everything to live for."

5

Grant pulled through the metal gates as they slid back and appreciated the scene before him as he did every morning. Dense with trees and shrubs, Altimate Pharmaceuticals's beautiful campus of one- and two-story buildings was barely twenty minutes from his house. It wasn't perfect, nothing was, but except for Payne's presence it had been a haven for Grant.

Grant hoped Altimate would work its magic on him this morning. After Angie's phone call, he needed something to lift his spirits before he confronted Payne.

When he got to his lab, Grant pushed open the door and paused on the threshold. He closed his eyes and took a deep breath. Labs had always been his sanctuaries and the familiar smells of chemical reagents an atmosphere he loved. The first time he'd walked into this lab, he had marveled at the generous high-ceilinged space, the gleaming glass and chrome installation, the new and sophisticated equipment—*all his*. Ali Baba's cave couldn't have held greater treasures for him.

He waited for his usual response to being here: feeling his muscles relax and a smile stretch across his face. But it didn't happen. Instead he felt a strong uneasiness, a premonition that something bad was going to happen.

What did he expect? he asked himself. After Payne's memo and the dead raccoons, anybody would be gloomy.

"Grant!" It was Nathan Horcroft, president of Altimate.

"Hello, Nathan."

A number of thoughts ran through Grant's head when he saw Nathan here: Why was Altimate's president in his lab; did it have anything to do with the memo Payne had left for him; was there any more bad news in the offing... But the thought that stayed: This was the man who had given him the revolver he didn't have to use on the raccoon this morning. Nathan had given him the gun when Grant and Dena had gotten engaged, and Dena had moved in with Grant. He had told Grant to use it to protect his daughter. Grant felt a familiar lump in his throat.

"How are things going?" Nathan asked.

"So far, so good," Grant answered. Where was Nathan heading?

"Preliminary results on the white twin looked good," Nathan said. "I expected nothing less from you, Grant."

He was smiling like a father, Grant thought.

"We should be able to send the purified drug to animal testing today or tomorrow," Grant said. "We're on schedule."

"Good, good." The smile stayed on Nathan's face. "You're very capable, Grant. That's important."

What did that mean? Grant wondered. I'm supposed to be competent.

Then Nathan's face changed. "About tomorrow night's dinner," he began. He seemed awkward now, almost embarrassed.

Grant indicated the lab with his hand. "I have to be here for the photo shoot for the annual report," he said. "Probably on Saturday, too."

Nathan looked relieved. "It's just that Daniele will be there, and..."

Grant understood. He and Daniele had always been like oil and water, and it had only gotten worse when Daniele thought he was competing with her for the presidency of Altimate. Still, he had a pressing reason to mend fences with her.

"Take care," Nathan said.

When Nathan got to the door of the lab, he turned. From the look on Nathan's face, Grant thought he was going to say something about the memorial service Grant had arranged for Dena this coming Sunday.

"You've done good work for Altimate, Grant. Consistently. Always follow your intuition. Every good scientist is smart. Every great scientist follows his inner voice. Intuition is what separates the plodder from the one who finds the Holy Grail." He nodded at Grant and left.

Grant wondered why Nathan had given him a pep talk now. The last time Nathan had used those words was when he was recruiting Grant to come to Altimate. Since then Grant had had to fight tooth and nail to do the research he wanted and to get funding for it. If Grant hadn't believed in the research that led him to make the black and white twins, his drugs would never have been created. No one but Grant had had any faith in his work.

Grant mused about the fact that a pharmaceutical company might test *ten thousand* chemical compounds to successfully bring one new drug to market. For the past three years it had felt to Grant as if he had gone through those ten thousand chemical compounds himself. The hours of book and computer research until his eyes and brain ached, the laborious chemical lab work, the blind alleys he had found himself in, again and again. And then, when he had a compound that was ready for testing, the long wait, holding his breath and hoping that test results would be encouraging.

The repeated failures.

All of that blood, sweat and tears had led to the white twin, Grant's Holy Grail. Grant wasn't giving up on it. Period.

Grant walked over to his section of the lab. Before he got to his office, Angie met him. His twenty-four-year-old assistant was wearing her usual crisply starched white lab coat over a long skirt and white blouse. Grant thought she always looked like a parochial schoolgirl. She pushed curly dark hair back from her face, and Grant saw her hands.

"Good morning, Dr. Fraser."

"Don't worry, Angie. Everything will be all right."

"How do you know I'm upset?" she asked.

He pointed to her chewed, pink-painted fingernails. "They're an infallible barometer, even if your calm and cool exterior threw me off."

She made a face and followed him to his office. Payne's memo was in the middle of Grant's desk.

Grant hung up his jacket and put his briefcase on his desk without looking at the memo. He wanted to find Payne and talk with him, but Angie was standing anxiously in front of his desk.

"We're in pretty good shape with the timetable for this project," Grant reassured her. "We've got the purification process down.

We should have enough purified white twin to send to animal testing by tomorrow at the latest."

Angie nodded her head. "But Payne will ask me questions at the review. He tells me to be there, and then he asks questions I don't know the answers to so you and I both look bad. I want to be prepared. Please help me." Tears started in her eyes.

Angie was smart, Grant thought—she'd graduated at the top of her class and was now working toward her Ph.D.—but like many unusually bright people she had failings in other areas: She was insecure. She was an excellent assistant who had helped him greatly. Grant did his best to encourage Angie—he had believed in her so much that he had even loaned her money for college—but it was an uphill battle. Payne's constant hounding had turned her insecurity into anxiety.

Grant shook his head. He had to talk to Payne now.

"We'll review, Angie, but later."

The lab door opened, and Grant braced himself.

6

Grant expected Whitney Payne to storm in. But when he heard a low whistle from one of the techs, he knew Joss Avery was on her way. A beautiful woman with flaming red hair in a tailored green suit strode into the lab.

Although the director of communications was his colleague and confidante, Grant was slightly disappointed. He wanted to get the confrontation with Payne out of the way so he could work.

"Hi, Joss," Grant said.

"Hope I'm not interrupting," she said with a smile. "I just wanted to remind you—the photo shoot for the annual report starts tomorrow at 5:00 p.m. The publicity will be good for you."

"I'll be here," Grant said. Count on Joss to keep my interests in mind and support them, he thought.

"Great." As Joss turned to leave, she paused and told him, "I was just in Horcroft's office. Payne was there, and he's on his way here."

Grant shrugged. So he would have to wait after all. Grant would have preferred to use the time to get ready for Payne, but Angie looked pleadingly at him.

"It looks as if we have time for a short review after all," he told her.

Angie beamed.

"If you've got a few minutes, Joss, please stay," Grant said. "Angie and I are preparing for a meeting with Payne next Tuesday on the white twin. He will do his best to punch holes in everything. I'd appreciate it if you'd listen and play devil's advocate. I want to be prepared for him."

Grant wanted Joss's reactions. She heard every word you said and her logic was flawless. No surprise. She had a Ph.D. in biochemistry.

"I'll be happy to," Joss said. She pulled two stools over, and she and Angie sat on them. "Anything to help the white twin become a blockbuster drug."

"Thanks," Grant said. He appreciated Joss's confidence. Still, Grant couldn't help worrying that Payne was heading for his lab this early. He usually didn't come by before 11:00 a.m.

Grant began by holding up his hands so they faced each other. "The drug we developed exists in two forms, which are mirror images, like my hands."

"Which means that even though they look the same, they are different molecules," Joss said.

"Right. In the lab, there is only one way we can tell the drugs apart—dissolve them in a liquid," Grant said. "One rotates polarized light to the right, and the other rotates it to the left."

Joss tapped a high heel impatiently on the rung of the stool. "Is it me or is this presentation on the basic side?"

"You're right," Grant said. "Payne wants review presentations to be self-contained." Grant's stomach tightened as he wondered what he could say that would make Payne postpone the white twin's review.

"Well, that's logical," Joss said. "Not all of the scientists at the review will be familiar with the research. You have to bring them up to speed quickly—what you're trying to accomplish and how."

"I agree," Grant nodded. "The problem is that Payne's grasp of the science is limited. So you end up having to define every scientific term and the presentation…"

"Has to be simple enough for a six-year-old to grasp," Joss finished. "Because he gets angry and abusive when he doesn't understand something. I know his reputation… You were saying that in the lab the twins seem identical."

In spite of his anxiety, Grant smiled to himself. Joss was a beautiful firecracker; brilliant, often impatient. He thought her mane of red hair was a warning signal more than a color.

"Right," Grant said. "But inside a living creature shape is crucial. Molecules bind to each other and react because their shapes fit together—like a lock and key. Inside a living creature, the two mirror image molecules usually act differently so that only one of them is effective."

"Like D-penicillamine is useful while L-penicillamine is toxic,"

Angie put in, looking pleased with herself. "That's why we're still working on the white twin, and why they canceled work on the black twin."

"Right. Preliminary tests show that the white twin helps the immune system to fight pathogens like bacteria. The black twin didn't." Grant winced, remembering how much pleasure Payne had taken in telling him the black twin had been canceled.

"Invaders like bacteria do their dirty work outside the cells in our bodies," Angie added. "Invaders like viruses get inside the cells. So there are two different mechanisms which the immune system has developed to deal with them. The white twin helps the immune system wipe out things like bacteria."

Grant nodded, smiling.

"Wait a minute," Joss said.

"What's wrong?"

"Why should the immune system need any help from drugs?" Joss asked.

"Timing," Grant said. "The immune system might get antibodies in the bloodstream maybe three days after the first encounter with bacteria. But bacteria can reproduce every twenty minutes. That's an enormous head start."

"And it could be deadly if someone were infected with really virulent bacteria," Joss said.

Grant nodded. "After specific cells of the immune system recognize the bacteria—by binding to it—they are stimulated to release antibodies, and to reproduce and release more antibodies. The white twin seems to speed up the whole recognition and response process significantly."

"Significantly!" Angie said indignantly. "Animal testing said preliminary results were amazing, even *staggering*. And they never talk like that."

Joss smiled wryly. "Is there nothing wrong with your white twin?"

There was something in the look on Joss's face and the way she said this that bothered Grant. He frowned.

"Nothing that we can know right now, Joss. We've done the standard checks. And there's *no* history of chemicals in the white twin's family causing any problems in the human body. But could a metabolite—a molecule that the body breaks the white twin into during metabolism—have any negative effect? We can't possibly know that until we give the white twin to a person—and clinical tests are down the road."

"But—" Joss began.

"Whoa!" Grant said, laughing. "We're still just talking about rats right now. There's plenty of time to worry about side effects."

"Side effects?" Angie asked.

"Every drug has a side effect, Angie," Grant said. "Even aspirin. Sometimes it's as simple as nausea or heartburn. It's any action of a drug other than the one you intended."

Angie held up a molecular model of the white twin. "Why can't we tell what it can do from this?"

"If we could know everything about a drug from its structure, we wouldn't have to jump through hoops for the FDA to give us approval. But we have to go through years of animal and human testing to know what a drug will do. Even after all this testing, we still don't know everything.There are drugs we've used for years—including aspirin—and we don't know exactly why they work."

The lab door slammed open, and Joss and Grant started.

"Your introduction was simple, quick and good," Joss whispered. "And this is my cue to leave."

7

A short, stocky man with pouched eyes made a beeline for Grant. Payne's hands twitched at his sides as if he were ready to strike someone.

"Animal testing is waiting for purified *white twin,*" Payne said. "But you have time for socializing?"

Grant couldn't believe that Payne was talking to him this way, but he didn't want to antagonize the director just days before a review.

"Angie and I were going over our work on the white twin in preparation for next Tuesday," he said. "Joss was listening."

"*Ms.* Avery doesn't do reviews of my department," Payne said. "I do."

Grant didn't respond. He didn't want to make Payne any angrier than he already was.

Payne added, "Just because the impure drug seemed to have some positive effect doesn't guarantee that the pure form will have the same results."

That was one of the longest comments Payne had ever made in scientific terms, and it made Grant uneasy. It almost sounded as if he had been coached. And Payne seemed to be enjoying himself today even more than usual.

Grant's sixth sense warned him, but he wanted Payne to postpone the review. "The review is only five days away," Grant said. "And we haven't yet sent completely purified white twin to animal testing. We need to give them more time to evaluate the drug, so we know what it can do."

Payne stared at Grant with a disdainful expression. "So why is it taking Altimate's star researcher so long to purify this compound? Are you trying to postpone the inevitable—finding out the white twin isn't the white knight that will save the world?" Payne sneered.

He always goes for the jugular, Grant thought, grinding his

teeth. "We've been on schedule since the beginning of the project," Grant said. "At the latest, I'll have it ready tomorrow."

"Why can't you have your work done on time, Fraser?" Payne said, his color rising. "That's what you're paid for."

Grant nearly choked with anger. Payne was like a vicious dog who wouldn't stop lunging at you. It was impossible to get anywhere with him. "I'll complete the purification on schedule," Grant said. "But that still doesn't give animal testing enough time to come up with data, even for a preliminary review. If we can reschedule for two weeks from now..."

Payne cut him off. "The only problem is that you aren't doing your part of the work. This is a team effort. Animal testing has other drugs to test besides yours. Don't blame it on them."

"But Altimate expanded their animal testing capabilities to make sure that they thoroughly test each drug," Grant said, just barely keeping his voice calm. "To be sure they don't miss any of the drug's potential. It's in everyone's best interests if animal testing has enough time to do the job right."

No matter what he said, he was angering Payne. Payne said, "You don't decide what is in the best interests of Altimate. I do. And no one is going to miss the white twin."

Payne made a dismissive gesture and stomped out of the lab.

Blood was pounding hard in Grant's head. He turned toward his office. Standing in front of him was Tom, one of the technicians who shared the lab. Tom must have been in the lab during the fireworks, Grant thought.

"It's demoralizing to listen to that guy," Tom said. "I've been on the receiving end myself."

"I don't know how to deal with him," Grant said. "Reasoning doesn't work. He doesn't know the science and just pounds away at you no matter what you say."

"I think the problem is he's jealous," Tom said. "He knows you're smarter than he is. Maybe he thinks you're after his job."

Grant shook his head. "I just want him to let me do my job. This morning I was trying to get him to postpone the review, to give animal testing time to test the white twin. And he refused, as if I were asking for a personal favor. Of course I want this drug to succeed. I developed it. But it belongs to Altimate. If it has what it takes to be a great drug, Altimate is the winner."

"The craziest part," Tom said, "is that Altimate lets him get away with it."

No, Grant thought. The craziest part is that even *Nathan Horcroft* lets him get away with it.

8

Grant had work to do, and if he didn't push what Payne said out of his mind—at least for now—the words would just play over and over like a broken tape until Grant choked Payne or quit Altimate.

So Grant did what he had been doing in the nearly four years since Payne became director; he did the work, meticulously but woodenly.

By 1:00 p.m., even though Grant and Angie had purified enough white twin for animal testing and Angie had sent it over, he felt no sense of accomplishment. He couldn't get out from under the pressure of the cloud Payne had created.

Grant needed to get away from Altimate, if only for a while. Normally he grabbed a sandwich at the in-house cafeteria. There was always some scientific journal or some experiment he wanted to get back to. Right now he didn't want to see or hear anything having to do with this place.

He decided to go out to lunch and was on his way out the door when he remembered the raccoons. Despite the attitude of the animal control warden this morning, Grant hoped that someone in the department examined the raccoons and found what one of the animals was clutching in its paw. He wanted to call the department before they disposed of the animals.

The phone rang ten times before someone answered.

"Yeah?"

"Is this the Animal Control Department?" Grant asked.

"Yeah."

The voice sounded young and preoccupied, but Grant continued. "This is Grant Fraser. Someone from your department came to my house this morning to pick up a couple of dead raccoons."

"Yeah..."

"I want to know if anyone checked what one of them had in its paw. I think there's a chance they were poisoned, and the contents of the paw may have caused their deaths. If someone is putting out poison in my neighborhood, I want to know. There are a lot of dogs around, including mine."

"No kidding."

Grant interpreted that as interest, because he heard what sounded like a book dropping.

"What did you say your name was?"

"Grant Fraser."

"When did you say the guy picked up the raccoons?"

"About 7:00 a.m. today." Grant suddenly thought he should find out who he was talking to. "Who are you, and what do you do there?"

"Dave. Odd jobs. But I'm in vet school, and poison, well, that's *interesting*." He lowered his voice. "Nobody else here will do anything about it, I promise you. But I'll take a look at it."

"Thank you," Grant said. He hoped there was still a chance he would learn what killed the raccoons. He gave Dave his office number. "When do you think you might call me back to let me know something?"

"Depends," Dave said. "On if and when I can get to the animals, what lab facilities are available and what my schedule is. As soon as I have something for you, I'll call," he promised.

Grant hung up. He hated to have to go through other people to get information that he wanted.

He heard a knock and looked up to see red hair swinging around the face leaning in his door.

"Lunch?" Joss asked.

Grant was about to say he wouldn't be good company when Joss held up her hand.

"You want to be alone," Joss said melodramatically. "That's okay. I want to take my car anyway. I'll meet you where?"

Grant relaxed. Joss could be pushy in the best way.

"The little seafood place in South Norwalk," he said.

Joss nodded and left.

Grant was picking up his briefcase when his assistant stuck her head in the door.

Her dark curly hair was unrestrained today, and she kept brushing it back from her face with her hands. Grant noticed that her fingernails were more chewed than usual.

"Is it okay if I read in your office during lunch?" she asked.

"Angie, you always ask that, and I always say yes," Grant said. "It's a standing okay."

9

Angie was sitting cross-legged at Grant's desk, her face and book hidden behind his computer. She watched Daniele Horcroft sidle into Grant's office. She obviously thinks no one is here, Angie thought. What does she want here? There's something she's looking for. What?

For as long as she could keep up the charade, Angie pretended to be reading and to be unaware of Daniele's clumsy efforts to snoop.

She's not looking for his lab book, Angie thought. She's not looking for any of his papers or for something on his computer.

Angie's heart stopped for a second when she saw Daniele pull open a drawer that Angie thought was locked. Daniele reached in and lifted out a vial.

"Oh!" Angie said, "Dr. Horcroft. I was reading and didn't see you. I'm sorry. Can I help you?"

Daniele nearly dropped the vial.

If she hadn't been so upset, Angie would have been amused by the expression on Daniele's face. But all Angie could think was: If I hadn't been here, she would have taken that vial. The drawer was supposed to be locked, but it wasn't. And if I hadn't been here she would have taken it. Angie wondered if Daniele had ever taken something before.

There was no excuse for Daniele to be in Grant's office; Angie knew that. And Daniele clearly had no idea how to talk her way out of it. But being Daniele Horcroft, she probably thought she didn't have to.

With Angie still sitting in the chair, Daniele walked brazenly to the desk and put the vial down. She turned around and walked out of the office.

Angie's heart was beating like mad, and her hands were shaking. What did she want with the vial? Angie could imagine only one reason. She could never let that happen. Not if she had to sit here like a sentry day and night.

10

She was angry. Grant was relentless. He kept coming back, again and again. In her mind she saw the TV commercial with the battery-driven bunny. Grant was worse than that stupid rabbit. All the preparation and rehearsing he had been doing for that meeting with Payne. He wasn't going to give up on the white twin or the black twin, she was sure. What did it take to stop him?

When the black twin was canceled, she was sure that that would slow Grant down. She would have been crushed, at least for a while. To have worked that hard, to be so sure that you were onto something real, something important. To have spent that much time on a project that meant the world to you, and then to have someone turn around and tell you it was nothing. She had almost felt sorry for him.

She shook herself. What she was doing was important. She had thought it out carefully, going over every step, and the logic was flawless. It would revolutionize the way these things were done.

She looked at the calendar. She was too close to getting what she wanted to take the chance that Grant would foul things up now.

She would have to take another tack.

11

Grant put his heavy briefcase in the backseat and drove out of Altimate's gates. About half a mile from the SoNo restaurant, the car in front of him stopped abruptly, and he came close to rearending it. His laptop computer flew out of the briefcase and slammed hard into the back of his seat. Grant heard it fall on the floor with a plastic thud.

It was another reproach, in a day full of them, he thought.

The laptop contained highly confidential information about the white twin and the black twin—all that was in his lab books at Altimate and more. Grant knew he wasn't supposed to take anything like this out of the labs. It was absolutely forbidden. He could be fired for it, even prosecuted.

But it was the only way he could work in peace and accomplish something. He had felt *forced* to buy this laptop. Payne always seemed to be in Grant's lab—criticizing him, taunting him. Despite Grant's training and his rigid discipline, he sometimes found it impossible to concentrate at the labs.

So he worked on the laptop at home, far from Payne's prying eyes and acid tongue. And he kept a constant, nearly paranoid watch on the laptop, to ensure that its precious contents never fell into someone else's hands. All of the stress was getting to him.

Grant hit the steering wheel with the heel of his hand. He didn't know how much more of Payne he could take. He had even been looking around, sending out feelers to other pharmaceutical companies. The only thing that held him back was the thought that if he left Altimate, he would be forced to leave the white twin behind.

12

When Joss pulled into the parking lot of the restaurant, Grant was already there.

He was leaning against his car, watching the small harbor with boats bobbing gently at anchor. Joss knew that this kind of setting had the same calming effect on Grant that labs did.

"Enjoying the view?" she asked.

He smiled at her and turned his attention back to the harbor. "I've always liked to be near the water. Not *in* it—even though I learned to swim I've never been comfortable in it. But I like to be near it."

Joss hadn't known that about him. She didn't think Grant was afraid of anything. "I like the water, too," Joss said. "One of the reasons I accepted Altimate's offer was because I could live here."

"Hungry?" he asked, opening the door of the restaurant.

"Starving." Joss smelled the mouth-watering aroma of frying seafood.

"Good," he said. "I don't have anything pressing for a while. We can have a leisurely lunch if you have the time."

Joss thought leisurely didn't apply to anything Grant ever did.

"Leisurely? The way you were driving, I thought the hounds of Hades were after you. If I didn't know where this place was, I would have been lost right after we left Altimate."

Grant shrugged. "I guess I was thinking about work."

Joss believed that. He was nearly obsessive about it.

"What looks good to you?" Grant asked Joss as she read the menu, written on a blackboard behind the counter.

"Lobster rolls."

"Is one enough?"

"Only if you intend to share, and I don't," she grinned.

"Three lobster rolls, an order of fries and two Cokes," he ordered.

Joss was looking for a table for them when she heard glass breaking. She turned around to look out the window. A man had broken Grant's back passenger window and was reaching for the laptop.

Before she could say a word to Grant, he had run headlong to the door like a madman and rammed it open with both hands. Joss hurried after Grant. Out of the corner of her eye, she saw several people in the restaurant watching from the window. Great, she thought.

Grant lunged at the thief, but the man saw him and swung the laptop at Grant. The blow knocked Grant off balance, back toward a nearby car.

Joss ran to Grant and grabbed his arm. "Let him go, Grant! He's bigger than you are and he looks desperate. Don't get hurt over a computer."

The thief, still holding the laptop, ran across the lot to jump into a dark-colored Jeep driven by another man. The driver gunned his engine and shifted into drive to tear out of the lot.

Grant shook Joss's hand off, and she heard him cry out in a roar of agony as the thief disappeared behind a slammed door. She knew Grant wouldn't let it go, but she wasn't ready for what he did next.

Grant leaped at the side of the Jeep, hitting it with his body, but landing on the running board. As the Jeep jerked forward he groped for a handhold and found the handle.

For a moment Joss didn't move or speak, because she couldn't believe what she was watching. Grant held onto the Jeep with one hand and smashed his free fist against the window, over and over again. The Jeep driver tried rapidly accelerating and braking to shake Grant off, but Grant clung tightly. He just doesn't let go, she thought.

Then Joss saw the man lift a gun into view and press it against the glass, aiming it at Grant's face. "Grant, no!"

She didn't think Grant was going to let go, but he released the door handle just in time. As the attacker squeezed the trigger, the driver accelerated and Grant fell backward. The bullet didn't touch him.

The Jeep roared away, leaving Grant lying in the parking lot.

Joss ran over to him. His hands were cut and bleeding, and he was panting as if he'd run a marathon.

"He took it." Grant got up onto his knees, his head hanging down.

Joss knelt beside him. "Are you all right?" she demanded.

He nodded.

Joss was taken aback at the magnitude of Grant's anger— she had never seen him do anything like this in all the time she had known him. Grant hadn't seemed to be able to stop himself— not until the end. If he had gotten to the man inside the Jeep, Joss thought Grant might have killed him.

"Then are you crazy?" Her face felt hot with anger. It must be as red as my hair, she thought.

Grant was still panting. "You're right," he said. "I should have let go. But I couldn't—it was three years of my life. Three year's worth of ideas and sketches and information. All irreplaceable."

Joss was suddenly anxious. "Why would someone want to steal your computer?" she asked. "What did you have on that laptop?"

"All of my work on the white twin and the black twin."

Joss was stunned. "What! You put confidential material on the laptop and took it out of Altimate. Why?"

"Because with Payne hounding me every day it's the only way I can work in peace."

All Joss could think was—how many copies had he made of his work, and where were those copies?

She watched Grant limp to his car and stick his hand through the broken back window. Then he opened the door and reached down, picking carefully among the glass shards.

Grant cried out in surprise and Joss saw him holding two Zip Disks—like floppy disks, but with seventy times the storage capacity.

"They're here, Joss. I can't believe it. All my information on the twins is on these. How can it be?"

Then he started to laugh, and Joss thought his laugh sounded strange.

"On the way here," he said, "the car in front of me stopped abruptly, and I had to slam on the brakes. The Zip Disks must have fallen out onto the floor."

"Do you think the people who took your computer knew what you were doing with it?" she asked him. Was there someone who suspected or knew about the drugs? She had to know.

"No. I'm sure of it. No one could have known about it. You're the first person I've told."

"Was the laptop an expensive model?" Joss asked.

Grant nodded. "Custom. Top-of-the-line with lots of extra power and memory. So I could run complicated programs."

"Something that expensive would be worth stealing," Joss said. "And theft at gunpoint is becoming an everyday thing."

Joss shook her head, still stunned by what Grant had done: He had taken *privileged information* out of the company. He was a walking security risk.

Joss looked at the disks in his hands. She didn't want all that information staying with him. "It would be safer if both disks weren't with you. Give me one," she said.

Joss was putting the Zip Disk into her purse when she saw a change in Grant's face. "What is it, Grant?"

"And no one is going to miss the white twin," he said.

"What does that mean?" Joss wondered if he might have injured his head when he fell off the Jeep.

"Now I know what Payne said to me this morning, in the lab," Grant told her. "I tried to get him to postpone the review of the white twin, so we could give animal testing more time to get data. And when he said no, I didn't pay attention to what he said just before he left." Grant stared at the Zip Disk in his bleeding hands.

"What did Payne say?" Joss asked.

"He said, 'No one is going to miss the white twin.'" Grant looked up at Joss. "He didn't mean that animal testing doesn't miss anything, Joss. He was letting me know that no matter how well it performs, he is going to bury the drug."

13

Watching Grant Fraser as he drove out of the parking lot was a man in a Ford. His hands were clammy. "Stubborn fool!" he said. Fred Brown was unsettled by his reactions to what he had just seen.

Up to now Fred's assignment to follow Grant had been a yawn. The scientist looked like just another creature of habit, but with a Ph.D. Grant's human barnacle routine on the side of the Jeep had been the first interesting activity Fred had witnessed—he didn't think the scientist had it in him. But when the man in the Jeep fired his gun point blank at Grant's head, that brought back memories Fred hadn't dredged up since his accident and feelings he was still struggling with.

Fred Brown put those memories out of his mind as he drove to his next destination, the Westport Library, disguised as an old man. Today he probably didn't need a disguise, but he liked to stay in practice.

Fred had become adept at disguises—in his job it was important that he not be noticed. He knew from both his work experience and his childhood that two categories of people, the old and the handicapped, were nearly invisible to most adults. They didn't see them or remember them. So Fred often appeared in one of those two guises.

Unconsciously, he brushed his upper lip. The gaping opening that had deformed him as a child was now an almost invisible scar.

His cell phone rang and he winced. He knew who it would be, and he was right. It was his boss, Smith, checking up on him. Fred listened and then turned the phone off. He didn't need Smith calling him up so often. This was an easy assignment.

The Westport Library was located next to the Saugatuck River. If Fred hadn't been working, he would have enjoyed just sitting in one of the reading rooms. The woman he approached for help was knowledgeable and helpful. Out of habit, Fred didn't want her to remember him or what he was reading, so he took the local newspapers and went upstairs to the Children's Reading Room.

Fred sat down at a long empty table. He liked to do his own research, even on simple jobs like this one. Normally it was the job of his employer's researchers to submit reports, the job of the actives to do the assignment. But Fred had hated that arrangement from the beginning and never accepted it. He had argued to his superiors that the researchers were intelligent, but they didn't think the way he did. And if they missed something important, it could mean he would fail. Which could mean he would die.

Fred did his own research for another reason—to protect himself. Although he didn't think his employers had ever sent someone to shadow him, he didn't know for sure. Fred had no intention of ever leaving himself open to second-guessing or betrayal.

He decided to start with the oldest newspaper issue, several months ago, and work forward. Fred wanted to get a feel for the town that Grant lived in. Everything about Grant Fraser was important to Fred right now—where he chose to live, what he did with his free time.

In a recent issue he came across a number of articles on a school referendum—which he found out was taking place today. The issue: Should the school budget be reduced by a million dollars? Fred noticed that Grant was mentioned in the article as one of the organizers of the referendum.

As Fred paged through the papers, his practiced eye noticed short articles on two recent deaths. An older woman had drowned in the Saugatuck River right next to this library, and a man had crashed his car into a bridge support.

The door to the reading room opened, and Fred looked up quickly. An elderly woman with a little boy paused on the threshold, like a startled bird when she saw Fred. But after a moment she came in and sat down at Fred's table. Apparently she felt an old man posed no threat, Fred thought.

She held the boy—maybe three years old, big eyes and all skinny arms and legs—on her lap as she turned the pages of the book. Fred could see the book. It was large, colorful, with a big picture of a rabbit.

"What's this, Michael?" she asked, in a soft, low voice. "What's his name, love?"

With an obvious effort, the little boy focused on the picture. He frowned, brightened and then looked confused, as if it had just been there and he'd lost it.

When he looked at the little boy, something in Fred tightened. He tried to turn his attention back to his newspapers.

"What kind of animal is this?" the old woman coaxed, putting her cheek next to Michael's. "You've seen him before. There's one just like him on your lap."

The little boy looked shyly up at Fred for a long moment and then smiled. The old woman had surprise—and fear—in her face.

"You know Michael Hor...Horcroft?" she asked, in a shaking voice.

Fred shook his head no, and the woman looked relieved. Without knowing why he did it, Fred got up and shuffled toward them.

"Hello, Michael. My name is Fred."

Michael smiled and put out his hand. "Hi, Fred."

Fred felt a warmth he didn't know was in him when the child put his small hand in his. For a moment he couldn't let him go.

The woman looked from Michael to Fred. "I'm amazed. Even normally he's not so friendly with strangers."

Fred thought that she caught herself on the word *normally*. "He's a little under the weather?" he asked her.

Tears welled in her eyes. "More than a little," she said with surprising vehemence. "He's been like this on and off for a couple of weeks. She doesn't want me to take him out, but I thought it would help him to come here, he loved me to read to him. He's so bright." She stopped abruptly, as if she'd already said too much.

Fred watched her curiously. He wanted to know more about the boy. "Surely it's not so serious?" he said. "He looks all right to me."

"All right! Just look at him. Normally he's chattering like a magpie, naming everything in the book, telling *me* the story, squirming on my lap to turn the page, running around to find other books." She paused for a breath. "And he doesn't even smile or laugh the way he did. Although he did smile at you—I wonder why."

Michael looked up at Fred. "You like to dress up," he said.

Fred jumped inside. Had Michael seen through Fred's disguise?

"Well, to go someplace special, yes, I do," he said.

Then Fred got to his feet and made his escape before the little boy had a chance to expose him.

14

As Fred drove away, he found himself thinking about Michael. And that made him think that his boss, Smith, might be right about something. Smith had given Fred this easy assignment because he feared that Fred wasn't ready yet for anything more. Fred had reassured Smith that he was as good as new.

Actually, since his accident, Fred had felt *better* than new. Getting shot in the head had turned out to be a blessing; the brain surgery had been a passage to a new world. Fred had noticed the changes when he first awakened in his hospital bed.

Smith had been waiting for him, and Smith had always made Fred uneasy. But that morning in the hospital, Fred felt slightly detached, an observer as well as a participant. The usual emotions and thoughts that Smith called up in Fred were still there, but Fred was *aware* of them without being overwhelmed or *controlled* by them. It gave him a wonderful new freedom of observation and action.

Fred shifted uncomfortably in his seat at the recollection. There was one slight problem with his new perspective that he still didn't like to acknowledge—even though incidents like the theft of Grant's laptop were rubbing his nose in it.

Fred told himself that you couldn't expect anything to be all good or all bad. It was how you used it. But the fact was that Fred's new awareness not only allowed him to see and experience things with a wonderful objectivity. Fred was beginning to feel an affinity with other people.

And that could be an inconvenience to someone who killed for a living.

Fred had always been good at what he did, and since his accident he was better. Smith had been pleased. He'd even hinted that Fred was in line for his position.

It was just that discovering this vista inside him had given Fred a new appreciation for his own mind. For the human mind.

Fred smiled a tight smile. It was the first time he'd actually put it into words. And it was funny, he thought, when you realized what his employer did.

Both Smith and Fred worked for Massachusetts-based American Research Laboratories, A.R. Labs, which received funds from the military (like many other research organizations) to come up with contributions to its chemical warfare arsenals. This was not widely known, and of course A.R. Labs wanted to keep it that way.

Like any good organization, A.R. Labs recruited the best people it could find. Dr. Grant Fraser had been high on their list of candidates, Fred understood. And they knew he was unhappy at Altimate.

But how to approach him? Given the sensitive and secret nature of much of A.R. Labs's work, it seemed most appropriate to follow Grant and learn as much as possible about him before any job offer was made. A.R. Labs wanted to know their candidate would say yes when they asked him. Besides, following Grant around might turn up something useful that would help them persuade Grant to join A.R. Labs.

Fred smiled to himself. He never thought he would be an executive recruiter.

15

"About time you showed up!" the elderly man grumbled. "Hardly four more hours till the polls close."

"What's the matter, Ed?" Grant asked. He had just walked into the school gymnasium where the vote on the referendum was being held.

"All the people who signed the petition against this damned school budget increase, I hope they show up tonight."

Grant understood how Ed felt. Ed had been a driving force in the Westport Taxpayers Group; he lived in a trailer court and couldn't take many more tax increases.

The issue that surrounded this referendum was personal to Grant; it struck at his roots. Raised by an aunt who had had to work far past retirement, he had been a boy when she died prematurely. Grant would never have missed this vote; he had even helped organize the WTG. But Grant had an even bigger reason for being here.

Grant was facing Ed when he saw the reason walk in. It was the blonde woman in the photo in Grant's foyer. For a moment Grant's heart caught.

"Daniele!" the old man called.

Daniele saw him and smiled. "Hello, Ed."

Daniele Horcroft. Dena's sister.

Her blonde hair wasn't streaming like Dena's was; it was tightly wrapped in a shiny French knot. Grant saw she wore square glasses and an expensive but stiff-looking wool suit. Daniele was a very attractive woman, but she somehow always looked hard and cold. The techs called her the "ice princess." Grant thought she had no sense of humor. He remembered that once she had needed to mail something before a deadline, but she had refused to use an available stamp because it had a cartoon character on it.

Daniele walked into the gymnasium as if she owned it. She crossed her arms, and Grant saw nine perfectly manicured, painted red nails. The little finger of her left hand was visible, with the fingertip missing. She registered at a table and got in line for the voting booths.

Grant wanted to talk with Daniele, *had* to talk with her. But he wanted to approach her when there were fewer people around. He decided to wait and watch for an opening.

"The WTG is so grateful for your help on this," Ed said.

Daniele shrugged it off. "It wasn't that much," she said.

"It was," he insisted. "You made calls, gave money… Why, you got most of the names on the petition. I don't know what we would have done without you."

Daniele's gaze slid to a nearby woman and little girl. "Well, hello!"

The mother seemed torn between two conflicting impulses. "Hello, Daniele."

"I hope there are no hard feelings about the referendum," Daniele said. "We both just tried to do what we thought was right."

"It's important to keep the quality of our schools up," the mother said.

A big woman whom Grant recognized chimed in. "Of course it is," she said. "One of the biggest attractions of this town is its school system. If it goes downhill the prices of homes will fall. I can't believe they wanted to reduce the school budget—and by a million dollars!"

"One million dollars is just two percent." The solemn small voice came from the little girl. "Daddy said so."

The big woman glared at her.

Ed's mouth twitched with resentment and anger. "The little girl's right. That budget goes up every year without a word from the board. A lot of people who've lived here for years wonder if they can afford to stay."

From his vantage point, Grant could see the faces of everyone in the gym as they watched this exchange. He thought he could guess how each of them would vote. Everyone seemed to register a strong emotion.

Everyone, that is, except Daniele. She looked totally uninterested. So why had she gotten so involved in the referendum? Grant wondered. More to the point, why had she gotten involved with the people who wanted the school budget *decreased*—the retired, those on fixed incomes? Grant guessed that it had to do with impressing her father, now that he was getting ready to name his successor at Altimate. Everyone at Altimate knew that Daniele wanted to be the next president.

You aren't being very charitable, Grant's alter ego told him. *When someone is kidnapped because her father is rich, and is tortured and has part of a finger cut off, she can have a change of heart.*

The little girl piped up. "What's wrong with Mike again?"

Grant's head jerked up. Again? Had Michael been sick again? He strained his ears to hear Daniele's answer.

"He had a virus for a day or so last week," Daniele said.

Grant's anger flared. She's not taking care of him, he thought. Grant missed the child. The last time he had seen him, two months ago, Michael had left behind his small terrycloth rabbit. The one Grant had taken away from Bailey this morning before he left for work.

Whoa, his alter ego said. *Even if Daniele isn't taking good care of him, where did all that anger come from? Michael Horcroft isn't your business.*

Not my business! Grant thought. I've probably spent more time with him than Daniele has. I know I changed his diapers more than she did. Her housekeeper is with Michael all day. Most evenings Daniele is out. All of us have been Michael's babysitters. Dena and I took care of him many times. So did Joss. Even after Dena died I saw him a lot. Then Daniele decides that I'm her competition for president of Altimate. And she punishes me by not letting me see him.

He's just a little boy, his alter ego said. *Another man's son.*

Grant didn't care. He's been like *family*, Grant thought. Aside from Nathan Horcroft, Grant was the only man in Michael's life. The little boy and he had bonded. He's special, Grant thought. I want to be part of his life, help him grow up. That was why he was here tonight: to mend fences with Daniele so she would let him see the boy again.

"How is your campaign at Altimate going?" It was a female voice that asked Daniele.

The question grabbed Grant's attention. He didn't know that Daniele's ambition was public knowledge.

"Right on track," Daniele answered. "And when I run Altimate the first thing I'm going to do is get rid of dead wood."

Daniele was looking right at Grant.

16

After he voted, Grant got Bailey and took him to Winslow Park. He sat at a picnic table in the middle of acres of grassy meadow with towering pines. The park was popular with people who wanted to exercise and play with their dogs. But Grant was oblivious to everything—even Bailey racing around, doing his "crazy dog" routine—but a replaying of his run-ins today with Payne and Daniele. While neither of them had been explicit—Payne hadn't said, "I'm going to get rid of your drug no matter how good it is." Daniele hadn't told him, "I'm going to fire you, first thing."— Grant was sure he had understood their messages.

Was he paranoid, stupid or crazy?

This couldn't be happening, Grant thought. Altimate was a respected pharmaceutical firm. Its business was to come up with successful drugs that would make money for years to come. And Grant was a well-known pharmaceutical chemist with a better than good track record. They had no reason to be unhappy with him.

Besides, Grant was still getting offers from pharmaceutical companies all over the country. If something happened at Altimate and he had to leave, he had lots of alternatives. What did he have to worry about?

He would have to leave the white twin behind.

That was like saying to someone who had spent years acquiring a house, car, possessions, investments—"Sure you can move anywhere in the world you want. You just have to leave with the clothes on your back."

Just thinking about it made Grant feel as if he had a hole in his chest.

Right, Grant thought. And none of that hole is because Daniele isn't likely to change her mind about Michael. Grant didn't even want to think about not having the little boy in his life…Well, he wasn't giving up on the white twin or Michael. He would see Daniele on Sunday at the memorial service. He would talk to her then.

Friday
October 24

17

When Grant got to his lab, he closed the door softly behind him so the technicians wouldn't hear him come in. He had prepared a new argument to convince Payne to postpone the review of the white twin, and Grant was sure he would sway Payne this time. Grant wanted to rehearse his argument without any distraction. The techs were loud this morning. Since Grant decided that he would just alert them to his presence if he said anything, he ended up overhearing their conversation.

The half-dozen men were ranged in front of the picture windows which ran the length of one end of the lab. Wearing lab coats and holding steaming mugs of coffee, they were commenting on one of the heads of the departments, an electronics engineer who carpooled with three other engineers.

Tom, the senior technician and leader of the pack, pointed at the parking lot. "Here comes Sharpley," Tom said. "Thank God his spot is empty, or he'd be stuck down there all day, figuring out what to do."

"Give good old rat-face a break," said another tech named Dave. "Anyone who is allowed to fix Daniele's computer deserves a reward. Besides, he's going to fix my VCR."

Sharpley must be really good, Grant thought. Daniele usually didn't let anyone near her equipment.

"VCR? I didn't know we got VCRs here. I want one, too." Another tech was ribbing Dave. It was an open secret that Sharpley would repair non-Altimate equipment on Altimate time, just because he couldn't say no to an electronic challenge. Especially when you knew how to get to his ego.

Voices laughed.

"You'd better take it easy on Sharpley."

"Why?"

"He nearly freaked the other day. Two guys coming from opposite ends of the lab were bringing him their VCRs. All of a sudden, Sharpley turns white, nearly falls off his lab stool and yells, 'Don't bring them together!'"

"Sounds weird," someone offered.

"No," another voice said. "It's because Sharpley doesn't just *fix* the VCR. That would be beneath him. If he agrees to work on your VCR, you end up with a machine that can do everything but fly. So he probably didn't remember what special features he put in those two VCRs, and he just didn't want to take a chance they'd blow up on him!"

The others laughed.

"Taxiing into his spot," Tom said. "Can you believe this? They have to be engineers. All four of them open their doors and lean out to measure how far the car is from the two white lines!"

Grant chuckled to himself. There was silence for a while, and he thought the group had broken up, but then someone spoke.

"Whoa! There's another one."

"What are you talking about?" Tom asked.

"The Westport Weekly. There was another death. Some girl was jogging and dropped dead."

"If I jogged, I'd drop dead too!" someone said.

"It's not funny," the newspaper reader said. "This is number four or five in the past several weeks."

"Of jogging deaths?"

"Of course not! A bunch of different things. A guy ran into a bridge support, a woman fell into the river…"

"No kidding?" Tom said. "I haven't heard anything about this on television."

"Maybe you have to watch something besides the cartoon channels."

There was a lot of murmuring and a pause, and Grant hoped the techs were ready to go to work. But the group at the window had another item.

"Did you hear what happened at Angelo's last night?"

Grant knew Angelo's; it had been a popular bar and restaurant for years. It attracted serious drinkers from all over the area.

"They finally had the police there—they're still keeping it pretty hush-hush, but somebody had his nose seriously put out of joint."

"How did you hear about it? There wasn't anything in the paper."

"Nor is there likely to be. I heard it on the police band of my ham radio. The cop who let it slip got chewed out, I'm sure. They shut him up fast."

"But why would the police want to squash that?"

"Not squash, just not broadcast it. Westport is a pricey community. People don't want to hear that there's violence at their favorite watering hole. Getting away from violence is the reason a lot of people move here."

"I'm surprised the bar didn't just have the bouncer dump the guys out in the street," Dave said.

"Yeah," another voice said. "The Mothers for Expensive Educations could regroup as The Mothers for It Doesn't Happen Here."

Grant heard muttering and an occasional "bummer." Apparently some of the techs had been affected by the school referendum and were disappointed that the side that wanted to reduce the school budget had lost. Grant had been disappointed; he knew how many names had been on the petition. If these people had all voted, their side would have won. Instead, the mothers' group had won by a large number.

There was a quiet pause, and then the first voice spoke again, so low that Grant could just make it out.

"This time it may be harder for them to hush it up. A woman was involved, and the nose in question was Payne's."

"You mean it wasn't the woman who got the worse of it?"

"No, for a change."

There was a pause filled with murmuring.

"So tell us," one tech urged. "We have inquiring minds."

"The police got pretty graphic on the radio" the first tech said. "Apparently he was roughing her up, and she took out a nail file and slit his whole nostril open."

"Ouch!"

"And weird. But the really weird thing is that he didn't press charges. I don't know why, but he refused to cooperate with the police."

"Maybe he plans to get vengeance," someone said.

"So how did the police get involved if nobody saw anything and nobody's talking?"

"The story is that someone saw him dripping blood. The guy called the police before the owner or the bouncer had a chance to do anything. I guess we're not the only people who aren't particularly crazy about him."

There was a general murmur of agreement.

"Any fallout from the head office?" Tom asked.

Grant figured that Tom was asking about Nathan Horcroft, Altimate's president.

"I hear Payne is to report directly to the principal's office as soon as he gets to school."

"Hope your magic connection hears what's going on. I wouldn't mind being the proverbial fly on the wall to hear that conversation."

"Does that mean you won't take offense if we call you an insect?"

Amid good-natured laughing, the group broke up.

18

Angie arrived, and she helped Grant set up for an experiment. Just as they were about to start the experiment, Payne swaggered in and snapped his fingers at Grant. "Fraser. In my office. NOW."

Grant's heart sank; he didn't want Payne in a bad mood when he presented his new argument to postpone the review of the white twin. Grant couldn't help staring at Payne. Although the director had a big bandage on his puffed-up nose and his face was discolored, he marched into the lab as if he were a king.

A sneeze on the other side of the partition interrupted him.

Payne looked up, annoyed, then began talking again. "Bring your lab books. Something is wrong with the white twin. I want to see all notes…"

There was loud sniffing, then another sneeze.

"Shut up, you morons!" Payne yelled.

In response, there was a thunderous cacophany of sniffing, nose blowing, snorting, wheezing and sneezing. They varied in pitch, duration and repetition—producing every sound the human nose could make. You could hear nothing else in the lab.

A look of understanding slowly passed over Payne's face, and his expression changed from annoyance to blind fury. His face rapidly turned dark red, and a murderous look came into his eyes. He seemed ready to lunge into the next bay and kill whoever was there.

The phone rang on Grant's desk. He answered it. When he hung up, he said to Payne, "That was Dr. Horcroft's office. He wants to see you now."

If possible, Payne's face turned a darker, more menacing shade of red. He put his face near Grant's so just he could hear and spat through fury-clenched teeth, "You're going to lose everything, Fraser. I promise you. Everything." He slammed his way out of the lab.

When the door swung shut behind him, an artificially high-pitched voice from the next bay said, "It would seem that Mr. Payne's sensitive appreciation for music does not extend to the wind instruments." Then six voices were guffawing.

But Grant's heart had stopped early in his exchange with Payne. What had Payne meant aboout something being wrong? Was there any truth to what he said? Or was he just torturing him again?

Joss walked in and saw Grant's face. "Payne was just here," she said.

Grant nodded. "He said something is wrong. He wanted to see my lab books."

"Something is wrong?" Joss repeated. She shook her head, and her red hair swung around her chin. "What could be wrong? Preliminary testing was fabulous. And you just sent purified white twin to animal testing yesterday. There wasn't enough time for them to come up with any meaningful results, let alone for someone to translate them for Payne."

Joss put her hand on Grant's shoulder. "I think I know how important the white twin is to you," she glanced around the lab and lowered her voice, "even before your performance on that Jeep yesterday. Don't let Payne drive you crazy…Especially since you won't be able to talk to him at least until Monday."

"Why?" Grant felt like a man on a rack, slowly being tortured.

"I was talking with Horcroft. He's unhappy about Payne's incident in the bar," Joss said. "Not to mention that he doesn't want him running around with that bandage on his nose. Horcroft sent him home and told him to stay out of sight until he looks normal again."

Grant didn't tell Joss about Payne's threat. It didn't sound believable, and besides, talking or even thinking about it made Grant's stomach knot. Grant decided he would have to keep himself busy every minute until Monday to keep himself from going crazy.

"Look, I'll be out most of today. I have meetings, and then I have to attend the Westport House Tour. Altimate is one of the sponsors, and it's for the benefit of the Galway Rehab Center," Joss said. "But I'll be back before 5:00 p.m. for the photographers. Hang in there. Everything is going to be all right."

Grant didn't share her optimism.

19

Daniele had to remove an earring to answer her office phone; she dropped the earring, then the phone. By the time she picked up the phone and spoke, she was annoyed. "Hello?"

There was a pause. Daniele said, "Hello? Who is this?"

"I'm sorry," a young-sounding male voice said. "They must have transferred me to the wrong phone. I was looking for Grant Fraser."

Daniele frowned and was ready to slam her phone down. All that trouble, and a call for Grant. Then she wondered who the man was. It was obviously an outside call. Maybe Grant is looking for another job, she thought. Good. She glanced up to see if Grant were in his office. No. He must be out to lunch. His faithful assistant was sitting in his office, though.

"He isn't here right now, but I work with him," she said. "Could I take a message?"

"Sure. I mean I guess so. This is Dave from the Animal Control Department. He called me about a couple of dead raccoons that were removed from his property."

Oh God, Daniele thought. Is there nothing too mundane or pointless for Grant to stick his nose into? Everything intrigues him. Well, when he loses his precious white twin project, he'll need other interests.

Daniele thought Dave paused as if he were waiting for her to indicate some knowledge of the incident.

"Well, he's probably worried about his dog," she said.

"Sure," Dave said. "If the dog got into the poison..."

"Poison?"

"Yeah. He thought they looked as if they might have been poisoned, and he asked me to look in the paw of one of them."

Daniele had been making notes. She shook her head. "In its paw? What does that mean?"

"I guess the raccoons must have turned over his garbage cans, and Grant thought they ate something in his garbage."

"So you looked in its paw?" Daniele prompted impatiently. Suddenly she stopped writing and interrupted him before he could answer. "What did you find?"

She listened while he told her—it was a crumpled letter. Her hand trembled when he told her what the letter was.

"Why don't you bring it to me?" she said. "I have to go out now. I can meet you at the McDonald's on the Post Road across from the movie theatres in fifteen minutes. My name is Daniele, and I have blonde hair and a red car. Okay?"

Daniele hung up and frowned. As she left the lab, she noticed that Tom the technician was talking with Angie.

20

"Do you always write in your books?"

Angie spun in Grant's chair. She hadn't heard anyone else come in. She didn't like to be surprised, even by Tom.

"Usually," she answered him. "If they're worth reading they're worth thinking about."

"Well, that looks Greek to me," he said.

"That's because it is," she smiled. "I studied it in college, and I like to keep reading it. Actually, you have to keep reading it, or you lose the ability so fast. The characters are so different from ours that it's hard to make the connections. It's almost like a code."

"How are things going here?" he asked.

"Payne was in here today, threatening and screaming," she said. "And Daniele was skulking around yesterday."

"So are you hiding out or standing guard?" Tom asked.

Angie grinned. "A little of both."

Grant's phone rang and Angie answered it.

"Oh, no," a male voice said. "They did it again."

"Who are you trying to reach?" Angie asked. "I can transfer you."

"Well, I was just talking with Daniele. I'm going to meet her, but I'll be about ten minutes late, and I wanted her to know."

"I think she just left," Angie said. "Sorry." Then she had another thought. "If she calls here, who should I say you are?"

"Dave—from the Animal Control Department."

Angie hung up and wondered what somebody from the dog catcher's department had that would get Daniele to meet him.

"A call for Daniele?" Tom asked.

Angie nodded.

"She is one person you never want to cross," he said. "She doesn't forget, even little things. She finds a way to get back, long after it happened."

"I know," Angie said. "That's why everyone gives her and her office wide berth."

"I remember some engineer who worked here a couple of years ago. He said something once that had nothing to do with her, but she took it personally. She got him fired."

Angie shuddered.

"It's funny," Tom said. "Daniele grew up with a nice guy for a father, and she had everything she could ever want, and she's still unhappy. Go figure."

"What happened to her mother?"

Tom lowered his voice. "The story is that she ran off with some man she met when the girls were little."

"Maybe that had something to do with it," Angie suggested.

"It didn't affect Dena that way; she was a sweetheart. No, I think it's just Daniele's nature—she's like a scorpion."

21

Joss looked at her watch. It was 2:30 p.m., and she was at the next to last stop on the Westport House Tour, looking at yet another enormous house decorated to perfection. Joss was bored with the tour and ready to leave. She wanted to go back to Altimate and try to do the job that had made her leave biochemistry for communications.

"So there you are."

Joss recognized the voice and turned to face Daniele.

"Remind me of the name of the charity for this event," Daniele said.

"The Galway Rehab Center," Joss said. "They give training, therapy and social support to people with mental and physical handicaps."

"That's right," Daniele said. "Didn't you have a retarded uncle?"

Joss was annoyed. "Not retarded. He had an accident that damaged his frontal lobe. He had been a brilliant engineer, but he lost everything."

The image of her helpless uncle—having to justify to some uninterested person that he hurt or needed something—was engraved on Joss's memory. Joss intended never to be at anyone's mercy.

But Daniele had already tuned out and was looking at something.

"Why are you here, Daniele?"

"Altimate is helping sponsor this," Daniele said. "I'm a good-will ambassador."

Right, Joss thought. You don't even know what the charity is. "Well, I'm going to the last house."

"I'm going back to the labs," Daniele said.

"But aren't all the sponsors supposed to meet at the last stop?"

"I can live without it," Daniele said.

The daughter of Altimate's president was used to doing what

she wanted, Joss thought.

As Daniele walked away, Joss shook her head. Daniele was a piece of work. Daniele thought that Grant was her competition for the presidency of Altimate, and she had shut Grant out of Michael's life. But even though Daniele thought Joss was Grant's friend, Joss was still babysitting Michael.

Joss spent the next quarter hour going through room after perfect room. Okay, Joss thought, I've done my part representing Altimate.

She turned to leave, but by the time she reached the front door it was blocked by a clique of women. They were all turned toward the stairs, staring. Slowly making his way down the stairs was a tall, handsome man in a perfectly tailored suit with star quality written all over him.

The women were whispering and tittering. They all recognized him as the challenger for the upcoming gubernatorial race, Joss thought. You couldn't have missed the avalanche of newspaper articles and TV spots—they told everyone that he was the wealthy head of an international import/export business.

What a bitter campaign this has been, Joss thought. She couldn't remember one this vicious. The incumbent seemed ready to do anything to stay in the governor's mansion.

The man on the stairs seemed aware of the glances and comments following him, and Joss thought he looked as if they were his due. He looked relaxed and casual, but he missed nothing. And then he saw Joss and widened his eyes and gave her an enormous television smile.

It looks as if my ex-husband has spotted me, Joss thought. Damn.

Joss didn't want to talk with Dell. She was sure that he just wanted something from her again; Dell was a great manipulator. Besides, she had things to do.

But Dell held Joss with his dark eyes as he advanced on her. Thick light brown hair surrounded a face that had only improved with time. His tall, muscular body was still in shape. Joss was surprised that, even now, he had an effect on her—small though it was.

"Joss." He stopped and smiled, scarcely a foot away from her, but didn't touch her. He smelled faintly of the scent he always wore.

In the past, Joss had found his intensity and charm captivating. But not now.

"Hello, Dell. What brings you to a house tour?"

"Probably the same as you," he said. "Public relations."

Then she remembered. "The election is just over a week away."

He nodded, but said nothing. She remembered that he always spoke sparingly and never about things that were very important to him. Or to her, she thought.

"How is life at Altimate?" he asked.

It seemed clear that he wanted to direct the conversation. He would get around to the subject of the election, but in his own way. She could feel him subtly controlling her. She felt like a cow being shuttled down a chute. Well, I won't give you the satisfaction, she thought. "Great. How is the campaign trail?"

There was a slight flicker in his eyes that probably only she could see was annoyance. He didn't answer immediately, so she pushed it. "Is this a fundraiser for you or just an appearance?"

"I don't fundraise at other people's events, particularly those earmarked for rehab centers," he said. "I'm here as one of the sponsors."

Joss couldn't imagine Dell doing anything strictly for charity, but she let it go. "Have you had any events in Westport?" she asked.

Dell said quietly, "We've had fundraising dinners. Or private individuals have made their homes available for an evening of low-key mingling. I don't like to ask, Joss. If it isn't a spontaneous offer, I'd rather not engineer it."

Right, she thought. She didn't know when he hadn't engineered something. She had finally decided that he didn't like to leave himself open to chance. It suddenly occurred to her that that might be the only thing they had had in common.

She returned his gaze and was struck again by the purpose

behind the perfect brown irises. What does he need from me this time? But she knew. He wanted people—influential people—who knew and liked her to be introduced to him. As if she approved of him as a candidate, if not as a husband.

Dell, you divorced me, she thought, surprised at the anger in her. And now you want my blessing for your campaign? Forget it. She was about to say no when Dell looked at her with an expression that would have looked sincere on anyone else's face.

"I'm sorry," he said.

Joss knew that he meant about the divorce.

"I was angry, Joss."

"*You* were angry? You wanted the divorce. Why?" She could feel her cheeks getting hot, and it made her angrier, to let him think he still got to her.

"Because you were right."

Joss's face began to contract in a frown. What was his strategy now? Dell never admitted he was wrong.

"I couldn't make room for you in my life," he said. "I couldn't accept what you had to give, so I pushed you out."

Joss said nothing. For Dell to be self-aware, to see himself as others saw him, was a dream. For him to admit a fault was impossible.

"I wasn't a good husband to you, Joss. I can be a good governor. Please help me."

These were words that Joss had never heard him utter. She didn't believe him.

"Will you host a small evening for me next week?" he asked her.

"It's so close to the election," she said. "I don't know if there's time to prepare."

"People will come," he said. "Food is never a problem for you."

She was going to say no, but then she thought—God forbid, but what if he wins? She knew Dell better than to make an enemy of him. "I suppose a small group would be possible, late next week…"

"Thank you, Joss." His large warm hand enveloped hers. The

reward. Touching her, closing the gap after he had made the deal he wanted. "Thank you."

Joss pulled her hand away. Dell had gotten what he wanted. Again.

"Joss," he said, as if he had just remembered. "Thank you for the help you gave me."

"Help? Oh, that wasn't much. I'm not a professional."

Dell's face got serious. "Oh, no. You were better than anyone else I talked to. I checked things out. Your assessment and recommendations were far and away the best. Your logic was flawless, as usual."

Robbins, his second in command, materialized almost immediately, tapping his watch, apparently to remind Dell of another engagement. As Dell and Robbins walked away, Joss overheard Robbins say, "The talk at Town Hall is next. We need to leave now."

22

Joss headed toward her car—and realized that she was planning to go to Town Hall. Normally the last thing Joss would have been interested in was listening to Dell give a political speech. Why now?

I have to go hear him, Joss thought. I just promised to have a fundraiser for him. I need to know what he's going to say in my house.

Westport's Town Hall was a large, yellow two-story building. Tall white columns topped with a pediment framed the entrance. Joss parked in the lot behind the building and walked up the stairs to the auditorium.

Dell's p.r. photo was on an easel in the aquamarine-walled anteroom. How familiar Joss was with him. She knew every crease and wrinkle. Every laugh, every mannerism, every joke. Every opinion.

And she didn't know him at all.

When he'd asked for the divorce, *that* was what had taken her heart out. That she was losing him after trying so hard, and she had never gotten past the p.r. photo. Everything that she knew about Dell was what everyone else knew. She never saw him let down his defenses, never sensed that she was talking with, eating with, making love with, the person who was behind the flashing smile and searching eyes. Dell was always reaching out, pulling to him everything that he wanted or needed like a sump pump. But he managed to process all of it without getting personally involved.

The lingering anger didn't have anything to do with Dell. By now she realized that you can't regret missing something you could never have. The anger had to do with being totally clueless. How could she have been attracted to someone like Dell? How could she be certain that she wouldn't do it again?

Joss walked in toward the end of his speech and stayed against the back wall. The room had a good crowd. Dell was standing at the front of the room on the stage. He looked strong, confident, capable. He smiled as he spoke and a number of people in the audience laughed.

From the middle of the audience came an agitated voice. Joss was surprised. Everything had seemed so orderly, almost staged. But the voice was insistent and Dell paused. The speaker was an older man, maybe mid-seventies.

"You don't mean 'interfere', I think," the older man said. "The government doesn't interfere with people by contributing money to Medicaid. People who are retired or unable to support themselves couldn't survive without it. It isn't a luxury. Why take money away from the segment that can least defend itself? Why not try to cut spending in some area of government that has excess?"

Joss wondered how Dell would handle this question. More and more there seemed to be a polarization in Westport between these two groups. One was the group of aging couples who had lived here for years and raised families. The other was the group of young couples who had moved here for the location, for the schools. The former group was not necessarily poor, but many were on fixed incomes. The latter group was still overachieving and felt that nothing was too good—or too expensive—for them or their children. Two different sets of values and interests.

Dell began by giving a politician's response that didn't really answer the man's question but didn't ignore him either. Then he changed to a more hardline stance where he basically said that anyone who couldn't make his own way ought to leave the tribe and go out on the ice and stop making a burden of himself.

Joss didn't agree with Dell, but she thought she understood where he was coming from. She knew that he had made every cent he had. He had started out with nothing and had built an empire. He thought everyone should do the same. But how would the people in the audience take it? Joss wondered.

For a moment there was silence in the room. Then a woman stood up in the second row and began to slowly applaud. Gradually the applause was taken up by a man a little further back. Then another and another. Finally it was very clear the way this audience was divided, although you wouldn't have been able to tell beforehand by looking at them. Both the people who agreed with Dell and those who disagreed with him cut across all age and economic groups.

From the front of the room came camera flashes, and Joss was suddenly aware of photographers who were snapping pictures of the scene.

Joss was stymied. She would never have thought that Dell would so blatantly speak his opinion and take the chance of alienating a group of voters. Dell had always been the most calculating man Joss had ever known. He never burnt bridges until he was sure he never wanted to cross them again.

Well, it looked to Joss as if Dell had pushed a self-destruct button. Politicians were always looking for ways to avoid taking a stand so they wouldn't lose anyone's vote, and Dell had just deliberately turned off nearly half this audience.

Maybe Dell just couldn't help himself, she thought. He was used to stating his opinion, giving orders, getting his own way. Maybe he wasn't really politician material. And maybe his opponents were there to document it with pictures. Joss wouldn't be surprised. This had to be one of the most vicious campaigns she had ever seen. The present governor seemed to be ready to do anything to keep himself in office. Finally, perhaps, Dell was going to fall on his face.

That would be fine with Joss. She hated what Dell had managed to do to her relationships with men. She hadn't gotten involved with anyone after she had divorced him.

Joss no longer trusted men. More than that—sometimes she resented them or just plain hated them.

What Joss *did* was most important to her. Her work was everything to her now.

23

The Galway Rehab Center—the house tour Joss attended had been held for the Galway's benefit—stood alone on the corner of a block facing the railroad tracks and the overpass. A long, narrow red brick building, it looked seventy years old, at least. The brick had been cleaned, mortar repointed and the windows repaired.

Fred Brown glanced up at the two-story building. He had decided that he needed to see Grant in operation at Altimate. When he found out about the photo shoot at Altimate this weekend—and he figured out how to get in—he decided he could unobtrusively watch Grant close-up if he took the disguise of a handicapped assistant. So he came to Galway to brush up.

Smith hadn't authorized Fred's going into Altimate, and his boss had told him to do nothing without clearance. Fred hadn't even mentioned it when Smith called him this morning. But Fred felt up to the project and wanted the practice. He was anxious to get back to more meaty assignments than checking out job candidates.

Fred had just one reservation about visiting the Galway Center and going disguised as a handicapped man to Altimate. Handicapped disguises were too close to the life he had led for what seemed like forever when he was a child. Fred thought maybe his discomfort also came from a touch of superstition. He felt that playing the handicapped role might give God the idea to make it a reality—again. The thought of being physically handicapped again was unnerving. But the thought that something might happen to his mind was intolerable.

When Fred had called the Center, the woman who answered the phone had told him to pull into the parking lot across the street. It was a bumpy, wedge-shaped area covered with gravel, with a few small, scraggly trees and some weeds, and completely enclosed by a ten-foot high chain link fence topped with barbed wire. When he approached the entrance, a gate rolled back to the left. He drove in and parked the battered Toyota.

Fred glanced at the barbed wire. The predators apparently made no exception for the handicapped, he thought. Fred was mildly surprised at his disapproval. A car was a car. An opportunity. That's all. He of all people knew this.

He put on a pair of thick, black-rimmed glasses and combed his hair over his forehead. He straightened his suit jacket. It was slightly small on him, and the pants were not quite long enough. Perfect.

He crossed the street and went in the main entrance. The floor was a gray-green linoleum and the walls white. Directly in front of him was the receptionist's window. A large, plump black woman with a kind face sat behind the desk.

"My name is Ted Wheeler," Fred said. "The director said I should have you call him when I got here."

The outside door opened and a right leg stepped over the threshold. It was followed by a nearly useless left leg. Fred looked up to see the owner—a young man, late twenties. Down's syndrome. He had a blank look on his face until he saw the receptionist. Then his face lit up.

"Lamps today, Tommy?" she asked.

"Lamps today Tommy," he agreed. He crossed to the elevator by alternately dragging the left leg and leaning on it so he could move his right leg forward.

Fred watched the young man carefully, while not being obvious. He memorized the stance of the man's body; the weight distribution as he moved, how he held his arms and his head. Fred couldn't practice there, right in the middle of the Center. But he could tense and release his muscles as if he were moving along with the man. He had done this kind of exercise many times.

When the elevator doors opened, a man in a brown suit got off and came over to Fred.

"Mr. Wheeler?" he asked. "I'm John Bray. Where would you like to start? Shall I tell you something about the Center, and then we can go for a tour?"

"I saw your literature," Fred said, smiling. "Perhaps we could start with the tour."

But someone muttering near him caught Fred's attention. He turned to see a sandy-haired man trying to use a screwdriver to repair a lamp. But he was turning the screwdriver the wrong way. It was clear to Fred that the man knew he should be using a screwdriver, that it was the right tool, but he couldn't figure out what he was doing wrong. His shoulders drooped, and there were tears of frustration in his eyes.

Fred could see immediately that this man was not mentally retarded. There was awareness and understanding in his eyes, and a look of infinite loss. The man looked as if he were caught in a dream. Like Michael, the little boy he had seen in the Westport Library. Fred stiffened.

Mr. Bray guided Fred past the man. "It is heartbreaking," he said. "You never become used to it. But he will get better. He's come a long way since he arrived here six months ago."

Fred thought he wouldn't want to live if he couldn't even use a screwdriver after six months of therapy. An unreasoning swell of anger washed over Fred for just seconds, but it was as if he had been hit by a wave.

"I have to leave," Fred said. He had intended to contribute a hundred dollars. But when he opened his wallet he found himself counting out five hundred dollar bills.

Outside, Fred inhaled deeply. It had started out being a good idea to come here. He needed to prepare for a role; he had come here for role models. That much made sense. It was standard operating procedure. But he'd gotten more than he'd bargained for.

He crossed the street to the parking lot. Out of habit he scanned the street and the lot. There was a van parked right next to his car, nearly obscuring it. With all the other empty spaces in the lot, why had they parked there? Fred suddenly knew and smiled slightly. A small humming feeling of excitement started and grew in him, and he moved toward his car, almost as if he were now in a dance, and the coming movements were all choreographed. Fred felt powerful, yet fluid.

When Fred reached the driver's door of his car, a man materialized at the hood end between the two cars. He looked Fred up and down with a sneer. With just the slightest movement of his eyes Fred could see there was no one behind him.

Which meant...

With the grace and timing of an acrobat, Fred braced himself using one hand against each vehicle, and he swung both legs upward and kicked his standing assailant in his surprised face, snapping the man's head back and leaving him in a heap on the gravel. Fred used the resistance provided by the attacker's body to twist his torso, so he landed facing the opposite direction.

By now the other man had squirmed out from under Fred's car, where moments before he had been in position to slash Fred's ankles to the bone. Fred waited, his arms open as if to embrace the man who rushed at him with a knife, an ugly snarl twisting his face. Then Fred broke his attacker's knife arm with a kick and brought his own blade up between the man's ribs in just the perfect position. He dropped dead, like a rock, at Fred's feet.

It had all happened so quickly that Fred was barely breathing hard. He was not at all tired; in fact, he was energized. The feeling of uneasiness he'd had at the Center had been dispelled. He was filled with well-being.

Fred took a quick look around the lot. All of the action had taken place behind the van, just as the two men had planned it. Nothing had been visible from the street or the Center. Fred glanced down at his front. There was no blood on his clothes. He wiped off the knife and got into his car. As he drove out of the parking lot he was smiling. He hadn't lost his touch.

Now Fred was ready to make his first appearance at Altimate Pharmaceuticals.

24

"Grant?" It was Joss.

Grant glanced at his watch. It was 5:00 p.m. He had been at his computer for hours.

"The photographer wants to have something on a computer screen when she takes this shot," Joss said.

"But my computer faces the back wall of my office."

"Not your computer," she said. "Daniele's."

Grant shook his head emphatically. "I don't want to touch her computer, Joss. She doesn't want anyone near her equipment. Especially not me, since she's decided I'm her enemy in the race to be president of Altimate. We would just be asking for trouble."

Joss crossed her arms. "We don't have another choice, Grant. We need to get this shot. Besides, the computer isn't hers. It's Altimate's. And you know the policy."

"Did you check to see if her assistant is here?" Grant asked.

"He left. Grant, you know the policy," she repeated. "Only research files are confidential and require a password. All other files are accessible without one. Including email. Nathan Horcroft said if you can't send email that anyone can see, you shouldn't send it in the first place. Besides, email legally belongs to Altimate. So put an email message on the screen."

Grant couldn't tell Joss about Daniele's threat at the school referendum last night. What would he say? Look, Joss, Daniele said when she becomes president of Altimate she's going to get rid of dead wood, and she was looking at me when she said it? But even a day later, after he had had time to cool down and think about it, Grant had no question that that was exactly the message Daniele had wanted him to get.

With Daniele already so angry, why would he do anything to antagonize her? He had no intention of ruining what chances he had of seeing Michael again.

"If you want to use her computer, you turn it on," Grant said.

Joss looked at him for a long moment, and said, "I can't. Your computers use a different operating system than mine do. You're the only one here who knows how. Help me."

Grant realized he was being forced to make a choice—antagonizing someone who already hated him or alienating his best friend. Joss hadn't raised her voice or frowned, but her red hair had a way of nearly crackling with electricity when she was intent on something. Grant decided.

With great reluctance, Grant sat at Daniele's desk and turned on her computer. He held his breath, waiting to see if she had any email.

"Nothing," he finally said with relief. "You'll have to take another shot."

"No, look. Now it's blinking," said Angie.

Grant turned back to the screen. It hadn't been blinking a moment ago.

"Call it up," Joss said.

Grant exhaled gratefully when he saw the email message:
65ue6t0ku7i5g-l=ek80k395r70-k070rl8-=0k0-k7ie7t5r=07565 -6uek-ode70-k9k0h56re[u5k570gr0rr9jr7ekte6t65=-675krtrey756 t5756l0k0ku85e6[8=6-y07ry967i560ky-6le70-kehe0[ej[5e78-966 5395r7

"Okay," Joss said. "Leave it on the screen."

"You want this?" Grant asked. "It's gibberish. There must have been an error in transmission."

"That's all right. You won't be able to read it in the picture. The camera will just pick it up as lines of print on a glowing screen."

Grant left the email on the screen, and the photographer took the shot she wanted. Grant was certain Daniele would figure out he had used her computer. He hoped he didn't live to regret his choice.

25

Grant hadn't been back in his office fifteen minutes when Joss reappeared at the door, smiling.

"What's got you puzzled?" she asked.

Grant thought she wanted to mend fences, after the shot of Daniele's computer. He welcomed that. "How do you know I'm puzzled?"

"You always bounce in your chair when you're trying to figure something out," she said. "I could hear you squeaking from the other end of the lab." She walked behind his desk to see what he was doing.

On the computer screen, stick and ball diagrams of molecules in reds, purples and blues gyrated gently, like a child's toys, on a black background.

Joss's gaze darted over the screen. "You're doing molecular modeling," she said. "That's the white twin on the left side of the screen. I don't recognize the molecule on the right. What are you looking for?"

Grant wanted to tell Joss what he had been doing. He looked forward to her objective viewpoint and her encouragement.

Grant thought for a moment how best to explain the reasoning behind the work he had spent hours on today. He wasn't sure there was a line of reasoning. It felt more like leaps across chasms—with a tiger on his heels. But once he started talking, the words poured out of him like a torrent.

"First Payne threatens the future of the white twin when he comes in this morning," he said. "Then when I want to ask him what's wrong with the drug, he's sent home from Altimate until Monday. So I have no way of finding out from him if anything really is wrong with my drug. And I won't hear from animal testing until they issue their report.

"I've got to do something, Joss. I don't want to wait until Monday or Tuesday to find out there *is* something wrong with the white twin. I want to be ready with some kind of counter measure. I do *not* want to have happen to it what happened to the black twin."

Grant shuddered inside, remembering how whipsaw fast the rejection of the black twin seemed to come.

"Then I remembered what you asked me yesterday—was there nothing wrong with the white twin? And I started thinking. I decided I would start with the brain and go from there. Now I know that there isn't necessarily any worry about a drug getting in the brain—lots of drugs do and they don't do any harm, and some drugs, like anesthetics, *have* to get in. But *if* the white twin had a negative effect on the human body, and *if* that effect were in the brain, it would be an interference with normal brain function. And the way that usually happens is if the drug and a neurotransmitter are similar in structure, so that the drug *blocks* whatever function the neurotransmitter mediates."

Joss nodded. "So you're comparing the structure of the white twin to neurotransmitters," she said. "Okay. I can understand that. Show me what you've got."

Grant tapped some keys and the screen changed. There were two colored molecules—bulbous shapes composed of connected red, blue and green balls—gyrating on the black background.

Joss watched the glowing screen. "Unless I'm missing something, there's no similarity."

"I don't think you're missing anything," Grant said. He called up another candidate molecule and compared that one with the white twin.

"Again nothing," Joss said.

Rapidly Grant called up one after another. Nothing.

When Grant finished the series, Joss said, "Well, that's one thing not to worry about." She turned to leave his office.

"Wait," Grant said. He called up another small molecule to replace the white twin on the screen.

Joss looked closely. "That's the black twin. Why would you even check that one? It was canceled."

Grant shook his head. "I don't know why I tried it, but I did. Look at this." He went through the same sequence, pairing each of the chemical messengers one by one with the black twin.

"Nothing," Joss said. She exhaled as if she had been holding her breath.

"Wait," Grant said. "Then I tried a simple *metabolite* of the black twin—something the body might break the black twin into after it was ingested."

There was absolute silence, except for the sound of Grant tapping the keys as he went through the sequence again.

With the final pairing still on the computer screen, Joss said slowly, "What does it mean to you?"

Grant stared at the screen. "It seems there's some similarity of shape between the metabolite of the black twin and this neurotransmitter. And another metabolite of the black twin might be even more similar…But what counts is how it acts in a human body," he admitted. "That's the acid test." Grant shrugged. "And there may be other neurotransmitters that I haven't checked, that the black twin or its metabolite are more similar to or less similar to. I don't know yet."

"Yet?" Joss asked.

"The brain contains at least fifty and maybe as many as two hundred different neurotransmitters. I don't have their structures at my fingertips. I had to go through research sources on the Internet to get the ones I've checked so far—and it takes time. There are a lot more to check."

Grant realized Joss looked incredulous.

"I don't believe it," Joss said. "Do you know how crazy you sound? First you say you want to be ready to defend the white twin next Tuesday, because you want to make sure it isn't canceled. So you use some offhand comment I made to justify comparing the white twin to neurotransmitters. Fine—even though the computer people already ran checks on the white twin. And you come up with nothing—just like the computer people did. Then you start working on the black twin and its supposed metabolites and come up with—whatever." She waved at the screen.

This was not the response that Grant had expected. He opened his mouth to protest, to explain, but Joss interrupted him.

"Oh, no," Joss said. "I believe that Payne threatened you. I believe that you don't want to lose the white twin. What I don't believe is that you—a professional scientist—would start looking for deception and conspiracies when you're worried about the future of your drug."

"But I didn't say anything about conspiracies," Grant said, amazed.

"You didn't have to," Joss said. "What else does it mean when you compare the black twin and its metabolites to neurotransmitters? That you want to know the *real* reason the black twin was canceled. That means you think they lied to you. Why would they lie? What would they be covering up? Why wouldn't they want you to know?"

Grant couldn't answer her. He didn't know. His intuition had only pointed him in this direction. He didn't know yet where it led.

"You know that every drug has some side effect, Grant," she said. "What we do is try to modify the drug so the side effect is minimized while the beneficial action is retained."

Joss shook her head. "You know drug companies don't cancel drugs and lie about their side effects. They work to salvage the drug so they don't lose what could be a big winner for them. Grant, do you know why I think you're doing this? I think you seized on modeling studies because it's the only thing you can do right now— the white twin is out of your hands, and you can't do any animal studies by yourself."

Grant said quietly, "Something doesn't seem right. Right now it's just a hunch. But I need to know exactly why the black twin was canceled."

"You know why the black twin was canceled, Grant. It didn't perform in animal tests. If, *if* the black twin happens to have any similarity to a neurotransmitter, it is just a coincidence."

"I think it pays to do some animal tests on the black twin to be sure," he said.

Joss was angry. "All right, Granite. Yes, that's what they call you. You can be so stubborn, as if nothing can get through to you. If everything comes crashing down on you because you followed your curiosity, maybe you'll be satisfied." She threw her hands up in the air and went back to the photographer.

Grant didn't tell Joss that if he had listened to this kind of criticism for the past three years, the black twin and the white twin wouldn't even exist. Sure, going into the unknown frightened him. He could end up being wrong and waste a lot of time. But he didn't have a choice: the unknown was where new things were.

Grant turned back to his computer. Joss's comments had shaken him. He was used to her being blunt, but tonight he thought she had wanted to hurt him. That wasn't the Joss he knew.

26

Persuasion didn't work with Grant. Ever. She knew. She had got-
ten blue in the face trying to convince him to change his mind, to
change a course of action. It didn't work. Once Grant was con-
vinced of something, no one could beat it out of him. Not even
Dena had been able to do that.

Remembering Dena reminded her of the memorial service
Grant had arranged for this Sunday. She would have to be there,
pretending to mourn...

She pushed her hair back with her fingers and began to worry
again about last night. Even though she knew his routine, she
knew his habits, she had taken a chance going to his house. But
she needed to know if he still had it.

After she was inside, Bailey had acted as if it were a game. He
had jumped up on her and licked her face. In the tussle, she was
sure he had pulled out some hair. If Grant found the red hairs,
what would he think, what would he do?

She shrugged. What happens, happens. At least she had gotten
what she came for.

Well, she had set up what she intended to be a trap for him. It
was clever, the kind of thing that would appeal to Grant. She hoped
he would take the bait. It would make everything so much easier.

But if things couldn't be done neatly, then they could be done
messily. It didn't matter to her.

At this point she just had to stop him.

27

Her feet resting on an Aubusson rug, Daniele Horcroft sat at the polished mahogany table in her father's paneled dining room. Light from the crystal chandelier glinted off exquisite china and crystal.

Daniele was pleased with her performance tonight. She had been nice to everyone: her father, Nathan; his wife, Anne; and the motley crew they had assembled. She mentally reviewed the guests.

At the head of the table was her father, the reason she was here. For months, since she'd had an inkling that he was getting close to naming a successor, she had stayed as close to him as possible. She wanted to block any move Grant made toward the presidency. After what Daniele had had to do for this job, she wasn't letting anyone else get it. She constantly applied every bit of leverage, guilt and threat possible to get her father to give Altimate to her.

Tonight as leverage she had let him keep Michael for the weekend. As guilt, she had made sure she grasped him with her little mutilated finger pressing into his upper arm, to remind him of what she had lost because of him. She was seated on Nathan's right; she planned to miss nothing.

Across from Daniele, on Nathan's left, was Dr. Eve Mallet, the internationally known and respected French infectious disease researcher. She was working on another book.

On Eve's left was Mrs. Perot. Dr. Perot sat on Daniele's right, facing his wife. Dr. Perot was a surgeon at University Hospital. Perot's wife was chair of the hospital's fundraising committee, which included Nathan's wife, Anne, so they were both here.

John Simms, grizzled and stocky, sat between Mrs. Perot and Anne. He had lost his wife several years ago, and he was here alone. A powerful and politically-connected lawyer, he was an ex-Marine who had been a friend and counselor of Nathan's for years.

Anne sat at the foot of the table. She had seated Dell Midland on her left. Dell had come alone tonight, too.

Dinner was over. Finally, Daniele thought. They were sitting over dessert; some with a drink, a few of the men with a cigar. Dr. Perot seemed to be looking for an opening. Daniele hoped he would keep it to himself. He always brought up a subject that was unpleasant.

But it was Anne Horcroft's voice that Daniele heard. She had been talking with Simms about her volunteer work at the hospital. The other voices at the table happened to drop just as she said, "Right now they can keep the virus under control and they think an AIDS cure is close."

Dell was sitting right next to her and must have been listening to her conversation because he responded immediately.

"An AIDS cure being close?" Dell said. "That seems unlikely. The virus gets into human DNA—how can anything reach it without killing the cell that contains the DNA?"

Dell shook his head. "Most of the people who have the disease refuse to take any responsibility. They act as if they're martyrs, and a lot of politicians buy it. Sometimes I wish we could send all of them back to Africa, where AIDS started!"

The conversation distracted Daniele from thoughts about herself. She stared at Dell. This was just a dinner party, but it was crazy for a politician to talk like that in front of the kind of influential people who were here. Most of them looked shocked.

Dr. Mallet sounded amazed. "AIDS was first introduced into this country on July 4, 1976, when ships from fifty-five nations poured sailors into Manhattan. It seems clear that AIDS was brought *to* Africa, as well as to the United States, from Europe."

Dell didn't contradict her. He didn't even look at her.

"Well, it's here now and we have to deal with it," Simms said.

Daniele heard murmurs of assent.

"Regardless of how or when it came here," Dell said, "it is sweeping the country. Many of the infected don't tell their partners when they're sick or use protection. Innocent children are born with this plague."

Heads nodded here and there around the room.

Daniele thought Dell's face looked intent. "The cost of hospitalization, drugs, workmen's compensation, insurance. All of these will eventually financially cripple the country," he said.

Dr. Mallet interrupted, "But they've made advances. Using a combination of drugs, the cost per individual can be reduced to maybe fifteen thousand dollars per year."

Dr. Perot added, "And it looks as if these drugs can keep people healthy. They reduce the amount of HIV in blood to levels that can't be detected by the most sensitive test available."

"So where is the good news in that?" Dell asked. "A lot of the people on this treatment no longer look or feel bad, so they've given up safe sex or even telling people that they're sick. So there's a larger population which will be alive longer to infect others."

No one contradicted him and more smoke filled the air.

"Starting treatment early means that they'll take a whole group of people who aren't showing symptoms, who were costing almost nothing to treat, and now they cost fifteen thousand dollars a year," Dell said. "There's an estimate that there are twenty-eight million people living with HIV, and nearly six million more being infected each year. What does that add up to?"

"But the cost may not be as bad as anticipated," Mrs. Perot said. "Medicaid—which is paying for treatment for probably fifty percent of the nation's AIDS patients—spends only about two percent of its budget on AIDS."

"Only?" Dell asked. "Two percent of their budget is nearly four billion dollars. And the cost of effectiveness doesn't even take into consideration lack of compliance. The treatments can involve fourteen to twenty pills a day. If the patient stops taking the drugs, the virus can break loose."

There were more murmurs of assent. Dell had a great deal of information at his fingertips, Daniele thought, and he was persuasive. Most of all, *he seemed so sure he was right*.

Nathan spoke for the first time. "Actually, there's another layer to the problem, more important even than the spread of the disease."

"What could be worse than this plague?" Anne asked.

"As we come up with new drugs, drug-resistant forms of the disease will be developed in the infected people," Nathan said.

"Simply by trying to control this disease, we will be contributing to the creation of more virulent strains."

Daniele recognized the words as Grant's, and she hated her father for parroting him.

"But there are people who are ill who engaged in no high-risk behavior," Anne said softly. "People who have gotten it from a trans—"

Dell interrupted. "Sometimes you have to make a clean sweep. Leave something behind, and you never know if it will start again, anywhere." Dell shook his head. "It seems we are driven to the point where there is no real choice," he said. "Whether treated with drugs or not, infected people will spread the disease; they can't control themselves. It is clear that any plan to control this disease has to include controlling the carriers."

Daniele looked around the table. Everyone stared at Dell; they seemed shocked, even frightened. Dell didn't seem to notice, let alone care.

Finally Simms said, "I know how you feel. The way this country works, they let a problem go until it's totally out of control. Then they try reasoning and campaigns, a dollar short and a day late. But I think you'll agree that monitoring, quarantining or getting rid of people—because that's what you really mean by 'controlling'—is illegal."

"How can you even talk this way?" Dr. Mallet said to Dell. "This is a democracy. A way of life can't be imposed on the country by a small group of indignant or outraged people—even if they think a minority group is making a mistake."

As the guests left, Daniele saw Dell go out of the door. What did she care about Dell's comments? Let the people he was after worry. All that she thought was that if Dell kept alienating people, he wasn't even going to make a decent showing in the election eleven days away.

Saturday
October 25

28

"Careful where you walk!" One of the photography assistants caught Grant's arm as he tripped over some shutters and tripods stacked outside his lab.

"Thanks." Grant recognized the assistant. It was the man with a limp who had been here last night.

Grant had arrived early, planning to get a head start on some molecular modeling. He didn't expect to find the lab jammed with people at 7:30 a.m.

Joss breezed past, stopping long enough to whisper about the photographer, "She's going to take a number of black and white polaroids until the composition and lighting suit her. Then she'll do timed exposures with color film." Joss was cordial and professional, but cool.

I'm still in the doghouse, Grant thought unhappily. He was still stinging from Joss's criticism the night before. He didn't want to alienate her. Besides her intelligence and insight, he valued her friendship.

Grant dodged photography assistants to reach Angie, who was blocking Grant's lab equipment with her body. Her crisp, white lab coat contrasted with her dark curls and her face, pink with indignation.

"Dr. Fraser! I'm so glad you're here," she said. "They want to take a shot of the set-up, and they're trying to take some of the equipment out of the hood. They say it's too *busy*."

Grant saw his plans to work in his office during shooting evaporate. He would have to stay here and guard his lab until they were finished.

"The equipment stays unchanged," Grant said. "If you can't work around it, you'll have to find another shot."

The limping assistant seemed to get the message. He moved quickly to the hood and made some adjustments to the lighting and dragged over a lab stool so part of the equipment wouldn't be visible.

By the time they wrapped up the last shot in his lab—hours after Grant had hoped to start working—he was champing at the bit to get to his computer. Yesterday he had contacted another research service over the Internet, in order to obtain more neurotransmitter structures. He wanted to compare the black twin's metabolite to them.

In spite of Joss's urging him to drop his interest in the black twin, Grant couldn't do it. He had to know if it—or the metabolite he had checked yesterday—were similar to any neurotransmitter. If it were, it might mean that the black twin wasn't canceled because it didn't work, but for some other reason. He had to know what that reason was.

When he walked into his office, he saw the number of the Animal Control Department in the middle of his desk. They were open from 8:00 a.m. to 4:00 p.m. today, so Grant called. He got a recorded message and he hung up. If he hadn't heard from Dave by now, he wasn't going to. It was three days since they'd taken the raccoons; they must be disposed of by now. Grant was disappointed. He wasn't going to find out why they died.

Grant unlocked his desk drawer to take out his lab book, and a small glass vial rolled toward him. He held it in his hand, rotated it with his fingers, watching the powder shift inside the vial. Grant held it gently, almost reverently. The vial contained a small amount of black twin, left over from the purification he'd completed the day before.

"This may be the last black twin I'll ever see or work with," Grant said quietly. He put the small vial down on top of the desk, in front of the computer screen. Then he took another vial out of his desk, a sample of white twin that he had purified. He put the two vials next to each other.

"The distillation of the past three years of my life," he said aloud. Grant shook his head and smiled wryly. That sounded melodramatic.

Grant sighed and sat forward in his chair, and picked up the two vials. These two substances, now sealed in and separated by glass, had been born together, more identical and intimate than human twins. *He* had separated them, using other molecules to reach in and sort them.

Grant suddenly had a premonition that the fate of these two molecules was linked. He shuddered, making the vials clink in his hand. He had already lost the black twin because they said it had no potential. Did that mean that the white twin would soon follow suit? For a long moment it terrified him to think that the sum total of his efforts was contained in his left hand, and that half of it had already been pronounced a failure.

Grant shook himself and turned his attention to his computer. His email showed there was one new neurotransmitter molecule waiting for him. He downloaded the information. He wanted to check its structure against the black twin's metabolite.

"Grant!" Joss's fearful voice carried from the other end of the lab. "Come here!"

29

Thrown off balance by the urgency in Joss's voice, Grant jumped up out of his chair. Without turning back to his computer, he ran through the lab. As he turned a corner and arrived on the scene, he saw a man standing in the middle of the floor, as if he were frozen, his face a mask of terror. The rest of the people ringed around him with grim faces. Grant asked, "What is it, Joss?"

"Acid."

The one word summed up the situation. Grant took one glance at the bottle and the chemical formula identifying it, and his breath died in his throat. Concentrated sulfuric acid. Grant had seen acid burns—deep and ugly and scarring. Twenty years later the scarred skin still looked twisted, pitted, stringy.

Trying to keep the fear out of his face, Grant turned his attention to the rigid assistant, staring in terror at his shirt and slacks which were wet with an almost oily fluid. A thin smoke rose from the spilled liquid. Immediately Grant pulled the man to the shower against the wall, caught him as he stumbled over the lip of the catch basin and turned the shower on. The water sprayed out, soaking the man, who stood unmoving under the torrent like a wet dog.

The only sound in the lab was the rushing water. None of the onlookers moved. Standing in a semicircle, their faces were solemn.

For long minutes Grant kept the man under the shower until his clothes were drenched, making certain that the force of the shower was on the acid stains. When Grant turned off the shower, he had the man peel off his wet clothes. Grant poured a dilute solution of alkali over the man's skin. Then he tested the man's skin with pH paper, to determine if there were any residue of the concentrated sulfuric acid.

Finally, Grant nodded his okay.

There was a huge sigh of relief and applause from everyone in the lab. The techs got enough spare clothes for the man to get dressed. The photographer told him to go home and he left, after thanking Grant profusely. The crew packed up and moved to the executive area.

Half-shaking, half-high from narrowly averted disaster, Grant returned to his lab. He still wanted to compare the new neurotransmitter to the black twin metabolite he had studied last night. Grant called up the modeling program, and then brought the new neurotransmitter molecule up on the screen next to the metabolite. Grant held his breath, but he didn't have long to wait.

"I can't believe it," he whispered. This neurotransmitter molecule was more similar to the black twin metabolite than was any of the others that Grant had seen.

The pressure inside Grant had been building up for months. Dena's death. The abrupt cancellation of the black twin. Payne's unending harassment and threats. He needed an escape valve. But while Grant's human nature felt the urge to *do something*, his scientific nature held him back, saying there was no solid lead to act on.

Well, now he had a lead.

Grant was halfway out of his chair, on his way to get Joss, when he remembered last night. Joss had blown up at him, insisting that it was just a coincidence that the black twin metabolite had any similarity to a neurotransmitter. There was no point in showing her the two molecules on his computer screen.

Grant turned off his computer. He needed to talk to *someone*.

He picked up the phone and called John Stedman, a close friend since graduate school. John worked for Pharmaplex, near New Haven. He was in his lab, as usual.

"I need your advice, John," Grant said.

"I know. What else is new?"

Grant didn't answer him.

"It's something important to you?" John asked.

"Yes."

John sighed. "Come on up."

30

Angie was watching the techs carefully clean up the broken glass and splashes of acid. As she listened to the clinking of glass shards falling in a wastecan, Angie was suddenly sure that something was wrong. It was just a feeling; if she had tried to tell anyone, she would have sounded ridiculous. She was a scientist, and she didn't have any proof.

But she had the strange feeling that the acid spill hadn't been an accident. She had seen the bottle of acid on a shelf. She had used it before; she knew how much it contained. It was nowhere near where the photography assistants had been working. So how had that man gotten it on his clothes?

Although she wasn't *sure* it hadn't been an accident, she somehow felt tricked, and that made her feel vulnerable and angry. She always tried to be prepared, to be on her toes. She never liked to be caught without having done her homework. It was why she had always been at the top of her class. She took pride in always doing her job and always being vigilant. Right now it was her job to watch and protect Grant's experimental set-up.

What did *that* mean? she asked herself. Her heart started beating faster. Had the accident really been a diversion? Had someone gotten Grant out of his office so they could go in?

Angie rushed back to Grant's part of the lab. Grant was gone. But Joss was standing at the doorway to his office. She looked surprised when she saw Angie.

"Has Grant gone out?" she asked Angie.

What was Joss doing here? Angie wondered. The photographer and her crew were already headed to the executive area. Joss was supposed to be with them at all times. She was never supposed to leave them alone. Angie felt like biting her ragged pink fingernails.

"I don't know," Angie said. "He didn't say anything to me before he left."

Joss shrugged and left.

As soon as Joss was out of the lab, Angie hurried over to the experimental set-up. Her practiced glance quickly checked it over. She had put the glassware together; she knew it intimately. It looked all right.

Then she went to Grant's office. She scanned the tops of all the surfaces, looking to see if he had left any confidential material out. Everything looked normal.

Then she got Grant's key to his desk. She had put the key in the lock before she realized it was already open. With trembling hands she pulled open the drawer and reached inside, searching for the vials of black twin and white twin that she and Grant had just purified. She froze in shock as she realized that both vials were gone.

31

Daniele leaned back into the car seat, her arctic white suit nestling into the soft grey leather, and adjusted her manicured hands on the steering wheel.

A man in a business suit was on her left, looking over the car. As if he knew a race car from a dog cart, she thought. He stopped in front, critically admiring the grille and apparently the paint job. Then he leaned over and rubbed his fingers on the hood.

She shoved the accelerator to the floor.

"Can I be of help?"

Daniele looked up. A kid was leaning his idiotically smiling face in the window, already intruding with his voice and his body. This underaged salesman would want to know all her vital statistics before he would even tell her what other colors the biggest Mercedes came in.

"Yes," she smiled sweetly. "To someone else."

Daniele had called ahead and spoken to the manager. She wanted his personal attention, or she wasn't going to buy a car from his dealership.

"Ms. Horcroft?"

As the pot-bellied manager scurried over to her, she eyed him critically. To start with, he was wearing a fake Cartier watch, and his slacks were a fraction too short and not cut generously enough.

Daniele didn't get out of the car. She rolled the window halfway down and moved the seat back. The manager came over and leaned over uncomfortably to speak in the window.

"We have the three models we discussed on the phone."

She had been planning to buy this car in a week or so, as a celebration present for herself. But a number of things had been stressing her lately, and she had decided to get the car early, to raise her spirits.

One of the stresses was Whitney Payne.

He was playing the part beautifully, she admitted. Putting Grant down and frustrating him at every turn. Lately, he was even sounding as if he actually knew what he was talking about.

And then he had to get involved in a bar fight.

She shuddered. If Payne kept getting in trouble, her father might do something stupid. And that would set off a chain of reactions that even Daniele couldn't anticipate. She needed to be appointed president soon.

"This is the most fully-loaded model," the manager was saying. "It includes...."

Daniele tuned him out. She didn't care about all the details; she just wanted the best.

At least the referendum had turned out well. Nathan had even called her, to tell her how pleased he had been with her efforts even though her side had lost. She snorted. *Her* side, she thought contemptuously.

"...and will you be using our financing package?" the manager continued.

"No," she said.

He looked flustered, as if his deal were going out the window.

"Cash," she said. "I'll pay cash."

32

It seemed to Joss that the photographer had been dragging her feet. It was only 5:30 p.m., but Joss had been up late the night before, and had then gotten up early this morning. She just wanted to go home, shower, sleep. She didn't even care if she ate.

"She would like you to look at this shot."

It was one of the photographer's assistants. Joss noticed that the man who held the polaroid was limping slightly. He was tall and seemed strongly built. He was wearing thick, dark-rimmed glasses and had his hair combed down, so Joss couldn't see his face well.

So the queen bee needs me? Joss thought, watching the photographer.

"Looks like the queen bee needs you," the man said.

Joss was surprised that he had spoken her thoughts. He looked as if he were surprised that he had said something candid like that aloud. Then his gaze slid away from her.

Joss crossed the floor, assuming that the photographer wanted her input on the composition of the shot. But all the woman wanted was someone to deal with some stained carpeting. Joss counted to ten and then made some helpful suggestions.

Joss returned to her observation post, regretting that she had chosen a career that involved *any* interaction with other people. She resented having to constantly adapt her demeanor, voice and conversation to the needs and whims of a series of prima donnas. Including Dell and Grant.

Dell's second-in-command, Robbins, had already called her. He was dictating every aspect of the event Joss had agreed to host. She wondered if Dell were going to give her a script to read as well.

And *Grant*. His experiences had taught him nothing. He still didn't know how to take no for an answer. She knew he wasn't letting go of the black twin—even though Altimate told him it was a dud.

Joss couldn't believe it was a matter of Grant's ego refusing to accept that he'd produced a loser. Grant had had losers before; he'd always moved on. But this time, far from letting go, he'd become *more* interested in the black twin after it had been canceled. Why? What did he suspect? No matter, she told herself. Grant's obsession was going to be his downfall.

To distract herself, she looked around the executive area. Like an anthill that had been kicked over, it was swarming with the photographer's helpers, running to and fro on missions that they treated as if they were life-and-death matters.

The limping assistant was approaching her again. Something made her curious about him. What was it?

"There's a call for you," he said. "Jane Zimmer from Corporate News."

Joss rose, wondering why Jane had called on one of Altimate's phones, when she could have used Joss's cellular phone.

The man glanced at her briefcase. "Maybe you turned off your cellular phone."

Joss had opened her briefcase to look—the phone was off—before she realized he had answered an unspoken question. She shrugged it off. Maybe she had glanced at her briefcase, and he was very observant.

He pointed behind her, almost around the corner of one of the conference rooms. "Could you please take the call over there?"

Joss glanced where he was pointing. It couldn't have been further from where the photography was going on. It was like being in outer Mongolia.

"I hope it doesn't seem like outer Mongolia," the man said.

Joss glanced up sharply. That was the third time he'd seemingly read her mind. Then she dismissed it, realizing she was dead-tired, and that it was no compliment to consider that the two of them thought in trite expressions or in the obvious.

He lowered his voice. "She doesn't like any noise while she's setting up a shot. She'll just wait until you're finished. Or longer..."

Joss got the hint. She would be punished for making any noise.

Both of them were watching the photographer. The limping

man spoke again. "I"ve already asked three favors of her today," he said.

Without thinking, Joss said, "Baba Yaga will eat you up if you ask for a fourth."

Now it was the man's turn to look surprised, and Joss realized that he had been on the point of saying those same words. Where had that come from? She hadn't thought of the old Russian fairy tale character in years.

The man was still looking at her. "Baba Yaga lived in a small house in a clearing in the forest," he began.

"The house was supported on chicken legs, which scratched in the dirt," Joss continued.

"And it turned all day to face the sun," he completed.

As Joss recalled, Baba Yaga could answer any question that you put to her. But there was a catch—she would answer just three questions. If you asked a fourth, she would fall upon you and devour you.

"It pays to be cautious," Joss said, smiling, "and well-read." Why was she smiling at him? Joss wondered. He was disarming, and not because of how he looked. There was just something... familiar about him. He felt like a kindred spirit. She shook herself. What was she saying? He was a photographer's assistant.

"When you deal with witches, you have to be cautious," he said.

"Do you deal with a lot of them?" Joss asked.

"I make a living out of it."

He was looking directly at her for the first time, and Joss could see something in his eyes, an openness. He wasn't used to being open, she thought, and he was surprised that he was being open with her. Joss shook herself again. She didn't know this man. What kinds of things was she imagining about him?

"I'll take the phone over there," she said quickly. "She can't take that long." I've discussed this article to death with Jane, Joss thought. It isn't competing for a Pulitizer prize. It's just a little public relations for Altimate.

After the call, the photographer plodded through two more shots. Joss got home after midnight.

33

Grant let up on the gas pedal. The Merritt Parkway wasn't particularly well-patrolled by the state police, but he still didn't want to take a chance on being stopped for speeding. He set his windshield wipers on high and clicked on the high beams for a moment, to make sure there was nothing up ahead on the road. Then he turned on the low beams.

As Grant drove north on the Parkway just south of Hamden, he passed through a tunnel. He was so absorbed in his thoughts that it took him a few moments to notice that something was different as he came out of the tunnel. Then it hit him with the combined force of shock and fear. All his lights were out! Headlights, instrument panel lights and brake lights. Grant wanted to get off the road. But when he tried to turn the wheel, he got a second shock. His steering column was frozen, turned slightly to the right. That meant no gas—but he had just filled up the tank this morning.

Grant tried his brakes, afraid they might not respond either. He felt a rush of relief as they held, but just barely. He started to skid, but he didn't let up on the brakes. He was afraid that if he did, he might lose them, too.

The frozen steering column was heading him into the right lane, and his car was still moving pretty fast. The car next to him would give him no quarter. "Move over!" he gestured. The other driver just lay on his horn.

Even with his brake foot all the way to the floor, Grant was still skidding into the right lane. He tensed, waiting to hit the other car.

Just when he was sure they were going to collide, the other car braked and veered to the left behind Grant. Grant's path was now clear, but he was headed toward the edge of the road and the roped barrier. He didn't have a choice: he hit the barrier.

Grant's face was knocked into the steering wheel. He saw stars from the pain and reflexively let go of the steering wheel as he felt for his nose. Then as the car dipped abruptly over the edge, he grabbed the wheel again, just to keep from being bounced around.

The car rocked back and forth, and Grant's head hit the driver's window hard. With the car jerking around in the dark so much, Grant couldn't see what was ahead. Though he was still pushing as hard as he could on the brake, it was friction from the unseen vegetation he was plowing through that finally brought the car to a stop.

When the car stopped, Grant still felt as if he were moving. The blood rushing in his ears made him dizzy. He closed his eyes and swallowed. Gently he moved his head, his fingers and his toes. He ached in a lot of places, but everything still seemed to function. Then he smelled gas.

Grant climbed out of the car and found that he'd somehow twisted his left ankle. Half-hobbling, half-running, he made his way back to and up the embankment, diagonally away from the car, up to the road. He stood, bent over and breathing hard.

Honking and yelling attracted his attention back down the highway, where he saw two cars hinged together, blocking both lanes. Both drivers had gotten out and were yelling at each other. Grant was grateful that it looked as if no one had been hurt. He was also grateful that they hadn't seen him—he was in no shape to face the irate drivers.

It was raining harder now, and Grant wondered if he should have stayed with the car. Had he done the scared rabbit routine, fleeing his car because he thought he'd smelled gas? And then an explosion hit him from behind, knocking him down, flat out on the wet shoulder. That did it. His stomach unsettled, and he was sick where he lay. He was shaking now.

Lightning flashed, and Grant had an ant's-eye view of the side of the road. The police would arrive soon, alerted by someone who had seen or heard the explosion. Who knew how they would react to a burning car by the highway? They might assume he was drunk or on drugs. They might insist on a breath test, even try to search him. The police weren't always rational or predictable. And they wouldn't be at their best now, when they were called out in the pouring rain.

Still lying on the side of the road, Grant pulled out his cell phone and dialed John's lab.

"Grant? I thought you'd be here by now."

"Listen, I've had an accident." Grant told John quickly what had happened.

"Where are you?" John asked.

"Right under the Exit 60, Hamden one mile sign." Grant smiled wryly—John didn't know how literally true that was. "Do you know where it is?"

"I'll be there in ten minutes," John said. "Can you hold on?"

"Sure."

Grant got up slowly and looked down at himself. His whole front was breaded with small, gritty, wet gravel. He wiped himself off as best he could and made his way to the side of the road, where he sat on a small stanchion, shivering and hoping that John would get there before the police.

34

Grant's hopes that the police would take a while to arrive were dashed when two cars roared up, lights flashing and sirens wailing. His heart started beating faster, with the first stirrings of fear.

The troopers in the second car headed for the twisted cars across the road. The two in the lead car approached him. One shined a flashlight on Grant while the other stood, with his hand on his holster, next to the first.

"Your car?" the first one asked, waving his flashlight toward the fiery heap.

"Yes," Grant said. Weren't cops even supposed to ask if you were hurt?

Haloed by the headlights behind him, only the trooper's outline was visible to Grant: the trooper's distinctive wide-brimmed hat, left hand holding the flashlight, right hand on his holster, legs spread. Grant reached a hand up to wipe his eyes and forehead, and the hand came back red.

"My forehead's cut, and my nose is bleeding," Grant said, surprised when he realized what had been dripping in his eyes and mouth wasn't just rainwater.

"What happened?" the trooper asked.

Grant reached for his forehead gingerly, searching for the cut. It was under his hair. "My electrical system died," he said. "Then my steering column froze." He didn't say anything about the explosion.

The trooper didn't say anything for a beat. Then, "The electrical system and the steering?" he asked.

Grant's fear increased a notch. He was already blinded by the rain; he didn't have the benefit of a wide-brimmed hat to shade his eyes. And he was blinded by having to stare into two sets of lights. "That's right."

"The steering wheel is on a different system from the electrical system," the trooper said.

Grant was wet, shaken up, blinded and getting angry. He was about to make an angry reply when he realized what a mistake it would be to set these two off. They probably looked for someone to give them an excuse to use their guns. He took a deep breath and wiped the rain out of his face. "I'm not a mechanic," Grant said. "I can't explain it."

The trooper didn't turn his head, but he said, "I don't know how much they'll be able to tell from your car when it's finished burning."

Grant didn't say anything.

"Can you walk?" the trooper asked. It was the first time he'd questioned Grant about his physical condition. He moved slightly closer to Grant, but didn't move the flashlight beam from Grant's face and hands. The second officer followed, still without a word.

Grant stood up slowly. What next? he wondered, his heart beating hard.

"Could I see some identification?" the police officer asked.

Slowly Grant removed his wallet from his pants and pulled out his license. The trooper asked Grant if he knew the license number of his car; Grant told him. As he moved toward the trooper to give him the identification, the trooper looked up sharply at him.

"You were sick," he said accusingly.

"I don't run off the road every day," Grant said. "It shook me up." Grant reached up again to wipe the blood out of his eyes.

The trooper didn't say anything for a second. He handed the identification to a third trooper who materialized out of the rain and then went back toward his car, presumably to call the information in and make sure Grant's car wasn't stolen.

Grant was oscillating between fear and anger. Why were they treating him like a criminal?

"Would you mind taking a breath test?" the first trooper asked.

Good Lord, Grant thought. Someone tries to kill me, and these idiots are intent on finding a drunk—or a drugged—driver. John, where are you?

"Why?" Grant asked. He knew he had to buy time.

The two troopers slowly began to advance on Grant, as if on a signal. "If you refuse to take the test, you'll have to come to the station."

Grant backed up a step. "I didn't say I wouldn't take one. Do you suspect every person who's had a car accident?"

Now both troopers began to slowly pull their pistols from their holsters.

Grant's heart seemed to stop. He began to sway. This was a bad dream. What were these two trying to prove? And what had he gotten himself in the middle of?

Both troopers pulled their guns. "I think you'd better come with us," the first said.

A car sped along the shoulder and pulled to a shimmying stop near Grant, spraying him with gravel. Two men jumped out. Grant recognized the first man as John. He didn't recognize the second man.

The second man went directly to the first trooper, his hands open and in front of him, holding what must have been identification. When he reached the trooper, he spoke quietly but forcefully, with sharply defined arm movements. John walked quickly over to Grant.

"Are you okay?" He looked directly in Grant's eyes. "You look terrible."

"I'm not hurt," Grant said.

John turned his attention to the man who had come with him. Grant watched the man's back. "Who did you bring?"

"Lawyer."

Grant was amazed. "You can summon a lawyer in ten minutes?"

John didn't smile. "He's a friend."

Grant's stomach was in a knot when the lawyer and the first trooper turned and walked toward him.

The lawyer glanced at Grant. "I've told Trooper Evans that the first order of business is to have you examined at a hospital. There's no one here who can make the determination that you weren't injured in that accident." He nodded toward the still burning car. "If there were any injury to your head or spinal column, minutes are vital."Grant was so relieved that his legs felt like jello.

"Let's get you to a hospital."

The lawyer turned toward the trooper. "If you like, you can follow us and take a statement there, after the doctors have assured me that Dr. Fraser isn't injured."

John and the lawyer helped Grant to their car. Grant slid into the back seat and sighed gratefully when the motor started and they drove away.

35

Fred watched Grant drive away with the two men. Fred couldn't follow them because he was behind the police barricade on the highway. What the hell was going on, he wondered?

Last night, disguised as the limping photography assistant, Fred had overheard Grant tell Joss there was a structural similarity between a metabolite of the black twin and a neurotransmitter. So Grant suspected that that metabolite might affect the brain! A mind-affecting drug would be right up A.R. Lab's alley, Fred had thought. If he could deliver both Grant and his drug, it would be a major feather in his cap.

First, though, he had wanted to be sure. Fred had planned to get a sample of black twin and send it to a friend of his at A.R. Labs, who would test it without saying anything to Smith.

But something had bothered Fred—the same thing that bothered Grant. If the metabolite affected the brain, why didn't the people at Altimate know? Or if they did, why hadn't they told Grant? Fred had decided that it might help to install a couple of phone taps.

This morning he had come prepared. While the photographer shot Grant's lab, Fred had tapped Nathan Horcroft's phone. Then Fred had tapped Grant's phone while Grant saved the man who had spilled acid on himself.

An acid spill was a helpful ruse when he had to work near people, Fred thought, because it never failed to capture the audience's full and undivided attention. Though, if anyone had tested the liquid, they would have discovered it wasn't concentrated sulfuric acid.

Fred had found the two labeled vials on Grant's desk and had taken samples. He had put the samples in a small box, and sent them directly to his friend at A.R. Labs.

———

But this evening…Fred shook his head, remembering. Nothing was what he had expected it to be. He had followed Grant because he wanted to know who Grant was going to see. Fred wouldn't be happy if Grant talked about the black twin with *anyone*, even an old friend like John Stedman. If the drug proved to be something Fred wanted to take to A.R. Labs, he didn't want someone else getting his hands on it.

And he never expected Grant's car to run off the road and explode. Grant had apparently called John Stedman for help. And the other man who came with him? Fred pegged him as a lawyer, based on everything from the way he dressed to the way he walked toward the cops. But why had Grant felt the need for a lawyer?

Fred's assignment was turning into more than a simple evaluation of a candidate for A.R. Labs. He was glad now that he had installed the phone taps. But he was uneasy about the attempts on Grant's life because he had no idea where they had come from or why. He didn't want to get caught in the crossfire.

36

When Grant woke up, he was lying on his back, strapped down, his head immobilized, inside some kind of machine.

"Don't move!" a voice commanded. He realized he must be in a CAT scan machine, and he was still. Otherwise he knew they would have to do the brain scan all over again.

Grant could hear two men talking. One of them was John. He assumed the other was a doctor.

"Looks okay to me," the doctor said. "Could be just a mild concussion, could be he was just exhausted by the experience. Listen," he told John, "someone should observe him overnight—awaken him occasionally to make sure he acts normally. And check to see if his pupils stay the same size."

"Okay," John said. "Thank you."

Right, Grant thought. Who was going to observe him overnight—Bailey?

They must have moved away or stopped talking, because Grant couldn't hear them anymore. He wondered how long he was supposed to stay in this machine. He was beginning to feel claustrophobic. He wanted to ask the doctor, but he knew that using his voice would move his head, however slightly.

Grant tried to breathe regularly, hoping that would calm him. Instead, as if to spite him, his heart rate increased, and the pounding jarred his chest.

He couldn't see anything or hear anything, and he began to panic. He wanted to move, to push himself out of this thing, but he knew they were just trying to help him, checking if his head or brain were injured.

Grant knew why he was afraid—he was being forced to confront his actions and decisions. As long as he was in motion, racing to meet John, running away from a burning car, he could avoid any thoughts that he didn't want to listen to. But confined in the dark of a brain-scanning machine, where he couldn't move, Grant's thoughts came home to roost like birds. He felt as if he were running headlong down a narrow road straight off a cliff.

37

The room was dark, except for the night light. She pretended it was for safety reasons, in case she got out of bed. But it was really to keep back the shadows that seemed to move in on her more and more.

She lay on her back, unmoving, staring at the ceiling. The more she stared, the more she thought she saw the dark move.

He had come through again. They had told her it was foolproof—a locked steering wheel, no lights and a bomb—but Grant had survived. If she didn't want to reach her goal so much she could taste it, she would laugh. Instead, she felt helpless and angry.

She stretched her leg toward the other side of the bed, her bare foot sliding under the covers. There was no one there. There hadn't been, for a long time. She told herself that she was glad to be alone, glad not to have to deal with someone else's uncontrollable habits and selfishness.

Tomorrow was the memorial service. They had told her to let it go, that they would take care of it. Right. She hadn't listened to them. She had a surprise for Grant at Dena's gravestone.

Sunday
October 26

38

It looked to Daniele as if Grant were the first person to arrive at the memorial chapel. Bright and early. No surprise—he had arranged for this service, and he probably wanted to make sure everything was perfect. What a brown nose.

Daniele had arrived early, by herself. She hadn't wanted anyone with a long face whimpering and climbing all over her as she made her way to a seat.

"Nathan will be sitting here." Grant motioned her to the front pew.

"So?" she asked.

He was always telling people what to do, she thought. What was she, an idiot? She couldn't find a place to sit without him? She walked to the end of the second row. That would be close enough to Nathan, and he could feel her eyes on the back of his head through the whole service.

"The Westport Taxpayer's Group was very grateful to you for all the work you did for them," he said.

Daniele looked at Grant.

"What are you, their official greeter and thanker?"

"No," he said. "I just heard them sing your praises at the referendum."

Daniele felt like giving him a nasty reply, but she decided to take another tack.

"Don't be so modest, Grant. You did a lot of work for them, too."

"Not as much as you," he said.

"Well, it's too bad we didn't win," she said.

Grant shrugged. "It seemed that they had the votes up until the last day."

What did he care? she wondered. He wasn't the dirt poor kid anymore.

"Elections are always unpredictable. Unlike you," she said.

Grant began to open his mouth, but closed it and didn't say anything.

"Aren't you going to ask me what I mean?" she asked. Come on, Grant, take the bait.

"Okay," he sighed. "How am I predictable, Daniele?"

Daniele waved an arm to encompass the chapel. "You arrange for a touching service, invite a hoard of mourners, sit the grieving family up front. Then you make your move. 'Daniele,' you say plaintively, 'can Mikey come out and play?'"

Daniele noted with great satisfaction that Grant's face had gone pale.

"Well, Mikey can't come out to play. Not today, not ever. Not with you."

Grant backed away from her, and Daniele noted with delight that he looked almost as stricken as the day he learned that Dena had died.

39

"Why so glum, kitten?"

Angie looked up in surprise at Tom. Why was he acting so familiar with her?

"It's a memorial service. Not a party," she said, frowning. "And my name isn't kitten."

"What?" Tom looked mystified.

"When you came over, you said, 'Why so glum, kitten?'"

"No, I didn't. I said, 'Why so glum, *gitten*.' Didn't you tell me the other day that means 'friend' in German?"

"No!" she said, stifling a laugh. "You're not even close."

"I give up, Angie. You're the one who has a natural ability for languages. Do you get your talent from either of your parents?"

Angie could feel her face get hot. "My father didn't like my ability with languages. He said it was 'getting above myself.' So I had to study in secret."

"Sorry, I didn't mean to pry."

Angie waved her hand. "It was long ago. It doesn't matter."

"Well, does your language ability include computer languages?" he asked. "I'd like to learn more about programming."

Angie shook her head quickly. "No. Just spoken languages." She didn't want to start a private tutoring service. "Look, I'm sorry I snapped at you. I guess I'm just upset today. It was a year ago that the accident happened, but this brings it up all over again."

"I understand," Tom nodded. "It was a terrible thing. Dena was one of the nicest people I've ever known. Smart, too. She was one of the last people I thought anything bad would happen to."

"Yes," Angie said. "It's like when famous people die, especially when they're young. They seem to have so much life, everything seems to go right for them, they're golden. As if nothing can touch them. Then they're gone, just like everyone else. It reminds you that none of us gets out of this world alive. No matter what you do."

"Wow, this place has gotten to you," Tom said. "I don't remember you ever being this serious." His eyes opened wider. "You used to work for Dena. I'd forgotten. So you must have been closer to her than I was."

"Yes, I worked for her when I first joined Altimate. I was supposed to work for Daniele, but Dena rescued me. She was a friend and a mentor. And it was a lot more interesting with her. Daniele doesn't come up with as many ideas as Dena and Grant."

The memorial service began, and Tom took his seat.

Angie hoped she hadn't gabbed on too much. She tended to do that with men. She started biting her nails again.

40

Fred stood at the back of the chapel, behind a stone column, watching and listening. Today he was playing the role of a caretaker—they attracted nearly as little attention as did the elderly and the handicapped.

Fred looked out over the gathering of mourners. The chapel was full. With a twinge, Fred watched Dell Midland, the gubernatorial candidate, bend over to talk to Joss. She seemed unwilling to talk to him, but he didn't look as if he cared. Politicians, Fred thought. You couldn't insult them or get rid of them when they wanted something.

It seemed that a lot of the people who had come to pay their respects worked at Altimate—including the president, Nathan Horcroft. So that was how things fit together, Fred thought. The little boy he'd seen at the Westport Library was Horcroft's grandson. All during the service Horcroft had held the boy; he acted like family.

And Daniele? She was the mother—but that was clear only from conversation, not from how she acted toward the child. Dena must have been very different, Fred thought. He couldn't imagine anyone coming to a service like this for Daniele. He'd heard her talking to her father. She was a grade-A manipulator.

The really interesting part, Fred thought, was when Grant saw Michael. The look he gave the boy—Fred wouldn't have guessed Grant was capable of so much warmth. And there was something else…But it was just conjecture.

Admit it, he told himself. You were impressed by Grant. His eulogy had moved a number of people in the chapel to tears.

Fred was now half-listening to the eulogy, when he heard something that caught his attention: a repetitive sound. Slowly the scene in front of him dissolved, and Fred remembered something he'd forgotten since it happened. When he'd awakened in the hos-

pital after brain surgery, *there had been another man with Smith.*
Fred hadn't been able to see the man because of his bandages.
But he had heard him. And the unseen figure with Smith had
made the same sound that Fred now heard in the memorial chapel.

Fred was alert, listening and watching for the source of the
sound. He scanned the area for movement as well as noise—the
echoing effect of the stone made it necessary. Finally, he found it.
In a corner of the chapel, a man was sitting at the head of a pew,
near a stone pillar.

The man was tapping his wedding ring, probably unconsciously, against the pillar. The shadowy figure with Smith in the
hospital had been tapping his ring against Fred's bed.

As the mourners brushed past Fred on their way out of the
memorial chapel, some sixth sense told him that it was very important that he find out who that man was.

41

"Grant?" Nathan Horcroft reached out and touched Grant gently on the arm.

Grant lifted his head slowly. He was still sitting in the pew in the memorial chapel, but he had been miles and years away. Slowly he realized that Nathan was holding Michael. Grant reached out eagerly for the boy and stopped when he saw he was asleep. Nathan held the little boy so Grant could look at him. How much he had changed in the months he hadn't seen him, Grant thought.

Grant had one question for Nathan. "How is he?"

"Much better now," Nathan said. "The doctor thought he'd picked up some infection." He looked down at Michael. "We're taking good care of him."

Nathan shifted the sleeping boy in his arms. "I'm going to try to take him again this week," he added.

Michael stirred in his sleep, and then his eyes slowly opened. He looked at Grant for a long, sleepy moment, with no sign of recognition. Grant's heart sank. Then the little boy's eyes opened wider.

"Grant." He stretched out his arms, smiling. "Grant." Nathan handed him over tenderly.

Grant cradled him, his eyes and arms devouring him. Through the sweater and pants, Grant could feel skinny limbs. Michael felt so light, as if he could float away. His skin was translucent and a fine tracery of veins was visible in his temples.

"How are you doing?" Grant asked.

"Great," Michael said. "Are you coming to visit?" He looked wistful. "And bringing Bailey?" he added.

"Sure. Soon," Grant said. He held the boy more tightly. Grant didn't want to let go of Michael. His hands and arms would not release him. He hadn't realized how attached he was. Grant didn't want to lose the child. He bent his head over Michael's and kissed his forehead.

Nathan interrupted, his voice husky. "Do you want to come out with us to…" He had never been able to say gravestone. "Before we leave."

Anne Horcroft spoke up. "I'll stay here with Michael, Nathan. It's too chilly for him."

Michael clung to Grant. "I want to go with Grant."

"We won't be long," Nathan said.

Some leaves had turned and were falling from the trees. Their path to Dena's grave was littered with crispy, papery shapes in red, yellow and brown. Grant carried the boy in his arms. He seemed to swim in his clothes.

Michael waved at the gravestones. "What are they for?" he asked.

"To mark the graves of people who have died."

Michael paused, as if considering. "Like Aunt Dena?"

"Yes," Grant said.

Michael took a deep breath and sighed. Grant could feel the small chest expand against his arms.

"But why do they have to be marked?" Michael asked.

"So people know where they are."

"Would they forget?"

There was something in the way he asked, a wavering quality in his voice.

"Not forget," Grant said. "It's just hard to find things in a place this big."

Michael leaned his head against Grant's chest and looked up at him. "If I was here," he said, "would you forget where I am?"

He said it so simply and straightforwardly that it knifed Grant in the heart. Tears sprang to his eyes before he could stop them. The scene in front of him swam as if he were looking at it through a kaleidoscope. He squeezed Michael tightly, tears running down his face. "You're not going to be here. You're not."

Nathan and Anne got to the gravestone first. Suddenly, it struck Grant how much Nathan had aged in the past year.

Ivy trailed over Dena's stone. Dead leaves and even dirt partly obscured her name. Nathan bent down toward the stone. Then he put his face in his hands. "She's gone," he said, his voice shaking.

Anne knelt down beside him, whispered in his ear and helped him stand up.

"I want to see the stone," Michael said. He wriggled out of Grant's arms and stood, wavering slightly, at the stone. His face was solemn. Then he kneeled at the grave and leaned forward.

Nathan's face crumpled. He began to sob softly, and his shoulders heaved. Anne took him in her arms.

Michael's attention was focused on the grave. He was still very solemn.

"The leaves are in the way. See, you can't even read her name. And I can spell," he looked up at Grant, "a little. 'D'... 'E'... There's a 'N' and a 'A' under the leaves."

He reached out a hand to the ivy and tugged at a leaf. A squirrel tore in front of him, scattering leaves. Michael started and his hand jerked. He fell back, a strip of ivy in his hand. He lay very still.

The three adults were frozen. Then they all reached for him.

Good God, Grant prayed, not Michael. Not Michael. Without realizing it, Grant knocked his hand against a tombstone in his haste to get to the little boy. He cracked the skin open over a knuckle and left a trail of blood on the stone.

But Michael looked up at them—and burst out laughing. He laughed until the laughter shook his small frame.

"The squirrel surprised me." He laughed again.

Grant scooped him up. "You scared us," he said, kissing the top of his head.

"Good." Michael laughed some more.

Even Nathan smiled. It was good to hear Michael laugh, Grant thought.

Grant carried Michael back along the path to Nathan's car. He didn't want to let go of him. Finally, Nathan gently pried him away from Grant. Nathan and Anne left with Michael, who gave a small wave.

Grant waved back with a lump in his throat. He fought down a fear that he wouldn't see the boy again.

42

She had watched the scene at the gravestone from a distance. She couldn't believe it—no one touched the stone! She had painstakingly set the stage: put a precious drop of liquid on each of the sharp edges of the stone. She had even pulled some vines over it to obscure the letters of Dena's name, and she had sprinkled some soil over the stone, too. But no one had tried to clean it off. Didn't they care what it looked like?

She was so frustrated that she was shaking. When she got this way, when something was blocking her from what she wanted, she just wanted to destroy something, anything. Anyone. It didn't matter who.

43

"What are those bruises from?" Joss took Grant's arm and turned his head so she could see the dark patches on his neck. "Did you have someone look at them?"

Grant nodded. "Last night."

Grant had needed a ride to and from the cemetery, but Joss waited until they were heading to her car after the memorial service before she commented on the bruises.

They were standing alone on the road running through the cemetery. The other people had left.

"What happened?" she asked. "Tell me."

"You know that the computer modeling I was working on last Friday showed some similarities between a metabolite of the black twin and one or two neurotransmitters," Grant said.

Of course she knew, Joss thought.

"Yesterday I compared it to another neurotransmitter. This one had enough similarity to make me think the metabolite really might affect the brain. Joss, if it actually took the place of a neurotransmitter, it might prevent whatever function the neurotransmitter performed or initiated. That means the metabolite could simply *stop* whatever activity that particular area of the brain controlled."

Joss shook her head. "That's a very big if, Grant."

Grant nodded. "Last night I wanted to talk to someone. So I drove up to Pharmaplex to talk to John."

Joss already knew that he had gone there; she had overheard him make the call. "Stedman? John doesn't deal in generalities. How much did you tell him about the black twin? You didn't show him a copy of your modeling information, did you?"

Grant interrupted her. "I gave him a sample of the black twin."

"You what?" She was shocked.

"I want to know for sure if metabolites of the black twin affect the brain, and what part or parts of the brain are affected," he said. "Testing rats is the fastest way to get an answer."

Joss was furious. "So that's why you rushed off last night after the shoot. This is the point of no return, isn't it, Grant? You've taken proprietary material out of the labs and given it to the competition." Grant was the last person she thought would have done something like this—this betrayal. It was another reminder that she wasn't a good judge of men.

"Why did you have to go to John?" she asked. "Couldn't you just have checked what that particular neurotransmitter did in the body?"

"That wouldn't have been conclusive, Joss; you know that. There's only one way to find out what the metabolite would do in a rat: give radioactively-labeled black twin to the rats, let it circulate in their bodies, then sacrifice them and examine prepared slices of brain tissue. The radioactive labeling would show—on photographic film—where in the brain the black twin's metabolite accumulated, indicating what kinds of activities it could block."

"*If* it affects the brain," she corrected him angrily. "I shouldn't have to keep reminding you that even if it gets in the brain, it isn't necessarily going to do any harm." Joss caught her breath. "And what if John decides he wants the black twin? It's two for one. He'd get the white twin, too."

"I trust him," Grant said.

And Altimate trusted you not to give away their secrets, she thought. If you gave it to John, who else would you give it to? There were penalties for betrayal.

"And *if* the black twin does have a side effect, then what?" she asked.

"If there were side effects, I want to know why they were never reported."

"Grant, I've told you repeatedly, even *if* side effects exist, they may not have been reported because animal testing *didn't even know about them*."

"If there's nothing to the black twin, Joss, why is someone trying to kill me?"

Joss narrowed her eyes. "Kill?"

"On the way to meet John, all my car lights went out, and my steering wheel froze. I ran off the road. I smelled gasoline, so I got away from the car. Just before it exploded."

Joss was chilled. Did someone else know or suspect what Grant was doing?

Grant shook his head. "Before last night, I wasn't sure something was wrong. I just had a hunch that I should check out the black twin. If it turned out to have a side effect, I thought I might be able to use it as leverage to reopen work on the white twin. But last night when I saw my car burning, I *knew* something was wrong. I think someone is afraid of what I'll find out about the black twin."

Joss stared at him. She had tried to head something like this off. It was a mess she didn't need. When she witnessed the theft of Grant's laptop computer, Joss had warned him that taking proprietary material out of Altimate would make him a magnet for violence. He hadn't listened to her. She had been right. But who had tried to kill him?

"Look," Grant said. "First the black twin was canceled. Then my laptop was stolen. Last night my car went out of control and exploded...All these things can't be coincidence."

"Are you going to tell anyone else your suspicions?" Joss asked.

"Absolutely not," he said. "Right now I don't have any evidence of what the black twin can do or who tried to kill me. If I say anything, I'd just be alerting them—and putting myself in more danger."

"How long are you going to leave the black twin in John's hands?" Joss asked. Grant might get impatient and try to give it to someone else, she thought. She had to try to contain this.

"John said he should have some answers for me by tomorrow."

As they got into her car, Joss glanced at Grant. He had always been driven; it was one of the qualities that made him a good researcher. But he had turned into a runaway freight train—he had to go where his impulses were driving him. That made him a liability.

Monday
October 27

44

Grant was on pins and needles as he walked into his lab at Altimate. He had been waiting all weekend to talk to Payne, to find out what he meant when he said something was wrong with the white twin. Come hell or high water, Grant was going to confront Payne and make him lay everything out. His chest tightened in anticipation of that conversation, and his adrenaline began to pump.

"Angie?"

"Over here."

Grant walked around one of the lab benches to find Angie sitting on a low stool with the contents of the cabinet spread out around her. Grant knew something was wrong.

"What's going on?"

She kept her head down while she spoke. "I thought I would get this drawer in order—so we can find things without a lot of trouble."

"You don't usually rearrange drawers when we have work to do," he said. "What happened here?"

Before she had a chance to say anything, the lab door slammed open, and Payne barreled in.

Payne's face alternated between looking angry and nervous. For the first time Grant wondered if Payne took drugs. Grant's heart sank. That was all he needed: Talking about the future of the white twin with someone who not only hated him, but who was high.

"I was in two times already today," Payne said, and he slurred his words. "Where were you?"

Grant's hackles went up. Since when did a senior researcher have to account for every minute of his day? Now Payne was sniffling.

"I've been on site for the past two hours, in a couple of meetings," Grant said.

Payne wasn't satisfied. "I expect to be able to find you whenever I want you, Fraser, not run after you."

"Did you check with my secretary?" Grant asked.

"No, I didn't ask your secretary! I'm director. If you're not going to be where you belong, you tell me where you're going."

Now Payne was completely irrational. Out of the corner of his eye Grant saw Tom wave from behind a partition. Great. If the techs are watching this, it will be all over the labs. Grant sighed; he felt very tired.

Grant hoped for his sake that Payne wasn't on drugs. He was going to try to have a conversation with him.

Grant said quietly, "I want to talk with you about the white twin. Last Friday you said…"

Payne didn't let him finish. "Your precious project," he sneered.

Grant watched Payne walk unevenly to an adjacent lab bench.

"The whole world doesn't revolve around your lousy project," Payne said. He waved a hand dismissively over the lab bench, and he knocked over some glassware. It shattered on the floor.

Grant said nothing for nearly a minute. He was barely containing a fury that wanted to grab Payne by the throat and choke him. So much that was important to Grant was at stake. He had worked for so long and done good work for Altimate. He didn't deserve to have it destroyed by a moron on drugs.

Finally Grant spoke. His voice was even, but his pulse beat so hard in his throat that it punctuated nearly every word. Grant didn't want to put off this discussion; worrying about the white twin had been eating at him all weekend. But with Payne in this condition, what could he accomplish?

"Maybe tomorrow would be a better time to discuss this," Grant said. "I have a lot of work to accomplish today."

Something in Payne must have snapped. He spat out in a loud voice, "You'll talk now. You'll talk to me now."

Suddenly Payne's hand flashed in front of Grant's face, and Grant jerked his head back. Glass! Where did he get it? If he'd been an inch closer, he would have slashed my throat, Grant thought. His legs felt wobbly, and he felt the blood drain from his face.

Now Grant was shaking with anger, but he knew that anger would be a mistake with Payne, especially now. Grant calmed himself before he said, "Look, I don't know what your issue is, but it's not my project or my not being here. Let it go. Tomorrow my schedule is less crowded."

At those words Payne gave a high, broken laugh and threw away the glass. "You bet it's less crowded tomorrow. There's no project tomorrow. As of now, it's canceled. Tomorrow your schedule is wide open."

Grant was stunned. The walls started to move in on him, and things began to go dark. Grant shook himself. Payne *must* be drunk or on drugs, he told himself. "What are you talking about?" he finally said. "The review is tomorrow."

"The latest animal lab results on the white twin were less than encouraging." Payne said it in a singsong voice.

"How can that be?" Grant's brain seemed thick as sludge. "It's too soon to have received any negative test results." He didn't believe Payne, couldn't believe him. He had to be lying.

"The project is canceled. Period." Payne's voice said he was enjoying this.

Grant couldn't have been more shaken if the earth had opened up under his feet. He took a step backward, as if he could get a better perspective with distance. It didn't help.

This was the last straw. He had been put down and had his work obstructed by Payne for years. The only reason he'd put up with it was because of the white twin. And now this monster was shutting down his project—his life—and all it meant to Payne was another chance to lord it over him.

"What do you mean, my project is canceled?" Grant's voice was low.

Payne's voice was demeaning, almost taunting, but Payne took a step backward. "Watch your mouth, Fraser. The decision was made by your superiors."

He wants to enjoy every bit of the torture, Grant thought. Grant knew there was little point in talking with Payne, but he tried anyway.

"This was the most promising immunological drug we've come

up with," Grant said. "Preliminary tests were encouraging. On what basis could the project be terminated?"

Payne was patronizing. "Fraser, you don't need to know the reasons—"

Grant cut him off. "This could be a big drug for Altimate. We can't tell this soon just how much promise it has. Why would they give it up, this early in the game? It doesn't make sense."

"It's their money and their decision, not yours," Payne said. "I want you to turn in all your lab books to me immediately."

Grant was thunderstruck. "Turn in? What is this, a homework assignment?"

"You will be given another project. You will stop work immediately on this project and submit all relevant information to me."

Grant was boiling. "I'll talk with Horcroft myself. I'll make him understand."

45

Daniele remembered once when she was a little girl and had gotten poison ivy. They had told her not to scratch it, that it would only make the rash spread. But she couldn't help it. It felt so good to rake her nails over the itching, blistered skin. It was so satisfying.

That was how Daniele felt now. She was enjoying watching Payne take Grant's heart out, even though she knew that Payne was destroying himself. Watching Grant's face as Payne told him that his precious white twin project was canceled was delicious. Daniele wished she had a video camera so she could capture it and replay it. And when Payne swung the piece of glass near Grant's throat, Daniele thought Grant was going to faint.

When Grant left the lab, the spell was broken. Daniele sobered when she remembered the pivotal role Payne played. What would happen when Grant reported this incident to her father? Payne had gone over the line with the broken glass. Other people must have seen him do it, too. Nathan's hand would be forced.

Things were already so complex. Daniele shuddered to think what might happen if Payne were no longer in his position. She counted on him.

Still, it had been so satisfying to see the changes in Grant's face. This was why a killer wanted to watch his victim die.

46

Joss soon heard about Grant's row with Payne and his exit to Horcroft's office; news traveled like wildfire in the labs. Joss paced her office, feeling as tight as a spring. What was Grant planning to do? He was already obsessed with the black twin, and now he had lost the white twin. If he blew up at Horcroft, he could lose his job. If he lost his job, would he go trumpeting his suspicions about the black twin?

Joss caught a glimpse of herself, reflected in her window, which stopped her in her tracks. She sighed. You couldn't control Grant; you could only stop him.

She returned to her desk and made herself calm down and focus. She had to do her work. After Dell called, pressing her with last-minute requests for the event she had promised to host this Friday, Joss told her secretary to hold her calls. She had just begun to be absorbed in what she was doing when her phone rang.

Joss looked up, annoyed. "Janet?" No answer. The phone rang again, loud and insistent. Joss picked up the phone. "Yes?"

It was the Westport Taxpayers Group. Joss was exasperated; it sounded like a fund-raising call. Joss wanted to hang up the phone, since the caller had started what was clearly going to be a long spiel. "Would it be possible for me to talk to you later, not here at work?" she asked. "You have my home phone. Right now I'm in the middle of a project."

"But you signed the original petition for the school referendum, and we need signatures for a new petition," the woman answered.

You are not being cooperative, Joss thought. Joss didn't want to hear it. After all, the WTG hadn't gotten their act together for the last referendum, and now they wanted another chance?

"What is this one for?" she asked, although she really didn't care to hear the answer.

"We don't think the first referendum was fair."

Joss was losing her patience fast. "You didn't get the results you wanted, so you want to do it over? What possible excuse could you have?"

The woman paused for so long that Joss didn't think she was going to answer. Then she said, "A lot of the people who signed the petition didn't make it to the polls."

"Maybe they changed their minds," Joss said.

"It wasn't that." The woman seemed reluctant to explain. "Lots of people said they were sick. That they tried to get to the polls, but they just couldn't."

Joss thought that older people could get tired or feel sick without it being unusual. But something made her ask, "Sick in what way?"

As the woman told her, Joss picked up her pen and made notes. Joss didn't hear anything else the woman said to her. She hung up and reread what she had written.

Was someone using her idea?

47

Grant headed to Nathan Horcroft's office, intent on convincing him to extend the work on the white twin.

But when Grant saw Nathan's face, his world started to crumble. Although Nathan greeted Grant with sincerity and an apology, Grant knew immediately that he wasn't going to give his drug a reprieve.

Somehow Grant couldn't believe he was losing it. Even though this had been his greatest fear, the drug had always seemed too real to him; it had too much life. He couldn't believe that there was no hope for it.

Grant was numb. He couldn't imagine what his life would be like without the white twin. Suddenly it struck him that a year ago he had felt the same way when he learned that Dena had died. Losing his drug felt like a death to him.

Even though Nathan's face was set, Grant had to try to make a case for the continuation of his project—for even a small extension to make sure the last series of animal tests was accurate.

"Let the animal researchers discuss the project with me," Grant asked, "or at least let them show me how and where the white twin failed. I can't believe that the animal tests could turn around and go from being promising to being total failures."

But Nathan was adamant. He looked straight at Grant. "You know that's exactly how it happens sometimes."

"But what about rerunning a series of the experiments?" Grant persisted. "What could possibly be the motive for refusing? Money? It would be a drop in the bucket, compared to what has already gone into this project."

Nathan made a cutting gesture with his hands. "This is a business decision, Grant. It's over; that's all there is to it."

For the first time, Grant noticed that Nathan's face was an ashen mask. He didn't look well. When Grant reflected for a moment on the short conversation they had just had, he thought Nathan had seemed to be doing this reluctantly. You're grasping at straws, Grant told himself. Don't try to fool yourself into thinking he doesn't want to do this, and you can somehow change his mind.

Grant tried again, anyway. Nathan's face was still pale, but he was adamant.

Dejected, devastated, Grant was waiting to be dismissed when Nathan dropped a bombshell, saying it as if the idea had just occurred to him.

"Grant, I'd like to make you a proposition," he began. "I'd like to offer you the position of director of research. Effective immediately. You would take over the supervision of research at Altimate, have a say in what direction it takes. You would also be able to pursue some research of your own."

It was so unexpected that Grant said nothing. He stared at Nathan and couldn't help noticing that the man now had some color in his face. It was as if he had had to swallow something bitter, and he'd gotten it over with. To be fair, Grant knew Horcroft didn't enjoy stopping projects.

Director of research? That must mean Payne quit or was fired, Grant thought.

When Grant didn't answer, Nathan added, "I believe you are familiar enough with the position that I don't need to describe it to you. You don't have to decide right away."

Grant was thrown off-balance. First he loses the most important research of his life, and then he is offered a promotion. Grant didn't know what to say; he hadn't thought once about what he might be able to accomplish if he were director, after he'd lost out to Payne several years ago.

Grant was about to say that he needed time to consider, when an image of Payne's computer came to him. Not because Payne used it a lot; in fact, the man had been as computer illiterate as they come. But the *access* Payne had as director; he must have been privy to much more privileged information than Grant was.

"Yes," he said to Horcroft, "I accept your offer." Nathan's face said that he was surprised at Grant's quick response, but he recovered quickly. "The office will be available today, although I expect you will want to make some changes, according to your own tastes."

Nathan paused, looking appraisingly at Grant. "Let go of it, Grant," Nathan finally said kindly.

Nathan had his hands on the arms of his chair. He was leaning forward slightly, and his eyes were riveted on Grant. Nathan measured his words carefully, "Altimate owns every bit of paper, equipment and idea that is generated here. I have made it as clear as I know how, what is the position of Altimate on the white twin project. The project is over, closed. That position will not change, Grant. There will be no further investigation here. This is a business, not a white tower."

"Your new position will require a great deal of your abilities to identify and pursue fruitful avenues of research," Nathan added. "There will be more scope for that now that you are the director."

Grant took a deep breath. Nathan put up a hand.

"I know I promised you that you could do research as part of your position. I will keep that promise. But, as before, it must be research that you clear with me. Do not try to use your position to restart any work on the white twin."

Nathan's face softened for a moment. Very quietly he said, "I'm sorry, son. That's the best I can do. For now."

Grant was almost dizzy; emotions swirled in him faster than the blood rushing in his head.

Nathan extended his hand, and Grant shook it.

"Congratulations, Grant. I know you'll do well."

Grant walked out of Nathan's office in a fog. He had accepted the new position with all of the conditions implicit in it. He felt as if he were being bought off—give up the white twin and become director of research.

Well, he wasn't giving up on the white twin. Or the black twin.

Grant hurried to his new office. Along the way he was congratulated by a number of people. News traveled fast in the labs.

Payne's old office had been vacated for barely two hours, but it had already been gone through and cleaned out. Grant paused in front of the wide desk. He had stood here so many times when

Payne called him on the carpet for imaginary transgressions. He could still see Payne sneering at him and making little chuckles. It was strange to think that he would now sit behind that desk.

He went behind the desk, turned on the computer and began tapping the keys. Grant planned to take whatever information he found on Payne's computer and use it to continue his research on the black and white twins—on his own time. If he came up with something promising, he would push to reopen the project.

Nothing.

The cleaners had wasted no time. Everything on the twins was gone.

Even though Grant should have expected this, he was so disappointed that he felt like crying. Not only had he lost his project, but he didn't know why it was canceled.

Nor was he likely to find out. So there would always be doubt in his mind about whether the white twin had really failed the animal tests. Just like losing Dena—loss and no closure.

His phone rang. When Grant looked at the time, he realized it was 2:00 p.m. How long he had sat in reverie he didn't know.

"Do you want to stop by here?" Joss said. "I want to show you something."

48

When Grant arrived at Joss's office, she waved him in to a seat. "Congratulations," she said. "I'm so happy. You've deserved this."

"Thanks, Joss. When you say it, I can almost believe it's a real promotion."

"That's a strange thing to say, when you've just gotten the job you wanted four years ago," Joss said. But she understood what he had lost today. She knew Horcroft had told him he *had* to give up the white twin.

"You know what I would have preferred," he said. "You said there was something you wanted me to see?"

She pushed a large envelope with a magnifying glass on top toward him. "These just came in, and I wanted you to see them."

She watched him pull out the eight by ten photos. They were the shots that the photographer had taken this past weekend. He picked up the magnifying glass and ran it over the first picture.

"It's like coming in for a close-up, isn't it?" Joss asked. "That's what the magnifier is for. I have to make sure there isn't anything objectionable in the photo before it is printed in the annual report."

Grant stopped at the photo of Daniele's section of the lab. Joss had marked a big red X across it and written 'for Grant' across the top. She watched him run the magnifying glass over the computer screen in the picture. He leaned closer.

"You were right," she said. "You can read the email message on the screen. I didn't think it would be legible in the photo. But it is."

Grant nodded. "What is the 'X' for?"

"It means we can't use that shot." Joss leaned over the photo. "Look at her desk. There's a folder with a title on it which makes reference to a proprietary process of Altimate's. I know you weren't happy that I made you turn on her computer. So now there won't be any record of it. All right?"

Grant shrugged his shoulders and nodded. Slowly he grinned. "You read me pretty well," he said.

She smiled. "Light reading. Hardy Boy mystery level." She leaned back in her chair. "I want to ask you about coming over tonight. A lot of the people here are really happy about your promotion. I promised to have a little congratulations party. Okay?"

Grant opened his mouth, and she thought he was going to protest.

Joss said quickly, "I know you're too modest to be the focus of attention, but this would be just a small thing, some close friends."

"Thanks, Joss," Grant said. "I'll be there."

"Good," she said, grinning. "Tonight at eight. Noblesse oblige."

Joss gathered the photos to put them back in the envelope. When she got to the photo of Daniele's computer, she pushed the shot and its negative toward him. "That photo isn't going in the annual report anyway," she said. "I don't see what harm it can do to give it to you."

Grant slid the photo and the negative into his suit pocket. "Well, at least that's the end of that," he said.

Joss watched Grant leave her office. He wasn't going to give up on the twins, she was sure of it. She sighed deeply. Things used to be so simple before, she thought. She used to be able to think of Grant as a friend.

49

Grant was still reeling when he got home. Too much had happened in one day for him to digest or make sense of it. The white twin was gone. Grant was the new director of research. People had come up to him all day, shaking his hand or thumping him on the back. They congratulated him for the promotion, but he still had more of a sense of loss than of gain.

There was one thread of hope.

Grant had taken a sample of the black twin to John Stedman's lab on Saturday night. Grant had called John this afternoon. John hadn't even been able to come to the phone; he'd been in the middle of testing. But he sent a message to Grant that he should have some news tonight.

Grant was nearly sure that a metabolite of the black twin affected the brain. If it did, Grant would use that information at Altimate to push to find out exactly why the black twin was canceled. He would also push to reopen work on the white twin.

How Grant would explain to Altimate why he had taken a proprietary drug out of the lab was something he wasn't even considering. Or the fact that what he planned to do smacked of coercion. Grant was becoming obsessed with resurrecting the white twin any way he could.

Bailey greeted him with an enthusiasm that Grant couldn't return. He half-envied Bailey as he tore around the backyard, running like mad, making fast stops and changing direction, his "crazy dog" mode. Bailey was just exhilarated to be alive.

Grant was making Bailey's dinner when the phone rang. The connection was filled with static, and it broke up from time to time.

"Grant, it's John."

Grant held his breath.

Time slowed down, and his senses became hyper-alert. Grant could hear every small sound in the house: The creaking of floorboards, the furnace kicking on, clicking in the water pipes, hot air hissing in the baseboard heaters and making the metal covers creak.

John took a deep breath and let it out. And Grant knew what John was going to say. It was almost as if they had been through this exchange before.

"I'm sorry, Grant," John said.

There. That was it. The words he hadn't wanted to hear.

Grant held the phone to his ear, listening. It felt as if the words John spoke were molecules of poison seeping into his brain.

"Did you hear me?" John asked.

"Yes."

"There was no localization, Grant. It was diffused. No 'neurotransmitter-mimic behavior.' The black twin and its metabolites don't affect the brain. I'm sorry, Grant."

Grant hung up the phone. Then he brought his fist down on the counter in anger. It had been his last hope.

If the black twin didn't have any affect on the brain, it meant that the drug really *had* been canceled because it did nothing for the immune system. And now it seemed the white twin did nothing, either. There was no conspiracy, in spite of Payne's viciousness.

For the first time in many years, Grant felt like a failure. In his head he heard voices that he hadn't heard in a long time. The voices weren't imaginative or articulate, but they didn't have to be. Like all negative mental tapes, they were never reviewed; they *did* the reviewing. And they were very effective.

Grant was still facing the kitchen window. It was darker now, and he could see his reflection. He felt as insubstantial as the image in the glass.

"I thought the black twin was the key," he said aloud. "I was sure of it. So sure that John's testing would find what I expected— that it went straight to the brain. And that would mean there *was* a conspiracy at Altimate. That was why the twins were canceled. That it wasn't true that they had no potential…"

"Director of research," he snorted. "I stopped caring about that years ago. I only took the job because I thought I could find something out about the twins. Now John has told me there is nothing to find out."

He abruptly kicked a cabinet door.

His eye fell on the clock, and he remembered with a start. He was supposed to go to Joss's for his congratulations party. He didn't want to go. It was the last thing in the world he wanted to do—be around people with grins on their faces, telling him he'd done great. That wasn't the way he felt.

Now it was official; he'd lost everything. Payne's prediction had been right.

50

Finally, Fred thought.

Fred had bugged Nathan Horcroft's phone on Saturday, while working as a photographer's assistant. So this morning he had heard a telephone conversation between Nathan and someone named *Walter*.

This whole crazy situation was beginning to make some sense to Fred. Nathan had never struck Fred as the kind of man who would be behind a conspiracy or who would try to have Grant killed. But Fred did think Nathan could be blackmailed into being involved in it.

From the conversation, Walter sounded like a power behind the scenes at Altimate. During his short conversation with Nathan, Walter had reminded Nathan that all he was supposed to do was cancel work on the white twin after it failed animal testing. That it wasn't up to him to fire Payne or replace Payne—especially with Grant.

Fred could even figure out how Walter might have wormed his way into Altimate: He must be the one who had kidnapped Daniele. Daniele wore her fingertip-less little finger like a flag; Fred had noticed it at the memorial service. She must have milked the kidnapping for all it was worth—never letting her father forget, keeping him feeling guilty.

Fred knew that two attempts had been made on Grant's life. And that Grant suspected that the black twin affected the brain. If the sample Fred sent to his friend at A.R. Labs confirmed Grant's suspicions, Fred would want to know if this Walter had any interest in the twins. Fred couldn't bring the black twin to A.R. Labs if someone else knew about it.

Fred's assignment to shadow Grant was supposed to be simple, but it wasn't. It troubled Fred that A.R. Labs knew nothing about the situation at Altimate. And yet, when he wanted to ask Smith about it, something held him back from making the call. Fred wanted to know more before he asked Smith any questions.

Fred wanted to find Walter.

But how to find him—through Payne? Fred had assumed that someone strong (like Walter) was keeping Payne at Altimate. Otherwise he couldn't understand how someone of Payne's limited resources and vicious personality could have remained for years in the position of director. But if Payne were connected to Walter, why didn't Walter reverse his firing? Maybe Payne's behavior, capped by getting his nose slit in a bar, had made him too dangerous to keep.

Still, Fred decided to follow Payne when he left Altimate in a rage after he was fired. Fred thought Walter might send someone just to make sure that Payne didn't make any waves and draw more unwanted attention to Altimate. So Fred found himself in the bar of the Toucan, an upscale restaurant in Westport, watching Payne drinking heavily.

If Fred had hoped to see a Walter-envoy at the Toucan, he was surprised and disappointed at the appearance of the sharp-faced, black-haired man at Payne's table: Sharpley. From what Fred knew of Altimate's electronics expert, he was the sort of mild-mannered man who thinks assembling a Heathkit is exciting. Fred was close enough to hear most of the conversation.

Sharpley hissed, "Grant did you in. What are you going to do about it?"

"What is there to do?" Payne said. "Altimate will never hire me back."

"Revenge."

"Right," Payne said. "Easy for you to say. What if I get caught?"

"You won't get caught. I promise you. Listen to me." But Sharpley didn't say anything more. He pulled something from his pocket and put it on the table with his palm covering it, and pushed it toward Payne.

Fred immediately decided that Sharpley either didn't work for Walter or was doing this on his own. Fred couldn't imagine Walter choosing such a public place for this kind of scene.

Whatever the two men were going to say was interrupted permanently by a buxom young blonde at the adjacent table. She leaned over toward Payne, her bosom falling out of a low-cut dress. "Do you have a light?" she asked. She arched her eyebrows at him suggestively.

Payne looked right through her and then turned back to his conversation.

She either wasn't used to men who were immune to her charms, or she was slightly drunk. The girl's companion grabbed her wrist, but she shrugged him off. She tried again, extending the cigarette to Payne. "Do you have a light?"

There were matches on the table; it wasn't so hard for Payne just to comply, Fred thought. Then he could get back to business with Sharpley.

But Payne's face curled into a contemptuous snarl, and he spat out a short reply to her which Fred couldn't hear. The girl was clearly taken aback this time. Her face contorted with fury. She grabbed a full glass and flung it at him. A red liquid and ice cubes splashed over his face and down his white shirt.

Payne's first instinct was to throw his hands in front of his face. When he did that, his hand hit Sharpley's hand. Something flew out of Sharpley's hand and landed on the table in front of the blonde's companion, in a small spray of splintered glass. Then Payne lunged to his feet. He reached across the table to grab the girl by the hair and fling her backwards.

The girl fell onto the side of a man who had just turned around to see what the noise was. His elbow connected with her nose and she screamed.

They both staggered. Her nose was bleeding. She moved drunkenly back to her table and reached for a glass, but it slipped out of her hand.

Sharpley's eyes were wide with fear, and his gaze was glued to the small object. He reached for it, but the girl anticipated him. She threw her body across the table and grabbed the object with a bloody grin of triumph. She slid back and landed in her chair, waving it in Payne's face.

Her companion's face turned white; he grabbed the girl's hand and tried to make her drop the object. She turned on him, her brows contorted in rage. He tried to take it out of her hand, but she closed her hand again, this time on his.

The effect was electric. As if they were two dancers linking hands across the table, their faces and bodies jerked in spasms. Then their body movements slowed and all expression left their faces except for a look of surprise. They slowly crumpled to their knees, their hands still linked across the table.

The entire restaurant became silent. It was clear to Fred that the two were dead. Sharpley looked at the two bodies in horror, and then backed out of the crowd that had already gathered around their table. Payne looked at the dead couple with contempt and walked away.

Fred watched pandemonium break loose as the wail of a siren was heard in the distance. Everyone in the restaurant scrambled for the nearest door, toward the parking lot and their cars. Even though they had had nothing to do with the deaths, these people did not want to get involved. Angry scuffling and swearing filled the room.

In the nearly empty restaurant Fred watched a man move across the floor *toward* the table and the bodies. The man looked around, then he leaned across the table and carefully pried the man's hand from the woman's. His gloved hand gingerly took what they had been holding—Fred guessed it was some kind of poison dart—and dropped it into a napkin he held in the other hand. He turned toward the side entrance and walked away.

Fred stopped speculating who the poison dart had been intended for, and turned his attention to the man he now dubbed "dart man." This man could be Walter's messenger. Although he had arrived too late to prevent what happened, he was in time to clean up.

Fred followed the man, who—probably pressed for time—stopped at a pay phone in the restaurant lobby. Fred caught him in the middle of his call. Whoever was talking to him kept interrupting him.

"...There was a blonde at the next table...The blonde and the guy with her...Yeah, just the two of them...Stiff...It all happened pretty fast...Look, there's going to be a lot of activity...*No, Walter!*...Because I wanted you to know that Sh..."

Fred strained to hear above the sound of the nearing siren. So it *was* Walter! Apparently Walter hadn't set this up. He was just making sure they cleaned up. But the last line. What was "sh"? What had dart man been trying to tell Walter? Was he going to tell him something else about Sharpley? If only Walter hadn't interrupted him before he finished that sentence.

The sound of the sirens got louder. Car doors slammed. Fred wanted to get out of there.

Now Walter must be yelling at dart man, because he was flinching. Eventually, with Fred breathing a sigh of relief, dart man hung up the phone with a bang, uttered a curse and headed out.

And what had Walter told him to do? Fred wondered. Probably not to come to him. Walter probably wanted to stay as far away from all this as possible. So where was dart man going?

51

As Fred left the Toucan, he thought there was something about the one-sided phone conversation that sounded familiar to him. On the surface, it was familiar because it was some hired guy doing his job and reporting to his boss. But there was something else...He couldn't put his finger on it.

The parking lot was nearly deserted. There was one car, a dark Oldsmobile; that had to be dart man's. Fred got the license number just in case. He was glad he'd had to park across the street. He got into his car and waited for the other man to come out. Then Fred started his car and followed him.

Fred had decided to gamble on dart man, to follow him—instead of Payne or Sharpley—until he led him to someone or something important. Even if it took all night and the next day.

Following dart man's car on the Post Road wasn't difficult. It was already dark, and there was a good stream of traffic. Fred was able to keep him in sight, even as he left the Post Road and made two turns on small side roads. But when he made the third turn, Fred had the feeling not to push his luck. He drove past the turn and waited a quarter-mile down the road. Then he came back. He drove down the road dart man had taken, but didn't see anything. He drove around for another twenty minutes, but the car was gone.

Fred swore. His first link to Walter, probably, and he'd lost him. He pulled to the side of the road and thought. What did he have? He had the license plate. He might be able to get a name. But what would that do? It could be a rented car, it could be borrowed, it could even be stolen. He decided he didn't need to know who was driving that car, but where he was going. Who he was going to deliver the dart to.

Fred looked around him. The evening was still young, and he had already lost his quarry. This was his fifth day on the job. Time was passing. He had to figure out another project, another destination for tonight. He remembered the flurry of activity to-day at Altimate. All the buzz about Payne's dismissal and Grant's promotion. Fred remembered that there was a congratulations party tonight for Grant, at Joss's house. A lot of people from Altimate would be there. Fred wondered if it paid for him to go over. He wouldn't be able to go in, of course, but he might learn something from hanging around the house.

Fred was surprised at the number of cars at Joss's. He parked his car at the end of the string. The party must be underway, he thought; no guests came or left as he made his way carefully to the house.

Joss's house had lots of trees and shrubs surrounding it. Fred had no problem finding cover as he walked around the entire perimeter of the house. Most of the people seemed to be in the living room. The curtains were all open, and he could watch the guests mingling.

By now he knew a number of them: Daniele was there. Fred was surprised; he knew she hated Grant. She turned toward the window, and Fred saw she didn't look upset at all. Fred also saw John Stedman; Fred recognized him from his appearance at Grant's car accident Saturday night. Tom was there, as well as some other techs. Angie was there, too.

When Fred saw Norman Horcroft, he couldn't help thinking about Michael. Fred didn't understand his reaction to Michael. In all his life he'd never been fond of children. Why should this one be any different? Fred shook his head. Why, for that matter, should he respond to Joss? And yet, he had. Since he had spoken to her Saturday night—even with all that silly stuff about Baba Yaga—the feeling of connection to her hadn't dissipated. In fact, it seemed stronger.

Fred looked for Joss in the room, but didn't see her. He worked his way around the house to the far end and came to a room with a large, nearly floor-to-ceiling window. The room was lighted by one small lamp, and the curtain was open. He peered around the edge. There were two people in the room—Grant and Joss.

Fred's chest clenched, and anger flared in him. He told himself to cool down and took several deep breaths. What had that been—jealousy because Grant was alone with Joss? They weren't doing anything but talking, but that hadn't mattered. Fred told himself this was not what he did; this was not what he was. He was a fixer, someone who got rid of people as easily as you might remove a stain.

Say it, he told himself. Say it now. "I kill people," he said aloud. His words startled him as much as if they had been said by someone else. In a way, he had kept the knowledge from himself. Fred was primarily a doer. It wasn't that he wasn't capable of contemplation. It was just that he thought about *how* he would do something, but not *that* he did something.

"I kill people," he said again. He stood, watching Joss through the window, feeling that more than glass separated him from her. And it profoundly unsettled him. This is crazy, he told himself. Involvement with subjects was a mistake. He'd better pull himself together.

Fred slowly straightened and, keeping his back against the house, edged to the corner, away from the window. The winding driveway curved closer to the house here. There was a car parked facing him—a dark car, an Oldsmobile. Fred's heart jumped into his throat.

The license was the same as the one at the Toucan.

There was no one at the car now, but Fred could hear approaching footsteps and voices. Two figures gradually came into view. Fred recognized one as dart man. The other man, taller, had his back to him.

The two men had lowered their voices so much that Fred could just hear murmurs, but couldn't make out the words. Then they seemed to argue. Finally the taller one raised his voice. "He doesn't," he said. "I'm sure of it."

Who was "he"? Fred wondered. The response from dart man was too low for Fred to hear.

"That doesn't matter. It didn't do any harm," the taller man said.

Dart man's response was louder, but Fred still didn't hear it.

"He won't stop us," the taller man said.

Dart man said something in a low voice, but it made the taller man flinch. Dart man got in his car and turned on the headlights. The taller man must have been blinded by them; he moved aside and put his hands up. The car backed up; as it did, the headlights illumined more of the man. When they reached his face, Fred saw it clearly. And he recognized him.

Grant's friend, John Stedman. *John Stedman worked for Walter.*

When the car left, John turned back toward the house and went in.

Now Fred understood why Grant had had at least two attempts on his life. Fred had heard the conversation Saturday between Grant and John, before Grant drove to talk to John. Grant must have told John everything: Grant thought a metabolite of the black twin had a structural resemblance to at least one neurotransmitter; he thought that it might affect the brain.

Apparently Walter and his crew didn't want Grant to find out what the black twin was capable of.

A light wind had sprung up, and it rustled the shrubs and trees, making a sound that reminded Fred of spectators settling into benches in a court. Waiting to hear the verdict. Except the verdict on Grant was already in. Grant had created the black twin. And whoever Walter was, he had some purpose for the drug and didn't want Grant getting in his way. Fred let the idea of Walter eliminating Grant sit with him for a while. Coming so soon after the scene in Joss's study, having a rival removed didn't make much of a ripple.

Fred shook himself. What was he thinking? Rival? Fred didn't even know Joss. Still, Fred kept thinking. Grant had created the black twin to help, not hurt. When it looked as if the drug might affect the brain, Grant pushed to find out. In spite of the fact that he was angering the higher-ups and even Joss. And he was hapless enough to have a confidant who had betrayed him.

As Fred walked back to his car, he took one last look at the house. Angie was standing by the window. She didn't look happy.

52

"Well, your boss got a richly deserved promotion, don't you think?" Joss asked Angie.

Angie didn't feel like celebrating.

Sure, Joss was happy, Grant was happy, Angie thought. But for someone like her, it changed everything. At least she had known what the ground rules were when Payne was in charge. Now, who knew what would happen?

"Sure," Angie smiled. No matter how she really felt about anything, Angie smiled.

"Angie, don't worry," Joss said. "I know how it is. When you're a junior person, every time there's any change you always wonder how things will filter down to you. But Grant is smart, and he thinks a lot of you. He's still going to do research, and you'll still help him. Things will still be interesting."

Angie thought that Joss meant to be nice, but she felt as if Joss were throwing her crumbs.

"He won't do nearly as much research as he used to," Angie said. "He'll have too many administrative responsibilities. It will be different."

Her job was over for her, she knew that. She started to bite her fingernails, right there in the middle of the party. She wasn't smiling, and she didn't care.

"I'm not good with change," Angie added.

53

She couldn't believe this. She was congratulating him! She was standing in front of him, telling him how happy she was that he was getting this promotion. She deserved a promotion more than he did. He had had two drugs canceled, and there he was appointed director of research! Somehow, no matter what happened, Grant always landed on his feet.

It was all getting too weird. What she had had to do to get what she wanted just wasn't fair. She shouldn't have had to twist herself into a pretzel of emotions. She shouldn't have had to be on guard every second, having to remember what she could and couldn't say. Sometimes she hadn't been sure which persona she was supposed to be in. It exhausted her and made her angry.

She kept telling herself that it was just a little more time. But it didn't help. Sometimes she felt as if she were going to explode.

Tuesday
October 28

54

"Angie, we're going to synthesize more white twin."

Grant was pulling his jacket off as he walked rapidly into the lab. He had been thinking about this on his drive to work. And he had decided that, whatever the consequences, he was going to know for himself.

Grant had been preoccupied with the loss of the white twin all last night, during the congratulations party Joss had given for him. In spite of the slaps on the back and the handshakes, Grant hadn't felt as if he had something to celebrate.

He was *sure* that the white twin wasn't a failure, in spite of what Nathan had said about reports from animal testing. Grant couldn't get out of his mind what Payne had told him last Friday, "And no one is going to miss the white twin." Grant was more convinced than ever that Payne had been instrumental in getting the drug canceled. Just how, Grant didn't know.

Angie was biting her nails in front of him, something she never did. Her face was almost frightened, Grant thought.

"But Dr. Horcroft told you that you can't do any more work on either of the twins. You told me that yourself. What will happen if he finds out? He may not fire you, but what about me?"

"If you don't want to get involved, Angie, I'll understand."

She sighed resignedly. "But Payne took all the lab books."

"That's all right. I can do it from memory." Joss's words from last night at the party came back to Grant. He had told her his suspicions about Payne, and she had said, "But Payne was fired yesterday; he left in disgrace. If Horcroft had had any reason to question Payne's canceling the white twin, he would have reversed his decision. But he didn't."

Unless Payne had been doing what Horcroft wanted, Grant had told her. Grant didn't want to believe it; he liked and admired Nathan Horcroft. But there must have been some reason for Horcroft to hire an incompetent person like Payne and then to keep him on for four painful years.

Which all sounded like some kind of conspiracy, and Joss had criticized him for that. "Why wouldn't Horcroft want a promising drug that could make money for the company he owned?" she had asked him. Joss had reminded Grant of his scientific training: To look for the simplest explanation that fit all the facts. She had said that incompetent people were often hired and kept, and that drugs that looked good at the beginning turned out not to have lots of potential.

Grant shook his head as he put on his lab coat. He knew that Joss made sense, but he had a feeling in his gut that the white twin had promise. That twinged his mind. Joss had always been outspoken, but she had always supported his gut feelings. Why wasn't she doing it now? Lately she seemed more of an adversary than a friend.

Grant shook himself. He always went with his intuition—even before Nathan Horcroft began giving pep talks on its virtues. Grant wasn't going to change his nature now. Stubborn or intuitive, he wasn't going to let go.

He was director of research. He could send a drug sample to animal testing and have them perform whatever tests he wanted on it.

Grant was taking a gamble. But his need to know was greater than even his need to have a job. Without the white twin, even the position of director of research didn't mean much to him.

55

Angie bit her pink fingernails the entire time she was setting up the equipment to do another synthesis of the white twin.

What was going on? she wondered. Yesterday she was sure that Grant had accepted Horcroft's conditions for his promotion to director of research: Stop all work on the twins. So why was he making more white twin? What had made him change his mind? Didn't he know he could be fired for this? Didn't he care that *she* could be fired for this?

A wave of self-pity came over her, and tears welled in her eyes. She shook her head angrily. Grant couldn't satisfy his curiosity, his relentless curiosity, in secret. Once he sent the sample of the white twin to animal testing, it would be public knowledge. And then everything would blow up.

Something else bothered her. When the vials of the twins disappeared from his desk drawer on Saturday, he had never said a word to her. Why? And where had the vials gone? Grant was nearly obsessive about the two drugs. And he always talked with her about what was on his mind. He couldn't hide something if it were bothering him. He was incapable of dissembling. So what happened?

She had said nothing to him about the missing vials. She didn't know what was going on with Grant, and she didn't want to take a chance on saying the wrong thing.

Angie watched Grant stride toward the equipment, a new spring in his step and a light in his eyes. Didn't he know what he was doing to her?

"All ready, Angie?" he asked.

Her smile trembled. "All ready."

56

Joss squeezed the steering wheel until the leather gloves she was wearing were so tight they hurt her knuckles. She hoped she was wrong.

After Joss talked with the woman from the Westport Taxpayers Group yesterday, she had been thinking about what she learned: A large number of the people who had signed the petition later complained about not being able to make it to the polls. Many said they were sick. When Joss pressed her, the woman told her the symptoms the people reported—they were classic for frontal lobe impairment.

The number of people involved and the similarity of the symptoms they reported made Joss think it couldn't be a wild coincidence. Joss had finally decided that some substance had been given to these people. And that substance could have been put in campaign letters sent to them just before the referendum.

If such letters existed, Joss should have received one. She had worked on the referendum, signed the petition and voted. But Joss had been so busy that week that she had thrown out a lot of "junk" mail without even opening it.

So Joss was going to interview as many people as possible who had signed the petition. She was going to ask them how they had felt the day of the referendum. And, if she were right, there *would* be a campaign letter, and one of these people would still have it.

———

Sasco Creek Village consisted of row upon row of closely spaced, well-maintained trailers lined up parallel to the Post Road. According to the mailboxes at the entrance, there were one hundred trailers. A large percentage of the residents had signed the petition. If there were something to be found, Joss felt she had a good chance of finding it here. As Joss drove along the horseshoe-shaped road that wound through the park, she reviewed the opening lines she had prepared.

At the first door she was met by an elderly man who removed his hearing aid as soon as he saw Joss. After saying, "What was that?" to every question Joss yelled to him, the old man abruptly said, "No!" and slammed his door.

The occupants of the next three trailers on her list were gone, or at least pretended to be.

An elderly man and woman, both neatly dressed, came to the next door. Before Joss finished, the old man began to close the door. His wife stopped him, saying, "There *was* a letter—from the Westport Taxpayers Group."

Joss held her breath. If someone had doctored campaign literature so it would make people ill so they wouldn't vote, Joss had figured there were two possibilities. The person or persons would have used genuine campaign literature or literature made to look genuine. Joss didn't know which might have been used, but she thought they would have more control over bogus literature.

"Do you still have the letter?"

"No," the woman said. "I remember throwing it out."

"Did you vote?" Joss asked.

"No." The woman looked embarrassed and shot an uneasy glance at her husband. "I just couldn't make it there. No get up and go."

Joss held out the twenty dollar bill. The old woman shook her head, but the man took it.

No letter, but an effect, Joss thought. Joss thanked both of them and moved on. The next door was opened by a young woman. She had long blond hair, shorter and spiky around the face. She had a small child on her hip and another clung to her sweater. She looked harried, but took the time to talk.

"Yes, I remember," she said. "The Westport Taxpayers Group sent a couple of letters. They wanted to remind you to vote no, and even had you call a number to tell them you would be at the polls for sure."

"Do you still have the letter?"

She smiled ruefully. "Why keep it? Anyway, where would I put it? There's hardly room for us. No. I threw it out at the polls."

"So you went?" Joss was surprised, and her heart lifted. Maybe there was nothing after all.

"I almost didn't," she said. "I could hardly get myself dressed, let alone them." She nodded to the children. "But I went. Little good it did. The other side won."

"Thank you for your help," Joss said. She held out the twenty dollar bill to her. The woman took the money.

Joss had made her way through nearly a third of the trailers, and she had no proof of a doctored campaign letter. She climbed the steps to the next door. This trailer had a deck with two wood outdoor chairs on it. The name on the door said Higgins. She had to knock twice before someone answered the door.

A neatly groomed white-haired woman in sweater and slacks opened the door tentatively. She looked unsurely at Joss. "What do you want?"

"I'm doing some follow-up research on the school budget referendum that was held last Thursday. I can pay you twenty dollars if you'll take just five minutes to answer a couple of questions," she added as the woman began to close the door. "We can talk on your porch," Joss said. "It won't take long." Joss sat on a wood chair on the porch and extended the twenty dollar bill.

The woman came out and eyed Joss warily. "What about the referendum?" she asked.

"I'm looking for a letter that would have been sent to Westport residents just before the referendum," she said. "Probably encouraging you to vote."

The woman's eyes narrowed. "Why do you want to know?"

"There's been a concern that various agencies might have tried to influence voters illegally," Joss said. "We want to collect samples of campaign literature that was sent out, in order to review it."

The woman nodded.

"So did you receive any letters?" Joss asked.

"I think there were several," the woman answered.

"What happened to them?"

"Some I threw out, the rest I don't remember," she said.

Joss extended the twenty dollar bill to her, but held onto it. The woman looked at Joss with a slow frown.

"Would you like to earn an additional fifty dollars by looking for any letters that had to do with the referendum, right now?" Joss asked.

The woman snatched the twenty dollar bill, and there was calculation behind the eyes. A small, shy smile crossed her face for the first time. "If I find them, and they're the letters you want, would it be worth one hundred dollars more to you?"

"Yes," Joss said.

It took Mrs. Higgins nearly ten minutes to find the letters, and the whole of that time Joss wondered what she would do if she found what she was looking for.

Mrs. Higgins returned, waving them in her hand. "They were in a wastebasket in my bedroom. You're lucky they're still here."

Joss went through the crumpled pieces of paper as if there were a scorpion in the pile, hoping she wouldn't find a letter. But it was there.

She smoothed the paper and looked it over quickly. At the top was printed "Westport Taxpayers Group." But Joss knew this letter was not genuine. Unfortunately, she was right. A bogus campaign letter *had* been sent out.

There would be no way of knowing whether the letter contained any chemical until she got it back to the lab, but Joss was already pretty sure that it did. Why else would someone send a letter pretending to be from the WTG?

The old woman was watching Joss, in anticipation. Joss pulled out one hundred dollars. "Thank you for your help."

Mrs. Higgins's face lit up as she took it. Then her cheeks got pink. "If I can find other people in the park who have that letter, would you want them?" she asked.

Joss was still staring at the letter in her hands. She looked up. "Yes. Of course." She had to be sure. To be safe, she had to have other letters. The one she held was wrinkled and worn. Even if there had been any chemical in the letter, by now it might be gone.

"How will I get in touch with you?" Mrs. Higgins asked.

Joss gave her a business card and wrote her home number on it. "Keep this to yourself, please," Joss said. "I don't want word of this investigation getting out. It could affect just what kind of information we get."

The wind whipped through the park—making a wheezing sound like an asthmatic old man—as Joss returned to her car. In her pocket was the letter she had hoped didn't exist.

57

Fred took the key out of his pocket and turned it in the lock. Right on time, he thought, satisfied. The stiff Express Mail envelope was in the mailbox. Fred walked down the steps of the post office and crossed the street. He decided to go via Main Street to reach his car.

There were a lot of women pushing baby strollers. A new wave of arrivals, he thought. What a nice place to be raised in. He looked in the faces of the babies and small children. Happy and alert, he decided, for the main part. Why not? Life must look good to them.

That made him think of the little boy, Nathan Horcroft's grandson, at the memorial service on Sunday. Why Michael should stick in his mind, he didn't know. Of course you know, he thought. There's something about him that makes you identify with him. A sense of openness and hopefulness that had been prematurely crushed. Fred had felt that way at the orphanage. Unconsciously, Fred brushed the scar on his upper lip.

The image of Michael stayed with Fred. He had listened to the conversation between Nathan and Grant on Sunday. So he knew that the doctor thought Michael had had some infection. Fred frowned. He didn't like the idea of anything hurting the little boy.

Fred reached Elm Street, crossed and walked up to the municipal parking lot behind Main Street. When he got behind the wheel of his car, he looked to make sure there was no one around him. He opened the Express Mail envelope and took out the inner envelope.

Fred put both hands on the envelope. He wasn't psychic, not even since his accident, but he thought he had a good chance of predicting what was in the envelope. He slit open the envelope and pulled out the paper. He read it through quickly. The friend at A.R. Labs who had sent it to him knew how to say something in plain English, so Fred knew right away how things stood. Fred had been right.

Fred made a call on his cell phone. "Go ahead on the other," he said.

He looked up, over the steering wheel, and stared into the distance. Gradually his eyes focused on an object directly in his line of sight, but much closer. Fred was startled when he realized he was looking at Michael.

On the other side of a split rail fence was a compact playground, with a small, gabled stone building with stained glass windows close behind. A bevy of young children pedaled around in brightly colored plastic cars or played in little groups with each other.

Except one. A little boy with brown hair and dark eyes stood by the rail fence that separated the playground from a side road. A torn stuffed rabbit dangled from one hand. He stared straight ahead, unmoving, as Fred watched him.

The day had gotten cooler, but the child showed no sensitivity to it. He might be shivering, Fred thought, and those women supervising the kids, have they noticed? They should button up his jacket. He's so thin.

The play period finally ended, and a woman led Michael back into the preschool.

58

Joss returned to Altimate late Tuesday afternoon. She headed directly for Grant's lab. She held her breath as she went in, hoping that no one was there. She was lucky. Even Grant was out. He must be at his desk in his new office, she thought.

It had been a while since Joss had worked in a lab, but she still remembered exactly what she had to do. She turned on the HPLC and waited for it to warm up. The High Pressure Liquid Chromatography equipment took up the space of a large desktop printer on top of a bench in one corner of the lab. Next to this equipment was a large tank of helium gas.

Joss put on rubber gloves and examined the letter she had gotten from Mrs. Higgins. It was in large print so it would be easy to read. But it was slightly complicated and had printing on both the front and the back. The reader was supposed to call a number to confirm that he would be at the polls on the day of the vote. In addition, there was a sticker on the back of the page that the reader was supposed to put on the refrigerator, or somewhere similar, to remind him to vote.

They were smart, Joss thought. They wanted to make sure that the readers handled it long enough to absorb whatever was in it through their skin—or to get enough on their hands to transfer it to their mouths.

She had seen and talked to half a dozen people who had seen and held a letter like the one she held. And in each case they seemed to have had temporary symptoms of frontal lobe impairment.

Joss cut narrow strips from the margins of the letter, wondering to herself if all of her efforts would be for naught. After all, the letter had been handled, and it had been in a wastebasket in Mrs. Higgins's bedroom for more than a week. Joss didn't know how clean the letter was, or how much drug or chemical—if there ever were something on it—might still be in the paper. After all,

Mrs. Higgins had touched it, and she hadn't seemed to be affected. Joss heard the chromatograph kick on. She hadn't used this equipment in a while, but she had watched Grant operating it to make sure the white twin he had produced was really pure.

The HPLC operated by passing an unknown substance over a column of special silica granules—at high pressures, close to two hundred pounds per square inch. Each component of the unknown substance would bind to the silica granules with a differing tenacity. Then a special liquid was passed over the column. Each component of the unknown substance would be carried by this liquid to the end of the column at a different time, depending on how tightly it had been bound to the silica granules.

The individual components that came off the bottom of the column were caught one by one and were recorded as peaks on a moving roll of graph paper. Joss would be able to identify components of the unknown chemical in the letter, by comparing the location of each peak *it* produced, with the peaks produced by known compounds.

First she wanted to dissolve out whatever might be in the letter without dissolving the paper itself. She decided on ethanol. Joss put the strip of paper in a small beaker containing ethanol.

While she waited, she ran a baseline by injecting ethanol into the equipment with a syringe. The rolling graph paper recorded the ethanol as a peak. Then Joss filled the syringe from the small beaker the strip of paper was in. She injected this into the equipment. Finally she followed this with an injection of the special liquid Grant had used.

Joss held her breath as she watched the graph paper coming out of the machine. The lab was silent except for the mechanical hum. The needle of the printer moved on the graph paper as it rolled past. Here and there was a tiny blip, but nothing identifiable. It was almost to the point that Joss knew was the transit time of the black twin.

As Joss watched, the needle of the graph slowly traced out a peak at the expected location for the black twin.

Joss heard footsteps behind her.

"What are you doing here?"

59

"What are you doing?" Grant repeated. He walked toward the equipment, frowning. Then his face slowly opened in amazement. "That's the black twin!"

Joss wasn't sure what to say to him. Maybe a good offense was the best defense.

"Why are you running the black twin through the chromatograph?" he asked. He looked totally mystified.

Joss held up the letter. "It was in this," she said.

Grant put his hand out for the letter, but Joss held it out of his reach. "I'd recommend that you put gloves on first," she said.

Grant stared at her and shook his head. Then light dawned. "The black twin *does* have a side effect," he whispered.

Joss nodded. "Apparently."

Grant quickly put on rubber gloves and took the letter. He read it through quickly. "What led you to this?" he asked. "How did you suspect?"

"Yesterday I got a call from the Westport Taxpayers Group," she said. "They wanted me to sign a new petition, to do a re-vote on the school referendum issue. They said that a number of the people who had signed the petition had been sick. The symptoms were classic for frontal lobe impairment."

"But how?" Grant said. "And why?"

"I would think you have a better idea than I do," Joss said.

Grant looked up, surprised. "What does that mean?"

Joss frowned. "You've been running around with information on the twins on your laptop. And you took a sample of the black twin to John Stedman."

"You don't think *I* put it in the letters?" Grant asked.

Joss shrugged. "If you don't exercise control over information, you are responsible for what happens to it."

Grant angrily waved his hand. "No one got the information I

had on my laptop. And I trust John; I've known him for years." He shook the letter. "Who could take the black twin from my lab? Who would want to use it in the referendum?"

Joss waited. She wanted to hear what he knew, what he suspected.

"Daniele," Grant said. "She was all over the place on the referendum."

"But she was working for the side that lost," Joss said.

"Which would put her in the best position to know who was against the budget increase," Grant said "The same people who signed the petition and who worked on the referendum."

"What would she gain from influencing a school budget referendum?" Joss asked. "I don't think Daniele's property value would have been affected by a school budget cut. Besides, her goal is to be president of Altimate. She's been currying Nathan's favor for months, volunteering for things she normally has no interest in. Daniele wouldn't do anything to jeopardize her chances of getting Altimate."

"How about Payne?" Grant said. "Maybe that's why he was so set on the twins being canceled. So he could use them for some other purpose."

"He's probably capable of something like this," Joss conceded, "but what would be his motivation?"

"Money," Grant said. "I know what was going to be cut from the school budget if the WTG won the referendum. There were some very lucrative contracts that would have been lost. Maybe someone who stood to lose one of those contracts decided to hedge his bets."

"Were the contracts big enough to justify using a *drug*?"

"The cuts would have stopped several ongoing contracts, as well as contracts that were just getting started," Grant said. "More than a million, over time. Somebody who had big hopes for the future might have wanted to be sure he wouldn't be disappointed."

Joss nodded slowly. It made sense, she thought. But if Payne had been the leak, now he was gone.

"I have to stop them," Grant said. "Once they know what the black twin is capable of, who knows how they'll use it next? Or if they don't have another use for it, they can sell it to someone who does."

"That isn't your responsibility," Joss said.

"Yes, it is. I made the black twin. But I didn't make it to be used like this. " Grant looked toward the door. "As soon as I find out about the white twin, I'm going to take this information to Horcroft."

"Find out what about the white twin?" Joss asked. That project had been canceled, she thought.

"Yesterday I authorized animal testing to rerun some tests on it," Grant said. "I should have at least some preliminary results soon."

Joss was furious, but she kept her anger in check. "You have a self-destruct wish, Grant. What do you think Horcroft will do when he finds out you went against his orders?"

"If the results are positive for the white twin, he should be happy that he didn't lose a drug with promise," he said. "If they aren't, Altimate still has a responsibility to account for the drugs it produces."

"And what if Horcroft is involved in this?" Joss asked.

Grant's face said he hadn't considered that possibility. "I should hold off telling him, then. That would blow everything up."

You don't want to make explosions, Joss thought. But you keep lighting the dynamite.

60

When Daniele opened the front door of her house, she didn't know which to do first—take a nice, long luxurious bath or open a bottle of champagne.

Michael came running toward her, with her housekeeper right behind him, smiling.

"Mommy, Mommy!" he shrieked. His face was beaming.

He had peanut butter on his fingers. Daniele could see it from ten feet away. She kept him at arm's length, as he tried to reach his hands toward her. She looked up with annoyance at the house-keeper. Can't she move any faster? "Mommy's busy now," she said. "Stay with Hannah, and I'll see you later."

Both Michael's and Hannah's faces fell. Too bad, Daniele thought. I want to savor this; I don't want to waste the evening talking to a kid. The housekeeper led Michael away; he kept looking back at Daniele.

Daniele crossed the foyer and walked up the stairs to her bed-room. It was finally happening, she thought. After all her plot-ting and efforts, it was all coming to fruition. Kissing up to her father and his stupid causes, and…everything. It had been worth it.

Today he had called her in her office. He had said that he had something important to discuss with her tomorrow. Something that affected the future of Altimate. It would just be a private meeting between the two of them.

She felt like jumping with joy. He was going to tell her that he was naming her his successor at Altimate.

61

Close to midnight, Fred turned onto Charcoal Hill Road, and took the winding two-lane road in the dark to Smith's house. He turned in the gate and followed the long drive to a semicircular loop in front of the house.

Fred turned off the engine and sat for a moment. His palms were wet. This was a first. Fear started to creep in on him. His skin felt chilled, and not by the fall night. "What is this?" he said. "This is a simple assignment. Why am I so tense?"

He got out of the car, but the feeling didn't leave him, in spite of his bravado. He knew why his palms were wet. Why his back was prickling with ice. Because his whole body was saying that something was wrong, and his mind was still saying that this was just a simple job.

The front stairs were broad and high, as if they led to a throne. Appropriate for Smith, Fred thought.

When Fred rang the doorbell, his coldness started all over again. Why was he walking into this house when his instinct told him to go? Because it's still my job, he told himself. Maybe all the good changes he'd discovered in himself weren't the only by-products of a new and expanded awareness. Maybe he had also acquired a supersensitive alarm system that was set off by little or nothing.

Smith opened the door. "Hello, Fred. Come into the living room."

Fred watched Smith's face. He was a tall, lean man, with almost white hair, sharp features and hooded deepset eyes. Fred followed him into a large, high-ceilinged room, with stone walls on three sides, glass on the third. An enormous fireplace dominated one wall. There was a fire tonight, and, on the large coffee table in front of it, a bottle and two glasses.

Fred walked toward the fireplace, glancing at the coffee table. And noticed the ring from a third glass. The hair stood up on the back of his neck.

"Drink?" Smith asked.

Fred declined. In all the years he'd known Smith, he'd never socialized with him. No time to start now.

"Sit down," Smith said.

They sat. Smith looked relaxed. The old professor-ness that had put Fred at his ease so many times in the past now made Fred's skin prickly. Smith had been so tense this past week, calling Fred every day, wanting to know everything. Now he was sitting as if this were a casual evening, with no other concerns in the world.

Fred thought over his reports to Smith. Since Fred had never gotten permission from Smith to get into Altimate, he couldn't now tell Smith about his discovery of the black twin. He couldn't tell him about Grant's phone call to John and about Grant's suspicions. Or the attempts on Grant's life. He *had* had to tell Smith what happened last night at the Toucan—when Sharpley offered Payne a dart—since it was a public place, and someone might have seen Fred there.

Suddenly Fred felt as if last night were a mine field, and he didn't know where the mines were. Maybe Smith suspected that he hadn't been honest about what he'd done, and what he knew. Maybe Smith was losing faith in him. Fred shuddered, knowing what that meant.

"I've been thinking about your report from last night," Smith began.

Fred nodded.

"You said that you saw Sharpley offer the dart to Payne, and that somehow it ended up on the adjacent table, in the hands of the man and woman."

Fred nodded again. He felt safer not speaking.

"How do you interpret that?"

Here was a mine, Fred thought. "It seemed clear that not just Payne is resentful of Grant," he said. "Sharpley has his own ax to grind, for whatever reasons."

Smith nodded. "Tell me again what happened after that."

"Everyone in the restaurant and bar left. Nearly as soon as

they were gone, the police sirens started. I left, too."

"Did it occur to you to follow any of the players?"

Here was another of the mines. Fred was sure of it. He hadn't followed Payne or Sharpley. He'd waited to see what happened, and he'd seen the dart retrieved by another man, who had led him to John. Should Fred tell Smith? He had to think fast. He couldn't take his time, as if he were weighing what he said. If Smith knew that Fred was lying, this evening could be Fred's last.

Fred's heart was beating so hard he thought Smith must hear it. He decided and said, "I was sitting further back in the bar, away from the doors. I had followed Payne to the bar, and I didn't know who he might be meeting. I didn't want to be out in the open where someone might see me. So when the stampede began, I was near the end of it. By the time I got to my car, the parking lot was in turmoil."

Only from long practice in this kind of subtle grilling was Fred able to keep his face and voice calm. And able to avoid fisting his hands into cold balls.

Smith seemed to be deciding what he thought of what Fred had said. Finally he nodded slowly. "You've done well," he said. "I know that this evaluation of candidate Fraser has become more involved than we anticipated." Smith smiled. "But I don't think you've minded that. You have probably been anxious to get back into harness. Am I right?"

Fred nodded and held his breath.

"I think it's time to wrap things up," Smith said. "Put together your report and submit it to me. We'll see if we can find something a little more interesting for your next assignment."

Smith stood up. It was the signal to leave.

So Fred left. Gratefully.

62

She tossed and turned in bed, struggling with a troubling dream.

She was in a large room with balloons on strings. The balloons were in a rainbow of jewel colors and gold and silver, and she knew they were full of treasure. They floated all around her, seemingly within her grasp. But every time she reached for one, it floated higher, just as her fingers were about to close on the string.

Again and again she tried leaping at the balloons and throwing her arms around them, but they all eluded her. Then she tried throwing a large cloth over one. She trapped a balloon. She could see its outline in the cloth, but when she lifted the cloth there was nothing there.

Finally, in frustration, she grabbed a knife and swung it around to puncture the balloons. They broke with explosions that elicited a high-pitched cry of surprise from her. But more startling than the explosion was what hung in the air where the balloons had been. They were the faces of the people who had received her letters and died.

Wednesday
October 29

63

"I don't understand it, Dr. Fraser."

One of the technicians from animal testing walked into Grant's lab around noon, shaking his head.

"We started running the set of experiments you asked us to, the ones we ran last week. And this time preliminary results are very encouraging. We're not finished yet, but I wanted you to know."

Grant's heart leapt at the news. Whatever happened to the white twin in the end, for this one moment he was grateful that a drug he had devoted three years to was not a complete failure.

Grant was debating what to do next, when Angie came toward him with another worried look on her face.

"What is it today, Angie?" he asked. Right now nothing could bring him down.

"Dr. Horcroft left." Angie looked at Grant, hesitating. "Michael is sick, and he took him to the hospital."

Grant went cold. Everything else left his head as he slammed the door of the lab open and sprinted to the executive area, nearly running into a dozen people on the way.

Horcroft's secretary was at her desk. She held up both hands as Grant hurtled toward her. "It doesn't look serious, Grant," she said. "You know how Dr. Horcroft is. He just didn't want to take any chances." She frowned. "Angie shouldn't have gotten you all upset. Dr. Horcroft didn't even want to tell you."

"What's wrong with Michael?" he asked. His chest was so tight he had trouble breathing.

"Just a chest cough," she said. "But he's been looking so washed out recently that Dr. Horcroft took him in."

"Where did he take him?"

"Norwalk Hospital," she said.

Grant wheeled on his heel, and she jumped up from her desk

to grab his arm. "No. Don't go. Daniele will be there, I'm sure. There will be a scene. It won't help Michael or Dr. Horcroft. He's calling in for his messages, so he'll tell me how things are. I'll keep you posted."

Waiting would be torture, he thought. But he didn't have a choice. "Okay. Thank you." He was leaving the executive area when he saw Joss coming toward him.

"I just heard," Joss said. "Angie told me. I know how much you love Michael."

They walked back together to the lab. The black twin was nowhere in Grant's mind. Nothing but Michael was. The little boy. The soft little boy.

Joss took his arm. "Grant, you're white enough to be having a heart attack. Are you all right?"

"I couldn't love him more if he were my own son," Grant said, his voice raspy. "But she won't let me be with him."

"Nathan will be there with him, Grant. He loves Michael, too."

64

Grant was in his office, staring at his computer, thinking about Michael. He hadn't gotten any work done this afternoon. He'd called the hospital several times, but there had been no news about the little boy.

He had to do something to occupy his mind while he waited. Finally, he decided to catch up on writing his personal lab notes—that was mechanical enough. Usually he wrote up the summary and review at the end of the day. But he hadn't had time in the past two days, what with the newness of the job and all the administrative work.

With his hands suspended over the keyboard, Grant tried to decipher his cryptic handwritten notes: "...and the earliest results..."

He flexed his fingers and typed: "...smf yjr rst;ordy trdi;yd..." Grant glanced at the screen and caught the meaningless letters before he'd gotten very far.

He was about to delete the line when it hit him. They only seemed to be meaningless letters because they were shifted, out of proper context. The image of the nonsense letters on Daniele's screen—the email message he'd called up for the photo session on Friday night—appeared in Grant's mind.

Something about that message had been bothering him since he'd first seen it. He hadn't totally believed, even though it had been his explanation, that there had been a mistake in the transmission.

Then, last night Joss had found black twin in a bogus campaign letter used in last week's school referendum. Grant had immediately felt that Daniele was involved. But he couldn't prove it. Now maybe he would discover something in her email message. He had to find out.

He pulled open a desk drawer and held his breath as he went

through the layers. It was there. The photo of Daniele's computer.

For only a brief moment—when his alter ego asked him—did Grant stop to wonder why the email message had captured his curiosity. It was his nature to follow his intuitive leads, without giving them the third degree.

Grant smoothed out the photo and carefully copied the email message visible on Daniele's screen. When you get proficient at typing, he thought, you don't have to look at the keyboard. Because your fingers know the positions of all the keys, once your index fingers are on f and j.

But what if the position of your fingers were shifted? When Grant flexed his fingers, they had been shifted to the right. Grant's fingers still made the right moves, only the wrong keys were under his fingers. Maybe that's how the nonsense message on Daniele's computer had come to be created.

On a regular keyboard, you needed three lines of keys to type any message containing letters; four, if you typed letters and numbers. Grant looked at the message in front of him.

65ue6t0ku7i5g-l=ek80k395r70-k070rl8-=0k0-k7ie7t5r=07565 -6uek-ode70-k9k0h56re[u5k570gr0rr9jr7ekte6t65=-675krtrey756 t575l0k0ku85e6[8=6-y07ry967i560ky-6le70-kehe0[ej[5e78-966 5395r7

He compared the letters and numbers to the keyboard and felt a small burst of excitement—they were all from the top three lines on the keyboard. That meant that his assumption might be right—the person had typed a normal message, but from a different starting place on the keyboard.

Grant moved to his next assumption: The person who typed this message would have started with his fingers on the second line of keys, not the third. Grant would have to try the four possible starting positions, starting with his index fingers on the r and u.

Now came the tricky part. With his fingers in each of the four placement possibilities, Grant had to do some transposing. He had to determine which finger was used for each symbol, letter or number in the message—and how far and in what direction the finger had to go to type each character. Then he had to take that pattern of finger movements and reproduce them, this time with his index fingers on f and j.

Grant started with the leftmost position, left index finger on the r, right index finger on the u. He memorized what each of his fingers had to do to type the message. Then he typed out the first ten transposed characters, using those same finger moves, but with his index fingers on f and j. He typed: 'ytjdygpju'. It didn't look promising, but he went through the rest of the message. Nothing.

He decided to try the next finger positions, with his index fingers on t and i. Again he went through the message, character by character. Nothing. If he had been writing on a sheet of paper, he would have crumpled it up in disgust. Grant rubbed his face and leaned back in his chair, stiff and disappointed.

He was about to click the file containing his cryptography exercise "close, do not save." But he stopped and stared at the screen for a while. "One more try," he decided.

He placed his fingers in the third position, index fingers on y and o, and began again:

regardingthecompanyinquestion

Grant was electrified. His hands were trembling as he carefully transposed the entire message:

regardingthecompanyinquestionitismyopinionthatdespitereorga nizationuniversalgeneticsissubstandardreportendsafterdeter miningyearlyprofitsfurtherinformationavailableatyourrequest

He added spaces and punctuation: Regarding the company in question, it is my opinion that, despite reorganization, Universal Genetics is substandard. Report ends after determining yearly profits. Further information available at your request.

Grant read over the message several times and felt like a fool. An exhausted fool. "Good grief," he said, leaning back in his chair. "I spent an hour decoding nothing. Daniele probably just didn't want everyone to know about her financial affairs."

Exasperated with himself, he made a copy—to remind himself the next time he looked for the obscure in the obvious.

65

Grant was nodding at the computer screen, all of the tension of the past week taking its toll. His eyelids slid shut, and he began drifting step by step down the stairs to oblivion, when his alter ego made an appearance:

Step by step, it said. A good way to proceed.

Grant was alert enough to tell it to get lost.

Each step takes you closer to your goal. It's so easy.

Grant reminded himself about the plan he had to prepare as the new director. He'd been spending so much time chasing down information on the black twin that he was neglecting the job he was paid to do.

You can't go back in this place. It is one-directional. Not like time.

Horcroft had said that he was interested in the ideas Grant had for directions for research. Bull, he had almost said to Horcroft. Why did they kill the white twin?

You need all the steps, and they must be in sequence.

Why hadn't they given him a chance to make some modifications to the white twin? The first set of results had been encouraging. And today, animal testing said preliminary results looked good on the retesting Grant had ordered.

It's like letters in a word. Words in a sentence. Unless they're in the right sequence, it doesn't make a message.

What a waste Payne's computer turned out to be. Like running to a safe deposit box and finding it empty, Grant thought.

His mind drifted to the photo shoot. Grant had an unwanted image of the message on Daniele's PC. He still felt like a fool about that.

One word for each step. No, not even a whole word. Just a letter.

Grant tried to drift off to sleep, but because he didn't want to think about Daniele's computer, his mind perversely brought the email message to the fore of his consciousness. Behind Grant's eyes the message hung in semi-luminescent letters, all caps: REGARDING THE COMPANY IN QUESTION, IT IS MY OPINION THAT, DESPITE REORGANIZATION, UNIVERSAL GENETICS IS SUBSTANDARD. REPORT ENDS AFTER DETERMINING YEARLY PROFITS. FURTHER INFORMATION AVAILABLE AT YOUR REQUEST.

He had reached the bottom and was drifting now. He was floating. The message seemed to be on a billboard, bobbing on water.

Soon the movement of the billboard dislodged the letters from their support. They wobbled and fell into darkness. Only a handful of letters remained, the first letter of every word. The message board stopped wobbling, and the letters seemed to glow more brightly in Grant's mind:

RTCIQIIMOTDRUGISREADYPFIAAYR
DRUG IS READY.

Grant shot bolt upright in his chair. The image of the glowing letters still burned in his mind. The sleepiness was gone, and he was all attention. He looked at the message, still on his computer screen, and made the first letter of each word bold.

It stood out: DRUG IS READY. He hadn't imagined it.

The message had been on Daniele's computer. Daniele *had* to be the link at Altimate.

Grant couldn't believe it. Even though this was what he had been looking for, now it seemed incredible. He knew—everyone knew—about Daniele's ambition to be the next president of Altimate. But how could her involvement in the theft of one of Altimate's drugs help her to take control of the company?

And how did she get Grant's drug? Grant couldn't believe that this was Nathan Horcroft's idea, or that he was willingly involved. So how did Daniele get access to Grant's research? How did she manage to shut his project down so there would be no trail leading back to Altimate? Maybe Payne had been in league with her. Grant's stomach went cold as he thought about the cancellations of the twins.

Although Grant didn't know how Daniele had done it, he trusted his gut reactions. And they told him that Daniele was capable of doing anything—absolutely anything—to get what she wanted.

He made himself stop and take a deep breath. He was a scientist. And he didn't have anything other than a coded message on Daniele's email. He needed real proof.

If Daniele were involved, there would be evidence in her house—Grant was sure of it. She was too arrogant to think that anyone would be smart enough to suspect her involvement, let alone look for evidence of it in her home.

Grant decided to break into her house.

His first step was to make sure she wasn't at home. Grant picked up the phone and punched in her number, praying no one would answer. When the answering machine picked up, Grant raced out of the office to his car.

66

It was starting to get dark, Grant thought. That would help. So would knowing Daniele's house and some of her habits. Her house-keeper wouldn't be there because Michael wasn't at home. The thought of Michael caught at Grant's heart. What would it matter if he found out about the black twin or reclaimed the white twin—if something happened to Michael?

Grant pushed thoughts of Michael away. He had to focus on what he planned to do. He knew it was illegal. And he knew if he were caught, Daniele would do everything she could to destroy him.

He parked away from her house and made his way carefully, hugging trees and shadows. He'd already decided in the car which window he would break into. Daniele had no alarm system. Frequently she didn't even lock her windows. "It isn't that kind of neighborhood," she used to say.

When Grant had squirmed his way through the ground floor window, he waited for a couple of minutes, listening for any warning sounds. Slowly he made his way through the rooms. He knew this place. When Dena was still alive, they'd both visited Daniele and Michael here. But where would Daniele keep any information on the black twin? Grant didn't think it would be in her library. Daniele must be using hi-tech devices, and she wouldn't let them mar the design of one of her public rooms.

He headed for her bedroom. The walls were composed of sections, either paneled in what looked like a rare hardwood or covered in heavy silk. There was a king-size bed, a sofa and two chairs, some tables and a walk-in wardrobe. Using his flashlight, Grant covered the room inch by inch, running his hands over the walls and even looking for a hidden space behind them. He found nothing.

Disappointed, he left the room and quickly checked each of

the upstairs rooms in turn. He went through wardrobes and clos-
ets, and scanned walls. There was no sign of any equipment or
information.

Downstairs, he thought, in her office. *Something* had to be
there. He had to move fast. He checked his watch. He didn't know
when Daniele would be coming home, and he didn't want to take
a chance on her finding him.

Quietly, nearly holding his breath in the dark, he came down
the stairs and walked through the living room to Daniele's office.
Like her office at Altimate, it was all top-of-the-line and painfully
neat; there wasn't a paper anywhere. Rapidly he went through
her desk, checked her files, scanned the bookcases. Finally he
turned on her computer. It was completely personal! Grant was
frustrated. This was the last place he could think of to look, and it
had nothing more than financial information.

Grant turned off her computer and cursed. She had to have
the information somewhere. There had to be some clue here as to
what she had been doing. There was too much for her not to have
used her house at all.

But there was no place else to look, and Grant was running
out of time. In the dark he recrossed the living room and went
back to the window he had entered. He had his hand on the window frame and was lifting the sash.

A hand came down on his forearm, and a barrel of a gun was
pressed in his ribs. The shock sent so much adrenaline through
him he could have hit the ceiling.

Daniele's cell phone rang as she sat in the hospital waiting room, where she tried to look like the devoted, worried parent while Nathan paced the floor. She was grateful for the interruption. She fluctuated between being bored to death and ready to burst from resentment. This was the day she was supposed to have her private meeting with Nathan. How long would it be put off?

"Dr. Horcroft?"

Daniele could hardly make out what the person said, because her voice was thick with tears. "Who is this?"

"It's Angie, Dr. Horcroft. I'm sorry...to bother you at the hospital...but your father's secretary gave me your number."

Daniele knew Angie was Grant's assistant. What was going on?

"The police just phoned," Angie said. "They found Dr. Fraser in your house. It must be some sort of misunderstanding. And they want you to go home so you can tell them. If anything is missing."

Daniele heard Angie's voice again dissolve into tears.

"*Please* don't do anything to him."

Daniele hung up on her. She was jubilant. She couldn't believe her good fortune. She was finally going to get rid of Grant. Forever, she hoped. What was the penalty for breaking and entering? She didn't know. But she planned to prosecute him "to the full extent of the law."

"I have to leave for a while," she told her father. He didn't say anything to her, but his face said he couldn't understand how she could leave for any reason. Tough, she thought. Michael would be fine. He always was.

She wouldn't miss destroying Grant for anything.

68

Angie couldn't believe the call when she got it. She never thought Grant would actually do something like this.

Her heart was beating like a triphammer as she put down the receiver after talking with Daniele. She had to steady herself. She couldn't get too unsettled. Angie looked around the lab and sighed with relief when she realized that no one was close enough to hear her conversation.

She had to think clearly. Now was no time to lose it.

With trembling hands she opened her purse, pulled out a mirror and checked her face. She couldn't walk around Altimate with tears and streaked mascara, or there would be no end to the questions and speculation. She wiped her face clean and took a deep breath.

She got up from the desk and walked out of the lab, down the corridor toward Joss's office.

69

"Joss?"

Joss looked up to see Angie standing in her office door, eyes red from crying, wiping tears away.

"What is it?" Joss asked.

"Grant is at Daniele's house. And the police are there."

"At Daniele's?" Joss asked. She couldn't have heard right. "What happened?"

"They say he broke into her house, and they caught him inside."

This is it, Joss thought. Grant has finally done it. He's gotten into something that he won't get out of.

"He wants you to come," Angie said. "He thinks they will listen to you. That you can confirm what he's telling the policeman."

He wanted her help. For one split second Joss thought she was going to laugh. After she had repeatedly warned him, he had still stubbornly pursued his obsession until he'd gotten into this mess. But she didn't laugh. She had to go. What might he say or do with his back against the wall?

"All right. I'll go," Joss said. "Just let me leave a message for my secretary."

Angie waved her hands. "I'll do it. You have to go now. Please. They're not going to wait. If you can't head this off, they're going to take him to jail."

Joss grabbed her purse and ran to the parking lot.

70

Grant saw the triumph in Daniele's face and knew that there was no hope for him to get out of this.

"That's the best I've ever seen you look," Daniele gloated.

The policeman came forward.

"Do you know this man?" he asked.

"Unfortunately, yes," she said. "Dr. Grant Fraser, who works—who *worked*—for Altimate Pharmaceuticals."

"He said that he was trying to prove that you have something of his in your house. Is there any truth to that?"

"He's crazy!" Daniele shouted. "I don't know what he's doing here, but it's not for any good reason. Look, I want to check my home to see if he's taken anything. Have you searched him?"

"Yes," the policeman said. "There was nothing on him."

"Good. Please keep him here until I'm sure there's nothing missing. All right?"

"I'll be right here," the man promised.

Daniele sped up the stairs. Probably going straight to whatever place I missed, Grant thought grimly. In no more than five minutes, he heard her footsteps coming down the stairs and sounding in the downstairs rooms.

"On first glance, everything seems to be here," she said, coming back into the living room. "Can I press charges now?"

She looked so eager, Grant couldn't hold himself back.

"You're not getting away with this," he told her.

"Getting away with what? You're the one in the handcuffs," she said with delight.

"You know what I mean," Grant said. "Stealing drugs from Altimate."

"You're hallucinating," Daniele said. "That is all fantasy. But breaking into my house is real. Give it up, Grant. There's nothing you can say that will explain what you're doing here. You're through."

Fred was in his car, watching Daniele's house. He had been sitting there since he followed Grant here from Altimate.

Last night Smith had told him to wrap up this assignment. "Just put together a report and submit it to me," Smith had said.

Fred was about as capable of letting go of this assignment as he was of flying.

Every hair on his head seemed to stand up when he thought about it. It wasn't just that he didn't know what was going on. Oh, sure, he figured that someone wanted the black twin so they could use it. Fred wanted the drug for A.R. Labs for the same reason. But the attempts on Grant's life, the involvement of a number of people. All this pointed to something big.

Which made Fred uneasy. If this were such a big deal, why didn't Smith know anything about it? Presumably there had been some preliminary investigation before Fred was assigned to follow Grant. Why hadn't they picked up on any of this? Why hadn't Smith told him?

Fred was feeling the same kind of mistrust that Grant had expressed toward Altimate over the cancellation of his drugs. Fred did *not* want to find out that A.R. Labs was holding out on him. He felt as if he had a tiger by the tail, and he wasn't letting go until he knew just what was going on.

When the police car had pulled up, Fred knew Grant was in real trouble. They had him cold. Then Daniele came, as eager as a fox in a chicken coop. When Joss got out of a car, Fred figured she was here to try to plead for Grant before the police took him to the station. It probably would have made more sense to call a lawyer.

Fred started his car. He already knew how this was going to play out. There was no way anyone was going to deflect Daniele from destroying Grant. From what Fred had heard, she had probably been waiting for an opportunity like this.

Fred decided he would have to pursue other leads to figure out what was going on—at least until Grant posted bail. What a shame. He was beginning to like Grant.

He was pulling away when he saw another car pull up to Daniele's house. This is getting to be a circus, Fred thought. How many more people are going to go into that house? And then he saw the driver, and his heart stopped.

72

You could never leave well enough alone, Grant! Joss wanted to scream when she walked in and found him handcuffed in Daniele's living room. But she held herself back. She couldn't say anything like that out loud, not now.

The policeman spoke first.

"Are you Dr. Avery?"

"Yes."

"We'd like to get this sorted out here," he said, "if that's possible."

"That's not possible. I'm pressing charges," Daniele said.

Joss thought Daniele looked rabid, as if she couldn't wait to destroy Grant. Joss wasn't sure what role she was supposed to play.

"Please, Dr. Horcroft," the policeman said. "Let's talk this out. Dr. Avery, Dr. Fraser said that you understand why he is here."

Let him explain it, Joss thought. She looked at Grant.

"Do you remember the email message on the computer?" he asked. "The one the photographer took a picture of on Friday night?"

"Yes," she said.

"We thought it was nonsense, that there had been an error in transmission. But it wasn't nonsense. It was a real message that had been typed with the hand positions shifted on the keyboard."

Joss saw that the policeman was frowning.

"Do you understand what he's saying?" he asked.

Joss nodded.

"The message in the email message was 'Drug is ready.' Someone sent that message to Daniele. It was on her computer. She must be the link at Altimate."

Joss saw Daniele's face change from a look of disbelief to anger.

"My computer? What were you doing with my computer?" she demanded.

Joss tried to head her off. She wanted to hear whatever else Grant had to say. "They were taking pictures of the labs for the annual report and needed a picture of a computer," Joss said to Daniele. "Yours was the only one that fit in the shot. It looked like a nonsense email message, Daniele. All letters and numbers. Just for a photo."

"Who gave you permission to touch my property?"

Joss could have told her that computers were Altimate's property and so was email. Daniele knew that as well as anyone. But it would only inflame her.

"Forget about who can touch your computer," Grant said to her. "We know you stole the black twin. But I had to find proof. So I came here."

Joss didn't say anything. Grant truly sounded crazy. A secret message? The policeman and Daniele must think Grant was delusional. Grant sounded like people who did violent things because they heard voices that told them what to do.

"You came here because of some email message on my computer?" Daniele said, shaking her head. "You're either lying or you're crazy."

73

Fred could clearly see the driver of the car. *It was his boss, Smith.* And Fred recognized the man on the passenger side, who got out of the car. It was the lawyer who had come with John Stedman to help Grant on Saturday night when his car exploded.

The lawyer stood by the car for a moment and tapped his hand against the top of the car in a staccato rhythm. With his ring.

Like the ring against the stone pillar in the chapel at the cemetery. Like the ring against the metal frame of Fred's hospital bed. Fred was suddenly sure that it was *this* man who had been in the hospital with Smith when Fred first awakened after his brain surgery. The lawyer worked for Smith.

There was such a rapid and violent restructuring of all the events and conversations of the past week that Fred felt as if a gale-force wind were ripping past him.

Fred had put all the pieces together: Smith wasn't checking up on him. Smith wasn't doing his job for him.

Smith had to be Walter.

Smith was the one who was masterminding the use of the black twin. Fred knew him as Smith, his boss. But Nathan Horcroft and John Stedman and dart man—and who knew how many others—knew him as Walter.

Fred suddenly understood why this assignment hadn't made any sense to him nearly from the beginning. Why Smith hadn't given him any background, why Smith had kept him on the edge and discouraged him from digging too deep.

A.R. Labs had never been interested in recruiting Grant. That had been Smith's ruse, to keep Fred busy while Smith covered his tracks. A. R. Labs must have gotten wind of what was going on at Altimate and sent Smith in to check it out.

Fred laughed grimly to himself. Smith had been sent to clean up a situation that *he* had created. And he had sent Fred in as a decoy and a fall guy.

Fred was both relieved and jelled with a cold fear. The relief came from finally knowing what was going on. The fear came from realizing that Smith intended to kill him along with all the other expendables.

For a long moment after Smith left and the lawyer went into Daniele's house, Fred stayed in his car, staring at the front door. When it occurred to him that Smith might have had him followed from the beginning—maybe even today—Fred froze. But when he looked around him, no one was there.

This was a whole new ball game. There was no place for him except under a mound, pushing up daisies. Smith had probably already set him up, so he would be put away by Smith or by A.R. Labs. Great.

Fred started his car, ready to drive away. Self-preservation came first. Even a thirst for revenge against the man who had betrayed him was secondary. Then he remembered: Joss was in that house.

"Not Joss," Fred said.

He knew he wanted to save Joss. But how? In his mind Fred saw himself approaching the house. Determining if anyone were outside, standing guard. Making his way in without a sound. Getting close enough to where the people were gathered so he could hear and see what was going on—without them knowing that he was there. Pulling his gun and changing the ending that Smith had originally written.

And an image came up in this scenario: He saw Grant ending up with Joss. Fred didn't like that.

And then Fred envisioned another ending to the story, one he liked better: He saw himself concealed, watching the unfolding scene with his gun at the ready. He saw himself wait, allowing the lawyer to shoot Grant. And then he saw himself burst into the room to cut down the lawyer before he could harm Joss.

Then only he and Joss would be left alive. He would comfort her. She would owe him her life. And since they both now had to flee A.R. Labs, they might as well flee it together.

74

"I'm not crazy," Grant said to Daniele. "And I know what you were planning to do with the black twin. I know about your referendum letters, how you used the drug on a bunch of innocent people. Joss found a bogus letter, and we tested it. It contained the black twin. Who were you trying to help? Who would have lost out if the budget increase had been defeated?"

Here we go, Joss thought.

"Was there such a letter, Dr. Avery?" the policeman asked.

"Yes," Joss said. "We tested the letter at Altimate last night and found the drug in it."

"Stop talking about the black twin!" Daniele was turning red. "I never want to hear about you or your damned drugs again. What would I want to use it for? To kill people like it killed your raccoons?"

Daniele turned abruptly to the policeman. "I don't want to talk to him anymore. I want him out of my house. I want you to take him to the police station so I can press charges. Now."

"Can't we work this out peacefully?" the policeman asked. "You're all professionals."

Grant couldn't believe what Daniele had just said. "What do you know about the raccoons?"

Daniele ignored Grant. "Professionals don't break into other people's homes," she told the officer.

Grant was sure that Daniele had just admitted her guilt. "If you know about the raccoons it proves you were involved," he said

Daniele threw her hands up in amazement. "You've got to be crazy. You're here in handcuffs, and you're trying to say I'm the criminal."

"But no one knows about the dead raccoons," Grant said. "I told no one. Only the person who was responsible would know."

Daniele shook her head slowly, a look of incredulity on her face. "Someone from the animal control center called you and got me by mistake," she said. "He said you wanted to know what was in the paw of a raccoon that died on your property; you thought it might have been poisoned. He said it was a letter from the Westport Taxpayers Group. I told him I worked with you, and I'd pick it up. I was afraid that you'd carry on about tainted letters in the referendum I worked so hard on. I didn't want that to happen; I did *not* want to work on another stupid referendum."

She stopped to catch her breath. "But that wasn't one of their letters," Daniele said. "I must have stuffed hundreds of the damned things; I knew. But I had the lab people test it. It contained the black twin." She laughed grimly. "So that's its side effect—it kills."

Something is wrong, Grant thought. Daniele sounds as if she didn't know about the bogus referendum letters. That isn't possible.

"I told you I want to prosecute," Daniele told the officer. "I don't want to talk anymore."

"But you're both prominent in the community," the officer said. "This won't help either one of you."

"I don't care what the community thinks," she said.

"Can't you try to resolve this peacefully?"

"I can't believe this!" Daniele said. "It's your job to prosecute criminals. If you don't want to do it, there must be someone else at the station who will."

"Please don't be hasty," the officer said.

"Hasty? I've been waiting for this for years."

Daniele crossed the room to the phone.

"I don't think this is advisable," the officer said.

Grant had picked up the change in the man's voice, and he glanced at Joss.

"Daniele, please," Joss said. "What difference will a few minutes make?"

"Go to hell," Daniele said. She picked up the phone.

"I think you should put the phone down," the officer said.

Daniele lifted the receiver and punched in a number.

"Please put the phone down," the man said.

Something is wrong, Grant thought.

"Hello. What is the number for the Westport Police Department?"

"Dr. Horcroft. I'm telling you to put the phone down."

"You're not telling me anything," she said. "I know my rights." She punched in a number.

The policeman lifted his gun and shot Daniele in the chest. Joss screamed.

Daniele crumpled to the floor.

75

Grant watched the scene as if it were happening in slow motion. Daniele collapsed heavily onto her oriental carpet, her face turned toward Grant.

He was mesmerized, watching her face. Death drained all of the anger and blackness out of her, and her rigid features softened into repose. Now she looked like Dena; more than she ever had in life. The gold hair loosened and fell around her face, like the picture in Grant's foyer. Only moments passed, but it felt much longer to Grant. Every instant was agonizing. It was as if he were watching Dena die for the first time. But it was as if he were losing her twice.

"What the hell did you do? You were supposed to wait for me."

The man's loud voice jarred Grant out of his shock. Grant looked up and recognized him at once. It was Jones, the lawyer who had come with John Stedman on Saturday night, who had stood in the rain in front of the headlights and argued with the state police to release Grant into his and John's custody after Grant's car had blown up.

"She was going to call the Westport Police," the other man said.

Grant was still reeling from seeing Daniele killed. Gradually it worked its way into his consciousness that the policeman wasn't a policeman and that Jones knew him. And Jones was carrying a gun with a silencer. Grant's insides got cold. He strained against the handcuffs, but they just dug into his wrists.

"They know about the referendum, about the email message—drug is ready," the fake cop said. "Probably they know about…"

"Shut up," Jones cut him off. "Get out of here. Go help Smith."

Through the thick, stupid haze in his brain Grant realized his assumptions must be wrong. I'm some kind of scientist, he told himself. Wrong about John Stedman, wrong about Jones.

Wrong about Daniele.

That shook Grant up. If Daniele weren't the connection at Altimate, who was? Someone had to have arranged this. Someone had to have followed him and set him up with the fake cop.

Jones turned to Grant. "What do you know about the referendum?"

"You treated bogus campaign letters with the black twin and sent them to people," Grant answered. "Enough got disoriented or sick and didn't make it to the polls. That was your idea, right?"

Jones didn't answer him, but he asked, "Did you tell anyone?"

"No."

Jones looked relieved.

Grant glanced at Joss. He expected her to say something; she had found the bogus referendum letter. But she said nothing.

"That's not the end of the story," Grant said. "The Westport Taxpayer's Group is suspicious. They've been calling people to sign another petition to do a re-vote. Because they say a lot of people were poisoned the first time."

Jones muttered under his breath. Grant couldn't hear what he said. Again Grant glanced at Joss. Why didn't she say *something*? Didn't she want to try to buy some time?

"If we figured it out, others will, too," Grant said. "A number of people who signed the original petition work at Altimate. They will have the means to find the black twin in the letters."

"If anyone else figures it out, it will be too late to do you any good. And they'll never trace it to us." Jones paused, smiling. "They never traced the plane crash to us."

Plane crash? For a moment, Grant didn't know what Jones was talking about. Then he understood, and his breath died in his throat. Dena's plane crash hadn't been an accident. Before today he'd told himself that he just couldn't face reality. But he hadn't been wrong.

"We got Sharpley to blow up her plane."

Dena. Trusting, happy-go-lucky Dena. Who wholeheartedly wanted to do her job the best she could, which meant knowing the truth. Grant could have screamed as he strained against the cuffs. And Sharpley. The mild-mannered engineer had killed her.

Grant blinked back tears, and Jones's face swam. "How could you justify killing her?"

"She guessed what was going on. She would have told Horcroft."

"Horcroft didn't know?" Grant didn't know how Horcroft couldn't have been involved.

"Smith told Horcroft he was only taking rejects." Jones laughed. "Horcroft, brilliant Horcroft, never guessed that we *made* them rejects."

"You bastards," Grant said.

Jones's face lost its smirk. Without another word, Jones lifted the gun and aimed it at Grant's head.

Grant knew he could expect no compassion from someone who had killed a planeload of people to stop one woman.

Grant tensed, waiting to die.

76

Fred had removed the silencer, so the lawyer would hear the gunshot. He had the satisfaction of seeing the surprised look on the man's face as he dropped at Grant's feet with a hole in the side of his head.

Fred was uneasy. Smith would have seen this through; he wouldn't have left the lawyer to do it alone. Why did he change his plans? Damn it, Fred thought. He had wanted to ask the lawyer where Smith was. But there had been no time.

Fred saw Grant staring at him and his gun. "It's okay," Fred said. "I'm the cavalry." Then Fred realized that this was the first time Grant had seen him out of disguise.

Crossing the room quickly, he bent to open Grant's handcuffs. "Rub them," Fred said, pointing to Grant's hands. "They're almost white."

Then he walked over to Joss. Her face looked uncertain and confused. She watched the gun in his hand and glanced from Grant to Fred.

"Who are you?" she asked. She looked at the door he had come through, as if she expected someone else to come in.

"Fred Brown."

Fred glanced over at Grant. He was rubbing his wrists and staring at the dead man with a strange look on his face.

"But why are you here?" Joss asked Fred.

"I was outside," Fred said. "I saw this guy go in, and I knew he meant you no good." That didn't explain things, Fred thought, but it was the truth. He watched Joss push her red hair back. How beautiful she was, even now.

What's wrong with this picture? Fred wondered. He'd always assumed there was something between Grant and Joss. But here the two of them were, having just escaped death, and they don't run to each other.

"I know you saved our lives," Joss said. "And I don't like look-ing a gift horse in the mouth, but what's going on? What were you doing here? Why did you come here yourself instead of calling the police?"

Fred stared at her. Joss had seen two people killed, had nearly seen Grant's head shattered and had narrowly escaped death herself. But here she was, giving him the third degree. She was a cool customer. "As a matter of fact," Fred said, "I do this for a living."

Fred's intended humor had no visible effect on Grant or Joss. No surprise, he thought, after what they've been through. He glanced out the window; he had to get them out of here. He pointed at the lawyer.

"We don't have much time," Fred said, "but you need to know who he was—a lawyer who worked for American Research Labo-ratories or A.R. Labs. Until tonight, I worked there, too, for a man named Smith. For years the Labs have had contracts with the government to contribute to its chemical warfare arsenals. But Smith was moonlighting. I found that out tonight. When this man got out of a car with Smith, it all fell together."

"His name was Jones," Grant said. "And we know only one of his connections at Altimate—Sharpley. They must have a lab. When they steal Altimate's drugs, they must manufacture them somewhere. We have to find it and stop them."

Fred noticed that, although Grant was talking to him, he was looking at Joss. She was still watching Fred guardedly. What was going on?

"Jones wouldn't have told us anything," Fred said. He decided to lay out what he knew. "You were right to be suspicious about the cancellation of your research on the white twin, Grant. My guess is that even before Smith used it in the school referendum, he tried it out to determine dosage. That would account for the unexplained deaths that happened in the weeks preceding the referendum."

Fred saw a tremor cross Joss's face, but he kept talking. "I figure those deaths must have been the red flag that got the at-tention of A.R. Labs. A. R. Labs must have suspected that someone was in competition with them—making and testing a 'persuasion drug' and screwing up royally."

Fred thought Grant's face said he was doing some mental calculations.

"How do you know about the referendum?" Grant asked. Then he paled. "How long were you outside this room, listening to Jones? You cut it pretty close," he said.

"Had to get the lay of the land," Fred said. Fred didn't tell Grant that he had considered saving Joss and not him.

"So A.R. Labs told my boss, Smith, to check things out here," Fred said, bringing the conversation back on track. "Ironic, isn't it? Smith was supposed to take care of a situation that he'd created. A.R. Labs didn't know about Smith's and Jones's moonlighting." Fred's voice got softer. "Neither did I."

Fred could swear that Joss sighed in relief.

Fred cleared his throat. "Smith brought me in. Told me you were a job candidate for A.R. Labs, and I should follow you to see if you would be responsive to the idea. Also to uncover anything they could use to persuade you to join."

"I've been following you at a distance since last Thursday," Fred said, "Then I got into Altimate to see you at close quarters. I was the limping photographer's assistant." There was a flicker of surprise and recognition from both Joss and Grant, Fred thought. But then they both went back to looking preoccupied with other things. *What were they thinking?*

Finally Joss spoke. "I still don't understand why you helped us," she said. "That wasn't part of your job."

"Maybe empathy for someone else who was betrayed," Fred said. He noticed that Grant looked hard at Joss when he said that.

"I tapped your office," Fred told Grant. "By Saturday I knew that you suspected that the black twin affected the brain. Even though it was no longer your project, you still had to know. You took a chance to take the drug out of Altimate. But you took a bigger chance to take it to John Stedman."

"Stedman," Joss said, frowning at Grant.

"John worked with Smith and Jones," Grant said.

Joss gasped. "So you handed it to them," she said angrily.

"Instead of handing it to you?" he snapped.

"What does that mean?" Joss asked. "You're sounding as crazy as Daniele said you are."

"Why else have you been so critical of me?" Grant burst out. "Why did you try so hard to get me to stop doing molecular modeling of the black twin? Why did you want me to accept the cancellation of the white twin? Why else have you been acting so proprietary about Altimate's drugs?"

Joss stared at Grant for a long moment. Finally she said, enunciating each word, "Nathan Horcroft chose me as his successor."

77

"Horcroft wanted to wait until next week to announce it," Joss told Grant. "He asked me not to say anything to anyone. He knew how much Daniele wanted the job. He was trying to figure out how to cushion the blow."

"I knew things were different at Altimate," she said. "Horcroft didn't have to tell me something was wrong. But I gathered it had something to do with him, and I would have free rein. I planned to change things, including doing some more research and testing on the twins. But you were getting so wild, taking confidential information out of the lab, taking a drug to a competing firm, that I was afraid whose hands it would fall into."

"I had to think about the bottom line," Joss said. "I had to think about the good of Altimate. That was going to be my job."

Grant felt supremely stupid and disloyal. What had he done? "I'm sorry, Joss," he said lamely. "Nothing has been what it seemed to be. I've been wrong all around. I shouldn't have suspected you."

Joss was still glaring at him. Finally she shrugged. "I was wrong, too. I thought you were crazy to suspect a conspiracy, but you were right."

"I hate to break this reunion up," Fred said. "But you two have to understand something. There is no returning to Altimate. You have to get out of here. Jones is dead, but Smith is alive and loose. He's got others here. And he knows where you live. When he knows Jones is dead and you're not, he'll come after you."

"Leave?" Joss said. She looked as if she were going to laugh. "My house and my job are here."

"Leave?" Grant felt fuzzy again. "I have to get Bailey." Grant turned toward the front door, and Fred put out his hand to stop him. Grant was pushing Fred's hand aside when he heard the front door open. He froze, fearful of who it could be.

"Jones? What's going on? Walter is waiting for you."

Grant shook his head as if to clear it. He couldn't be hearing right. He glanced at Joss; she had a funny look on her face. Fred stepped back, out of view.

Angie walked into the room.

78

For a moment, Angie looked unsettled when she saw the bodies of Jones and Daniele on the floor, but she quickly recovered. There was no nervousness or nail-biting, Grant noticed. Grant thought he saw a flicker of regret or shame in her face, but he decided it was wishful thinking. Angie looked with contempt at him and Joss.

Although Grant had heard her, he couldn't believe that Angie was the contact at Altimate. Even though she was pointing a gun at them.

With a shock that hit him in the chest, Grant realized it was his gun. She must have broken into his house. *Angie.* How long had she had the gun, had she used it on anyone? Grant felt numb. Stupidly, he had an image of the raccoons. He had been reluctant to use his gun on a dying animal. But something in Angie's face said she could pull the trigger.

Angie must have seen him staring at her. "Yes, it's your gun."

Grant shook his head as if that would help him to think. "But the email message was on Daniele's computer," was all he could come up with.

"Of course it was."

"And Friday night," Grant said, "you were the one who told me there was an email message on Daniele's computer."

She didn't answer him, but stared at him as if he were stupid. Finally Grant got it.

"It was *your* message," he said. "You wanted me to think it was Daniele's. You wanted me to break into her house. You wanted to get Joss here. You planned all of this."

Angie gave him a tight smile in acknowledgment. "It was so simple and it took you forever to figure it out," she said. "If you had been quicker, the 'police' could have picked you up days ago."

Grant felt as if his brain were working at a snail's pace. "How did they do it, Angie? How did they convince you to go along with their idea?"

Angie exploded, her face contorted with anger. "Jones told you it was *his* idea? It was *my* idea! It was brilliant. Using the school referendum to test the black twin. And there was a petition—so I had a *list* of everyone who was going to vote no. So I knew exactly who to send the letters to. All we had to do was wait for the results to come in, to know how well it worked. Then we knew how much we should use for the main event—to help Dell win his election."

Grant was rocked. *The black twin in the referendum letters hadn't had anything to do with school contracts!* The referendum had just been a testing ground. Grant glanced at Joss. Her face was wide-eyed and white.

"You tested it on innocent people," Joss said. "Before and during the referendum. People died."

"They weren't supposed to die," Angie said, sounding more annoyed than angry. "I don't know why they did. We didn't need their deaths. That just attracted attention. All we wanted to know was how much black twin to put in the letters."

It wasn't Angie talking, Grant thought. He didn't recognize the look on her face or her voice or what she said. It was all wrong. Grant couldn't believe that someone he knew was capable of such indifferent cruelty. "How could you do it?" Grant asked her. "You had a future."

"A future!" she burst. "Where? I graduated first in my class, and I almost didn't even get this assistant's job. Altimate told me I was too qualified to be an assistant, not qualified enough to be a researcher. Not qualified? I was smarter and had better ideas than ninety percent of the idiots working there."

"And what was my job?" she asked. "To spend nearly every moment running after you, Yes Dr. Fraser, No Dr. Fraser, and get no credit for what I did. I got a lousy salary that wasn't enough so I could save money for school, and not enough free time to go to school at nights."

"And they offered you more?" Grant asked.

SANDRA FEDER

227

Angie threw her head back. "I negotiated with them to get what I wanted. I have a top-notch lab with them. I send them samples of every drug that looks promising, and we evaluate them. When we find something we want," she paused, smiling, "I make sure that drug doesn't test well in Altimate's animal testing."

Grant was staggered. "You *sabotaged* drug samples? Compounds that I and other researchers spent years to create and purify." He had a moment of blind fury in which he could have throttled her.

"And Payne was always only too glad to stop work on the drug of any person he saw as a threat to him," she finished.

"Payne wasn't in on this?" Grant asked. He didn't believe it. He would have bet his life Payne was involved.

"No. But he couldn't have performed better if he had been," she said. "Daniele hated you so much. She did everything she could to make Payne hate and distrust you. She told him you were after his job."

Grant remembered Angie's act, full of loyalty and sympathy and tears, when in reality she had been so treacherous. It turned his stomach. Then he remembered the upcoming election. "How much is Dell paying for your help?"

"None of your business," she said.

"What about my car blowing up? Is that none of my business either?"

Angie's face got flushed with anger. "You screwed everything up. For us, for you. First, you took so long purifying the drug that we had to use unpurified black twin. Then they told you to forget about the twins, but you didn't. You had to do the molecular modeling! When you took so long to figure out the email on Daniele's computer, I told them to just shoot you. But Sharpley had to be clever with his damned electronics."

She paused, catching her breath. "When Horcroft let Payne go and put you in, we had to move fast. Especially when you sent the white twin back to animal testing."

Grant felt a chill at her callousness. He had thought he knew her. "Well, I'm still alive. You won't get away with this."

She had a disdainful expression on her face. "Spare me the platitudes." Holding the gun on them, she moved toward the phone. "Jones screwed up, but Walter won't. He doesn't make mistakes."

Angie looked at Grant's and Joss's hands. It suddenly seemed to occur to her that Daniele and Jones had been shot, and Grant didn't have a gun. She turned quickly toward the door, but Fred intercepted her and took the gun out of her hands.

Fred held the barrel in front of his nose and sniffed. "It hasn't been fired recently, maybe never," he said. "I don't think you have to worry about that."

Fred nodded toward the door. "Go to your house," he said to Grant. "I'll find you two later. Angie has a lab to show me."

79

Grant saw tongues of flame licking out of the upstairs windows as he screeched the car to a stop in his driveway. He flung open the door and ran for the house, Joss right behind him.

Smoke billowed out of windows. People from all over the neighborhood were standing on his lawn, open-mouthed, eyes wide with fear.

Grant searched the crowd for his next door neighbor, Carol. He found her and ran to her. "Where's Bailey? Is he with you?"

"No. He's not with you?"

Grant turned from her and ran around the side of the house. Hands tore at him when they saw what he was doing. But he threw them off and kept running.

Voices followed him: "Don't go in there." "It's suicide, Grant." "You can't survive, it's too late!" "It's only a dog!"

His gaze flickered over the house as he ran, trying to figure out where Bailey would be, and where he had the best chance of getting in the house.

He ran to the back, up onto the deck to the sliding doors. He grabbed one of the heavy deck chairs and threw it through the glass, turning his head away in case a blast of hot air or fire burst out. But though he could see flames in the hallway beyond, he thought he saw a path in. Grant smashed away more of the glass and stepped into the room, getting his bearings before smoke blinded him. He had decided that Bailey must be near his door. He was a smart dog. He must have tried to get out.

Moving cautiously but quickly, Grant headed toward the kitchen. It was only a matter of maybe thirty feet, but in a few seconds the smoke choked him. He had been planning to call for Bailey, but if the dog hadn't heard the breaking glass, he probably wasn't conscious. Grant wouldn't let himself think any further than that.

He smacked so hard into a wall that it stunned him, and his lungs choked with smoke. What wall was this? He must have made a wrong turn. Then he realized it was the door between the family room and the kitchen. He reached for the doorknob and turned it gently.

He couldn't see into the room. Hot smoke burned his eyes and seared his lungs. Grant stood for a moment with one terrified thought: Was he going to burn to death for a dog who might already be dead?

Then the smoke cleared, maybe because of the glass door he had smashed, and he saw a prostrate form lying against the kitchen door. His heart lunged. He threw himself into the room toward Bailey and reached the warm, furry body. There was no response. Grant didn't know if he should try to give Bailey air or get him out of the house. He was becoming too light-headed from the lack of air to do much, soon even to think.

With a supreme effort, he pulled Bailey away from the door, tore back the bolt and threw it open. As he pulled Bailey through and staggered through himself, everything went dark.

Grant heard a voice calling his name, over and over. He wanted it to stop. He wanted to stay where he was. But the voice was relentless.

"Shut up!" He finally got the words to his throat. Then he slowly opened his eyes to look up into Joss's face, white with fear. Immediately he remembered. "How is Bailey?"

Joss laughed and tears came to her eyes as she shook her head. "He came around before you did. The firemen," she nodded behind Grant, "crowded around him almost as soon as you brought him out. They've been giving him oxygen." She laughed again. "I guess they didn't want to chance bringing you around if they weren't successful with Bailey."

Grant leaned his head back to see Bailey's form, singed patches of fur, and his lifted head, mouth opened in a smile to the helping hands in gloves and coats and helmets around him.

Grant had to sit up slowly, because it made him light-headed and queasy. His shoulder hurt with a vengeance, and he winced. He focused only gradually on the scene around him. The firemen had finished spraying the house with water. It was gutted, the charred black interior visible through shattered windows. Everything must be gone. At that thought, his throat tightened so much he could hardly breathe.

He took a couple of deep breaths and looked back at Bailey with gratitude. The dog was trying to drag himself over to Grant, but he was too weak. Grant half-crawled, half-stumbled over to him and held him in his arms, hugging him, not letting go, the smell of singed fur and dog breath two of the best things he had ever inhaled.

Grant looked up at Joss. "I'm sorry, Joss. I've…"

Joss waved her hand. "Forget it. Anything you said or thought is going to pale in comparison to what A.R. Labs or Dell has in mind. I know Dell, Grant. He scares me more than anything. He never forgives, and he never forgets."

Carol, the next-door neighbor, came over and knelt down with Joss beside Grant and Bailey. "I called Dr. Helpern," she said. "He said he'd come over himself to look at Bailey, in case we shouldn't move him ourselves."

Grant cradled the dog, wincing as he looked at the burned skin and fur. The wounds looked serious, but Bailey wasn't complaining. He panted as his large, liquid eyes looked up trustingly at Grant.

Joss squeezed Grant's shoulder. "Do you have any idea who did this?" she asked. "The fire department and the police are checking the house—what's left of it—but I'm not sure anyone saw anything."

Grant shuddered and thought with bitter humor that he had a list of candidates: Fred's old comrades from A.R. Labs. But Grant had his money on Whitney Payne. The others would have killed *him*—Grant was the one who could make trouble. They wouldn't have burned down his house and trapped a helpless, living creature inside. No, this had Payne written all over it. Payne, in his irrational and jealous rage, wanted vengeance for having lost his job, by destroying every bit of Grant's life.

Grant lifted his gaze to the street, searching for Fred and his car. For a moment, Grant wanted Fred to help him find and kill

Payne. Grant was still slightly queasy and almost dizzy with the magnitude of his loss, and with how close he had come to death.

"Grant?"

Grant looked up to see James Helpern. He was a kindly, thin man with an English accent. The vet got down on his haunches to examine Bailey. When he saw the extent of the wounds, his face fell.

Grant's heart froze. "What? Is he all right? What's wrong?"

"Please do not worry," Dr. Helpern said. "I have not even begun. I was simply worried that when an animal is in pain he may bite without meaning to. I brought a muzzle."

"No," Grant said firmly. "I'll hold him, and he can chew my arm off before I make him feel more miserable by restraining his mouth. Go ahead and start."

But there had been no reason to restrain Bailey. Instinctively, he knew they were trying to help him. Though he whimpered when the vet touched his tender flesh, Bailey didn't move throughout the examination. Finally, the vet sighed. With relief, Grant thought.

"Well, as far as I can tell there is no serious or permanent damage. I may want to run a few tests when I get him back to my hospital. But I think Bailey is going to be fine. I want to keep him for a couple of days, to dress the wounds and to keep an eye on him. Is that acceptable?"

Grant nodded, not taking his gaze from Bailey. "I'll go with you and stay with him for a while."

Together they lifted Bailey into the vet's truck. Joss sat with the vet; Grant got in back with Bailey, holding him. "I'm sorry, Bailey," Grant whispered. "I wasn't there when you needed me." He shook his head. "I'm not going to leave you alone again."

As they drove away, Grant thought about something that only he knew. Payne had deliberately blocked Bailey's escape. Bailey's door had been nailed shut.

80

Grant carried Bailey in and put him on the vet's examining table.

"He has had oxygen, and he seems to be doing just fine," Dr. Helpern said. "But I am going to take a blood sample, to make certain his blood gases are all right. I also want to take an X-ray. He may have been jumping around quite a bit and hurt himself."

Grant knew what he meant. Bailey must have been terrified trying to get out of the house. Grant still wanted to get vengeance against Payne.

Dr. Helpern petted Bailey. "Leave Bailey with me. We should have some answers soon." He waved his arm around the spotless, gleaming surgery. "I used to send samples out to other labs for analysis, but I grew to have little faith in their turnaround times, let alone their accuracy. Fortunately, Westport can support my efforts."

As he sat in the waiting room with Joss, she put her hand on his shoulder. "Grant, he's going to be all right," she said. "Dr. Helpern just wants to do some tests to make sure. Don't worry."

The outside door to the waiting room opened, and a man walked in and identified himself as a Westport detective. The hairs on the back of Grant's neck stood up. Had the detective been to Daniele's house?

The man jumped right in. "I'd like to ask you some questions, Dr. Fraser. I hope you don't mind that I followed you here. But most people's memories are best right after an accident."

Dr. Helpern came into the waiting room. He'd apparently heard the detective. "My goodness, I should think there is no question that it was not an accident," he said. "There was no one in the house, and the dog wasn't likely to have started that blaze."

The detective ignored Dr. Helpern. "The fire department will of course examine the remains of the house for any evidence of arson."

Dr. Helpern spoke up again, repeating himself. "Oh, I think it is quite clear that the fire was deliberate."

Grant looked up sharply. There was no way that Helpern could know about Payne. What was he talking about?

"I don't think you are in a position to make that determination, Doctor," the detective said.

"Well, I think it is the only conclusion that makes sense under the circumstances."

"Under what circumstances?" The detective sounded annoyed.

Grant suddenly stood up. "Bailey—is he all right?"

Dr. Helpern made reassuring gestures with his hands. "He is fine. I have the preliminary test results, and I am quite satisfied that he will recover completely. That is not what I was referring to."

"Well, what *do* you mean?" The detective sounded exasperated.

"The dog was sedated."

"What?" Grant was horrified. Payne had sedated Bailey to make sure he would die in the blaze. Grant felt he could have killed Payne if he had been in front of him at that moment.

The vet shook his head. "I am not sure about the timing," he said, "since Bailey regained consciousness so quickly. Perhaps he had not had much sedative, and the effects had worn off. Perhaps it was the oxygen the firemen gave him as soon as he came out of the house. Perhaps he vomited and managed to get some of the sedative out of his system. But he *was* given a sedative. The blood analysis is quite clear."

Grant shook his head and muttered. Joss put her hand on his arm.

"Paradoxically, Grant, the sedative may have saved his life, in the circumstances," Dr. Helpern said.

"What do you mean?" Grant asked.

"If Bailey had not had the sedative, he would have tried to get out, one way or another. There is a good chance he would have hurt himself in the process. Instead, he was lying on the floor, where the coolest and clearest air is. His respiration and metabolism were depressed, so he was not breathing in so much smoke. And since he was near his door, he was in one of the only areas of the house that wasn't in flames when you arrived. I know it sounds strange, but it was lucky that he was sedated."

Grant was beginning to feel drunk from the battering he had taken. The revelation of the message on Daniele's computer, the confrontation and deaths at Daniele's house, plunging into his burning house, worrying about Bailey's injuries. Grant's body had been required to gear itself to life-threatening situations over and over. The adrenaline surges had left him drained. Not long ago he had been ready to track Payne down and tear him apart. Now Grant just wanted to go to sleep.

Sleep? Fred said he and Joss had to get out of here—tonight, now. Grant looked toward the door, on the other side of which Bailey was bandaged and resting. Dr. Helpern said Bailey needed to stay here for a couple of days. Grant clenched his jaw. He wouldn't abandon Bailey, no matter what.

81

Grant was staring at the door of the room where Bailey lay.

Joss came over to him. "Fred is outside waiting for us," she said.

"I won't leave without Bailey," Grant said. He had promised.

Joss looked tense. "Fred doesn't think we have much time. Carol said she would take care of Bailey."

"You go with Fred, Joss. I can't abandon him." Grant knew it didn't make sense, waiting for the dog when his life and Joss's were at stake. But Grant hadn't been able to save Dena or the white twin or his house. Somehow he had to keep Bailey.

Joss lowered her voice. "I'm not leaving without you. But if we don't go soon, Dell or Smith will get to us, and it won't make any difference."

Grant heard the crunch of gravel as a car drove up to the vet's. Maybe he had already waited too long.

Dr. Helpern opened the door to Bailey's room, and Grant heard a low whining. The vet stood in the doorway, looking back and forth between the dog and Grant.

Grant heard footsteps on the path to the front door. "How is Bailey, Dr. Helpern?" he asked. Grant's heart began to pound, anticipating who was on the other side of the front door. He saw that Joss was half-turned to the door, waiting.

"Under normal circumstances, I would say that Bailey should stay here a day or so," Dr. Helpern said.

The door opened, and a heavy woman carrying a Chihuahua walked in. A reprieve. Grant exhaled with relief. But he couldn't expect this to last. Too many people were after him. Grant's stomach tightened as he thought he might have to leave Bailey behind after all, if he were too weak to travel.

"However, what happened to Bailey was far from normal," Dr. Helpern continued. "I think it would actually do him more harm to keep him away from you. So I am going to release him to you, with some instructions and medicines."

Grant could have hugged the old vet.

Grant carried Bailey to Fred's car. Fred took a look at Bailey, but didn't say a word. Joss got in front with Fred; Grant cradled Bailey's head on his lap in the back seat.

As Fred drove away, it hit Grant. His home was destroyed. His belongings were gone—his computer, his books, even trivial things like mementos and clothing. Dena's things, too. All his bridges had been burnt. Including the Zip Disk, the one with all his information on the twins, the one that had miraculously not been stolen.

That was the last straw. The Zip Disk was all that he had. It represented the distillation of years of work. He could have started over again with it.

Started what over? Grant asked himself. What would he have done with it? He was running away. Where would he be able to surface to work on the twins, especially if they were both duds? In fact, what was he going to do anywhere?

"You look terrible," Fred told him.

"I'll try to avoid burning buildings in the future," Grant said without humor. "Did you find the lab?"

"Found it and got some people to do something about it," Fred said.

Grant didn't ask what happened to Angie. He wasn't sure he wanted to know. Grant noticed that Fred was even more tense than he had been in Daniele's house. He kept glancing in the rear view mirror.

"Do we have to run?" Grant asked, grasping at straws. "I don't want to leave everything behind." In one day he had lost his home and his job.

Grant thought Fred looked as if he might burst out laughing. Instead, he said quietly, "You're amazing, Grant. Your house and everything in it is charcoal, they canned your research projects, you were nearly blown up, and you're reluctant to leave 'everything' behind. If you wait much longer, you won't even have a mouth to protest with."

"A.R. Labs is not finished with you two, I promise," Fred added. "Or with me. Not as long as Smith is around."

Bailey whimpered when Fred hit a bump, and Grant stifled a curse. Fred caught Grant's eye in the rear view mirror.

"Forget about revenge on Payne," Fred said. "You can't prove he set the fire, and you'd just be getting your hands dirty. People like Payne tend to take care of themselves. His type ends up getting shot by some angry woman he's beaten up or by her husband." Fred gave Grant a look as he said this, and Grant didn't know if it were prediction or fact.

At this point, it didn't matter. Whether or not Grant got any kind of vengeance against Payne, he still had nothing. He didn't know where to begin.

"Any suggestions you have on what we should do would be helpful," he said quietly to Fred.

"Okay," Fred said. "Here's your advice. Ignore it at your peril. Don't use your credit cards ever again—they can trace you with them. Don't use your own cars. Rent a car, but use cash and other names. Stay in small motels, off the beaten path. If possible, one of you rents the room while the other stays in the car."

"Don't be highly visible as a couple," Fred said. "For God's sake, keep the dog out of sight as much as possible. And if you can, change your appearances. Unless people are trained to recognize certain unchanging features like ears and fingers, they will be fooled by things like color and length of hair, glasses, facial hair and so on."

Fred glanced in the rear view mirror again. "Don't look, dress or act in character. Stay away from places you have a connection with—like old home towns, where you went to college, that kind of thing. They can trace you from your resumes if you do. Don't ever forget that they're experts at getting information. Go as far as you can as fast as you can. Where you surface after that, and what you choose to do, is up to you."

"I'll get you started on the first leg," he said. "Then we part company."

Joss turned to Grant, and a smile trembled on her lips. "I feel as if we're getting five minutes of swimming instructions before we're dumped in the middle of the ocean," she said.

82

Fred drove the car down a long driveway of a house in New Canaan. The driveway ran between two rows of large trees, then swung behind the house, ending in front of a detached three-car garage not far from a beautiful pool. "We're going to change cars here," he said. He motioned to the car parked in front of the garage.

"Whose house is this?" Grant asked.

"Someone I know," Fred said.

Grant carried Bailey over and gently put him on the back seat. He covered him with a blanket. Joss got in and left the door open. Fred motioned for Grant to get in, but Grant stood outside the car.

"You have to get out of here *now*," Fred said. "No more delays."

Grant heard a car on the road behind them and thought it slowed down as it went past the driveway. Grant didn't want to stay there, out in the open, but he was determined to know the rest about A.R. Labs. It had cost him everything. He wanted to know why.

"I still don't understand why we have to abandon everything," Grant said, "our jobs, homes and identities. Why does A.R. Labs have to kill us? They must know that Joss and I aren't the ones who were using the black twin."

Fred's face was grim, almost angry. The day was nearly silent; the only sound Grant heard was the lapping of water in the pool.

"It's not what you did or might do," Fred said. "It's what *they* did. If A.R. Labs doesn't clean this up, someone will figure out what Smith and Angie were doing with the black twin. A.R. Labs can't let that happen."

Fred took a deep breath, looked around and cleared his throat. "A.R. Labs decided that if you want to influence people, the way to do it is to sensitize them first. So they developed a drug—a special excito-toxin—that has a way of unlocking the mechanism that keeps certain chemicals out of the brain. After administering an excito-toxin, it would take just minuscule amounts of a drug to affect the brain. And it would be virtually impossible to detect."

Sunlight breaking through the leaves made it impossible for Grant to see Fred's face.

"A.R. Labs is smart," Fred said. "They also know it's important to be flexible. You never know who's going to be your friend or your enemy. They wanted to cover all the bases."

Grant heard a car horn in the distance, and his pulse began to race. Fred glanced up and spoke even more rapidly and intently.

"But they wanted to test it first. They wanted to see how it worked. And they had to figure out how to ensure that people would ingest it. So they decided to put it into something that everyone would eat."

Grant didn't know what was coming.

"They put it in sugar," Fred said. "Starting with Connecticut."

Grant felt numb. But for some reason he heard wind rustling the trees, and he noticed that leaves were finally falling. They drifted into the pool.

"In sugar," Fred repeated. "From there it goes into almost everything you eat. Think about it. People are addicted to sugar. Each individual in this country consumes an average of half a pound a day. They *want* to eat it. It was a brilliant choice as a vehicle for the sensitizer."

Fred turned briefly to look at the driveway. "So now you know why they can't let anyone go who knows about the black twin. Not you and Joss." He paused. "Not me. The black twin that Angie and Smith sent in the letters made people sick. If they had eaten something sweet beforehand, there was a good chance they died. Remember, Angie and Smith used the drug before you had completely purified it. A.R. Labs is afraid that any investigation into it will lead back to their excito-toxin in the sugar. They can't let that happen—they have too much to lose."

Fred bent his head so he addressed both Joss and Grant. "So, I might add, does the government. This work was done for them."

"The *sugar*," Grant said. A.R. Labs had set them up, and Angie had pounded the nails into their coffins, he thought.

Grant shuddered as he remembered the dead raccoons, next to the remains of a package of cookies. One of the dead raccoons had been clutching one of Angie's letters in its paw. The raccoons must have eaten part of that letter, before or after they ate the cookies. That letter had been meant for Grant. Angie said they hadn't intended to kill anyone with those letters. But if Grant had eaten something sweet and then handled that letter...

"So why are we alive?" Grant asked.

Grant watched Fred's gaze stray to Joss. Then Fred looked at Grant. His face was tight. "You never let up, do you? Let's say it was a selfish decision. Let's just say that you—and Joss—reminded me in some way of myself. You try to do a good job. You give everything. You trust people. They betray you."

Fred's gaze slid to Joss again. "A lot of life is a sewer. That doesn't mean that everyone should be flushed down."

Fred put his hands on the car. "You have to listen to me so that you'll have a chance at staying alive. I don't want all this to be wasted action. I've told you about the sugar connection, but I don't want you to try to do something about it."

"But if there's something in the sugar supply," Joss began.

"There *is*," Fred said. "I told you there is. What will you do? Try to analyze samples of sugar, looking for some small molecule?"

Fred didn't wait for a reply. "The way they added the excitotoxin, it would be virtually impossible to dig it out of a sugar sample. Believe me. Don't you think they thought about this? Do you think they arranged it so you could just dissolve the sugar in some solvent, crystallize the solution to get pure sugar crystals and analyze the remaining liquid—like that?" Fred snapped his fingers.

Grant got the message—they'd probably chosen chemicals that would break down before they could be identified.

"I appreciate your help, Grant," Fred said. "Without it, I might not have found out about Smith before it was too late. But it's time to back off now."

"So it's like that?" Grant said. "You're big pushers with pure dope; they were small pushers with tainted dope. You both turn people into zombies."

"Don't push your luck," Fred said. "I appreciate a lot of things. But let's not pretend there was some great spiritual awakening on my part. A.R. Labs was just doing its job, making money."

Grant was incredulous. "But they hurt people. They killed people. This is a democracy. I still can't believe the government would do that to its people."

Fred snorted. "Of course not. Don't be naive, Grant. This country is run by people who have money and power and agendas. And you'd better hope you don't get in their way."

"Take what I'm offering you, Grant, and let it go," Fred said. "Life is a compromise. You know that. Besides, if you don't let go, someone will be back for you—someone like me. I can promise you that." He looked Grant squarely in the face. "Okay? That's the whole story. Now get on with your new lives."

Fred stood back from the car and tossed Grant a pair of glasses. "For your disguise," he said. "Use them. Make sure you use them. Now get out of here."

83

Joss watched Grant's hands gripping the steering wheel, and she thought: This is it. She felt as if she were on the edge of a precipice. When Grant got to the end of the driveway, she asked him, "Do you have a preference as to where we go?"

Grant shook his head. "The world is our oyster—didn't you hear Fred? As far as we can get, as fast as we can get there. I guess that means main, multi-lane roads. Do you have a direction in mind?"

Joss nodded. "As we get closer, I'll tell you. Take the Merritt Parkway to 287."

Between the house and the highway she was tense, watching every car that passed them. When they got onto the Merritt Parkway, she breathed a small sigh of relief. It was only two lanes in each direction, but there were plenty of cars all around them, and traffic was moving. Then things slowed down. Joss chafed as they inched along.

Joss wondered what Fred's plans were. He had let them go, but maybe he was planning to watch them to see if they led him to anyone else who knew about the black twin—someone he didn't know about. Then maybe he'd come back and kill them. Joss shook herself. He'd killed Jones and saved her life and Grant's. Besides, she couldn't afford to be paranoid.

Her hands were clenched in her lap. "We'll need money," Joss said. "Do you have any with you?"

Grant shook his head. "Not much. Just several hundred."

"I have one last source," Joss said. "Just before Dell and I got divorced, I got a safe deposit box in a small town in upstate New York—because I thought it was one of the last places Dell would look. I put bearer bonds, money, American Eagles, jewelry—anything portable that I could liquidate easily. I didn't know what Dell might do—or might bribe someone to do. I had my own money and didn't want to take the chance that he could somehow get it. Dell is incredibly devious."

Suddenly Joss put her face in her hands. "Oh my God," she said.

"Joss, what's the matter?"

"Dell has the black twin," she said. "And I told him how to use it."

Grant frowned. "What are you talking about?"

"I've been thinking about Dell since Angie told us. I couldn't believe her. A statewide election involves millions of people, not just a few thousand. But now I understand things that didn't make sense before."

"Tell me," Grant said.

"I saw Dell give a political talk at the Town Hall," Joss said. "He deliberately said things to divide the audience. And then, when the audience reacted, there were photographers who took pictures. I thought that Dell couldn't control himself, that it was an accidental outburst. I was sure that Dell had blundered and that his opponent had gotten it on film."

She laughed dryly. "He did it *deliberately*. And I didn't realize until now that I told him what to do."

"Joss, you're not making sense to me," Grant said. "What did you tell him?"

"Several months ago I ran into him at a fund-raiser. I tried to get away from him, but when Dell wants something, he gets it. So he picked my brain about elections."

Grant interrupted her. "What could you know about elections?"

"You remember recently when it looked as if drug costs might be threatened by government controls?" she asked. "You know how politically active Altimate got. That was my job. I met and worked with some of the savviest political advisors in this country."

"When I talked with Dell, I told him what I'd learned," Joss said. "That if you analyze each of the voting districts for how they voted, you find out that elections are won or lost by swing votes. A small number of votes that put you over the top."

Joss looked at Grant. "I should have known rule number one

with Dell: He never makes mistakes. He must have given talks in specially chosen locations—like Westport—that were probably just over the edge in the last election. He *wanted* to divide the audience at Town Hall, to find out who was for him and who was against him. So he said things that would make people react. And the photographers had to be his. He got pictures of everyone who was against him. Then he planned to send them letters laced with black twin so they couldn't vote."

Her eyes filled with tears. "He must have used that technique over and over again throughout the state." She felt Grant squeeze her hand.

"It isn't your fault, Joss," he said. "Dell has millions of dollars. He can afford the best. I'm sure that what you told him was good, but he must have gotten a lot more advice from his consultants."

"But I showed him what to look for. And at the Galway fund-raiser, he told me how much I helped him."

"He was trying to twist your head," Grant said. "You didn't help him. You didn't know what he was going to do with that information."

Grant looked as if something had just occurred to him. "When the Westport Taxpayer's Group called, and you found out people had been sick," Grant began.

"The symptoms were textbook for frontal lobe impairment," Joss said. "I figured it couldn't be a coincidence. I was afraid some-one had gotten their hands on one of our drugs, maybe the black twin. So I tested the bogus campaign letter."

"When I found you in the lab at the HPLC machine, I thought you might be involved," Grant admitted.

"You thought I put black twin in letters?" Joss could feel her face getting red with anger. "Why not? I was married to Dell. There must be something wrong with me. I must be capable of terrible things."

"A lot of crazy things went through my head," Grant said. "Who would ever have thought Angie would do something like this?" Grant reached for her hand, and she pulled it away.

"Don't you think I've told myself those things a thousand times?" she asked. "Why do you think I haven't had any relationship since I divorced him? I don't ever want to take the chance of being with someone like him again."

"He fooled a lot of people, Joss," Grant said. "A lot of people who think they're smart and discriminating. When someone like Dell is handsome, intelligent and successful, you assume he has other good qualities, too. It's human to do that. I liked him, too."

Joss was still stinging with hurt and anger. She didn't answer him.

84

Joss looked at her watch and the signs on the road. They wouldn't get to her bank today. Joss felt better when they got on 287. The Merritt had trees along both sides and in the middle, and she felt closed in. Route 287 was more open.

When they reached the Tappan Zee Bridge, she saw fog over the water and on the opposite shore. The swirling mist made her think of vampires lurking behind tombstones and moss-covered trees. She shook herself, but it didn't help. She wondered what was waiting for them up ahead. She was terrified to think of what Dell would do when he learned they had interfered with his plans.

How things could change. Two days ago Grant had thought his world was coming to an end because he'd had to give up his research project and spend more time in administration as director of research. She had been afraid that Grant's obsession with the black twin would make him lose his job and threaten hers. Tonight they had turned their backs on their careers and all of their worldly possessions, and they were only at the beginning of what she was sure would be a long journey. You never knew that things were good until they got worse, she thought.

Where would they go? What would they do? How could they start over? If A.R. Labs were as powerful and relentless as Fred said it was, both she and Grant would have to give up their names, their social security numbers. How would they survive without birth certificates and licenses?

It suddenly struck her that she had been thinking in terms of "they." Who was to say that the two of them should stay together? Maybe they would have more chance of surviving if they went their separate ways. Joss hadn't been part of a couple in a long time. She didn't know that she wanted to be tied to another person—even if it were Grant and even under these circumstances.

What was she thinking? she suddenly asked herself. How could she debate "me" versus "us" with herself when she didn't even know if they were going to get through today or tomorrow alive?

The first hint that it was far from over was the news flash she heard on the radio.

Joss had turned it on so they could hear any traffic or weather forecasts. She had been listening to the same news briefs over and over again, when the announcer broke in with an exclusive.

"Police have reported that Dr. Nathan Horcroft, president of Altimate Pharmaceuticals, has been found dead. No other details have been released."

Joss couldn't believe it. She shook her head, staring at Grant. This couldn't be happening to them. It was too much.

Grant gripped the wheel with white knuckles. "Nathan." He didn't say anything for a long time, but Joss saw tears in his eyes.

Joss knew Grant mourned Nathan Horcroft's death, even though Horcroft was involved with Smith. And even though Horcroft might have killed her and Grant if he'd been ordered to. They would never know.

85

"This one looks good," Grant said. They had gotten off at several exits, checking out the motels. This was the first one that wasn't too visible or close to the highway.

Grant pulled the car into the parking lot of a small, one-level strip of rooms with an office. He liked the location. Buildings were not close together; the next one was several hundred yards down the road. He noticed that the motel backed onto an area of trees and vegetation, and a clear strip just wide enough for the car.

"I'm going to drive around the back," Grant said. He sighed with relief when he saw the rear wall.

"A window?" Joss asked. "You think we may need an escape route?"

In the glow from the dashboard indicators, Grant could see her face. She was trying to look matter of fact, he thought, but her lip quivered. "I hope not. But we shouldn't stay anywhere where there's only one exit from the room. Not yet, at least."

"I'll go in and register," Joss said. "If I can, I'll get an end room."

Grant watched the parking lot while Joss was inside. He could still taste the fried chicken they had gotten for dinner, after they'd shopped at a local Ames where Joss had bought clothes and necessities for them. Only Bailey seemed to have enjoyed the food.

A few minutes later, Joss returned and slid into the front seat. "I got a room on the far end of the motel."

Grant parked around the side of the motel, right near their room. They carried in their bags in the dark. Grant pulled the drapes before he turned on a small light.

He surveyed the room. It was large, with a double bed and two chairs. There was a window looking out on the parking lot and another window in the bathroom. Though Grant checked the bathroom window and found it opened easily, he hoped they wouldn't have to use it.

When he returned to the room, he saw Joss emptying the bags

of clothes she had just bought. Sweaters, shirts, a jacket, socks, shoes and jeans tumbled onto the bed. He had never seen her wear jeans.

He didn't know what to say. "I'm sorry there's just one double bed," he finally said.

Joss looked up. "Don't worry. That's the least of it." She folded the clothes and put them in one of the big, nylon zipper bags she'd bought. Then she picked up a long, dark-colored dress with long sleeves and hung it up.

The dress looked completely foreign to Grant, not like something Joss had ever worn. But he was mystified when she took a wig out of a bag and shook it out. His surprise must have shown on his face.

"Part of the disguise," she said. "Remember what Fred told us." Joss patted a folded set of clothes on the bed. "Pajamas for you and clothes for tomorrow. There's a waist pack for each of us, too. For valuables and to keep our hands free." She looked around the room. "I guess that's all I can do now. I'll take a quick shower."

Grant was overwhelmed by how comforting and reassuring it was to have Joss with him. Somehow, he felt he could face anything with her. "Joss?"

"What?"

"Thank you."

She looked as if she were about to say something but changed her mind. "So far so good."

While Joss was in the bathroom, Grant hugged Bailey, pressing his cheek against the dog's neck fur. "Bailey, it's going to take some doing, but I promise you we're going to get somewhere safe. And I'm going to take good care of you."

Bailey licked his ear and his neck and wriggled happily.

After Grant gave Bailey his medications, he watched the front of the motel and the parking lot from behind the curtain. It was still pouring steadily, and he could only see the handful of cars that had been in the lot when he and Joss drove in. Nothing looked suspicious to him.

He was exhausted and had begun to nod off when Joss came out of the bathroom, wearing a flannel robe and toweling her hair. She was haloed by the steam that billowed out of the bathroom. "I haven't seen any activity in the parking lot," Grant told her.

She came into the room and sat on the double bed, rubbing her hair with the towel. "Okay. I'll watch while you shower."

Forgetting his promise to be quick, Grant stood under the spray, letting the hot water run all over his tired and bruised body.

It wasn't until he was toweling off in front of the steamy mirror that it hit him. Coming close to being killed at Daniele's house, losing his house and everything in it in a fire, nearly losing Bailey, running away—exhaustion and fear had numbed his heart and his mind. But now the thought rose up to break his heart: He had lost Michael. He would never see him again.

Grant stood for a long time in the bathroom, his head bowed and tears running down his face.

Opening the bathroom door slowly, he saw that Joss had draped a shirt over the one light so that there was just a dim glow to illumine the room. She was standing at the window, hugging herself and looking out from behind the curtain. When he closed the door, she turned toward him. Bailey, who was sitting beside her, turned his head, too.

He padded to the window and looked out over Joss's shoulder. The rain was still coming down. "The parking lot looks the same as it did an hour ago," he said. Grant patted Bailey's head. "Good boy," he said. "Keep alert."

Joss saw his face. "You've been crying."

He shrugged his shoulders. "I've lost Michael. I'll never see him again."

Joss put her arms around him. He felt her tears on his shoulder.

86

A shift in the bed brought Grant rapidly awake. After a moment of disorientation, he remembered where he was.

"Grant?" Joss whispered. "Are you awake?"

"Yes."

"All of a sudden I awakened," she said. "Is everything all right?"

In answer Grant got silently out of bed and crossed to the window. At the foot of the bed, Bailey lifted his head and looked at him as if to say: I would have told you if anything was wrong.

Grant looked out. "Still raining, still quiet," he reported. He got back into bed and lay there, near the edge. His body was tense. Without knowing why, he felt something was going to happen.

Grant heard a gagging and then a bubbling sound.

"Uggh! Oh, Bailey! How could you?" Joss's nose wrinkled and her eyebrows furrowed in astonishment as she sat up in bed.

Grant got a small penlight out of his pants pocket and trained it on the bed. Bailey had made a mess. Grant was flabbergasted. He checked Bailey to make sure he wasn't ill. But he seemed perfectly all right. He was wagging his tail as if he did this every day.

"This isn't like him, Joss. He's never done anything like this. Not even on the floor. And certainly not on the furniture. Maybe it's the stress of everything he's been through—he almost died tonight. And the medications he's taking. Everything that's happened has stirred me up. I guess it got to him, too."

Grant heard dismay in Joss's voice. "All over the bed! We can't clean these sheets, and it wouldn't do any good to change them. He must have wet the bed clear through to the mattress. Bailey! Either we get another room, or we have to go somewhere else."

Grant tried to get the motel office on the phone, but no one answered. "I guess we'll have to go over," he said.

They got dressed and picked up all their bags. Grant took one last look around the room to make sure they hadn't left anything, then they went outside, still leaving the light out.

It was so dark that Grant felt uncomfortable walking even the hundred feet to the motel office in the dark. "Let's get in the car and drive around," he said.

In order not to disturb anyone, Grant didn't turn on the headlights. As they were driving out from behind the office, an Explorer with no headlights pulled into the parking lot and stopped not far from the room they'd just left. The arrival at such a late hour plus the lack of headlights made Grant's chest tighten.

"Let's get out of here," Joss said. "I don't like this. Drive, Grant, now!"

Grant pulled out of the lot, his heart pounding in his throat, and drove away at what felt like an agonizingly slow rate. For a while they were in view of the motel parking lot and the other car. In spite of himself, he rolled down the window. He could make out figures jumping out of the truck and moving toward the room they had just left.

But that wasn't the end of it. He heard rapid gunshots and the sound of bullets going through wood and glass.

"My God, Grant," Joss whispered. "They followed us. How did they know?"

Grant searched the road ahead. "Tell me if any of them leaves the motel," he said. "We're not getting on the highway." Grant made his choice. Still with his headlights off, he made a left turn onto a small road. He hoped that night combined with a dark car would make it virtually impossible for the people behind them to follow.

Grant drove from one country road to another, until he had gone as far as he could with no headlights. He pulled over to the side of the road and stopped the car. He could just make out the road ahead of them. There was rising ground to their right and a fence—presumably a field—on their left. But he couldn't see more than thirty feet away.

"What now?" Joss asked. "I guess it's too dangerous to go to another motel?"

"I think so," Grant said. "Besides, we can't go anywhere without headlights, and I don't want to chance turning them on. If those people are anywhere around us, immobile headlights would be a dead giveaway."

"Without any lights we can't walk, either," Joss said. "Even if we don't run into anything, we could step in a hole and break a leg." She sighed. "I don't feel like spending the night in this car, but I guess we don't have a choice."

The windows were open a little. Grant stared into the night and strained to hear the smallest sound that would warn him of an imminent attack.

"Only a day of being hunted, and already I can't stand it," Joss said.

Grant took her hand and spoke quietly. "One day of running and having the room we just left shot to pieces."

Bailey stuck his nose into the front seat and nuzzled Grant and Joss.

"Yes, you're the one bit of good luck," Grant said. "For whatever reason you got sick, Bailey, it got us out of that room before they started firing." Grant sobered at the thought that they had once again narrowly missed being killed. For how much longer would they be lucky? He made a decision.

"We're not going to your bank tomorrow. The people following us could figure that we're here for a reason, and they could wait for us to show up. We'll have to keep going."

"We can't," Joss said. "We have no money. What will we use? Fred said we can't use our credit cards."

"I don't know. We'll think of something. We just can't go back into town. We have to get away from here."

Joss shook her head, and for a moment Grant almost thought he could see small sparks fly.

"*I'm* going back there tomorrow morning," she said. "To empty my safe deposit box in the Monsey Savings Bank."

Thursday
October 30

87

Joss was tense, waiting for Monsey Savings Bank to open at 9:00 a.m. She peered through the rain-splattered windshield at the street and shivered, thinking about what she intended to do.

Joss couldn't help noticing that the businesses along the street were worn, even shabby. The one- and two-story buildings were almost all in need of paint and repairs, and the display windows were not very inviting, not by big city standards. There was a store selling religious articles, another advertised comfortable walking shoes, next to this was a bakery. All of the businesses related, one way or another, to the community's religion. And everything was kosher, even a computer store.

She glanced at Grant; she thought the two of them were not easily recognizable. Grant had combed his hair over his forehead and was wearing the pair of glasses Fred had given him. He had his shirt buttoned to his neck and was wearing the jacket and baseball cap Joss had bought the night before.

"Isn't it nine o'clock yet? I want to get this over with and get out of here," she said.

When Grant turned to her, she saw his face was furrowed with worry. "Joss, I don't want you to go through with this," he said. "Not after last night. I feel as if we're sitting ducks."

"I told you that no one knows about the safety deposit box besides you and me."

"Then why the disguises?" he asked.

Joss was scanning the area. "Because you've got me seeing people from A.R. Labs everywhere. I don't want to take a chance. Even though there's no way anyone can know about this box. I told you—I took it out under another name."

"But this?" Grant motioned toward her outfit. "Why this outfit?"

Joss nodded out the window. "This is a Hasidic community, Grant. I've been here often enough to know that a designer suit would stand out like a sore thumb. The women all wear long, modest dresses and *sheitls*—wigs."

Grant gave her a questioning look.

"Their hair is cut very short. The idea is that they're only supposed to be desirable to their husbands," Joss explained. "So I thought if I wore this brown wig and a long dress and a pillow so I looked pregnant, I might pass...I'm scared to death, Grant. I've never had to run for my life." Joss felt Grant squeeze her hand.

"I can try to go in for you," he said.

"You know you can't do that," she said. "Your name isn't on the box. It would just alert the bank to something being wrong. No, I'll go in." She steadied her hands as she clutched the strap of an oversized purse.

As Grant drove down the street toward the bank, Joss watched the people and the cars they passed, alert for a possible pursuer. But the cars she saw were old, rusty and driven by men who looked the same as the ones walking along the sidewalk. The Hasidic men all wore black suits with white shirts under long black coats and black hats. The women—many walking in twos, or pushing strollers—were in simple, unpretentious long dresses, long coats and hats. Like what I'm wearing, Joss thought.

Then Joss saw something that made her heart stop. A modern car, nearly new, with two men. A.R. Labs, she thought.

Grant must have seen it, too. "We should forget about this," he said.

Joss's heart beat faster, but she was determined, angry determined. "I know two things," she said. "One, that we don't know who our friends are, and we can't trust anyone but ourselves. Two, that I'm going into that bank. I've left behind my house, my career and everything else I own. I'm not giving up this box. Enough is enough."

Joss heard Grant take a deep breath.

"All right. We'll go ahead with your emptying the box," he said. "But let me see if I can find anything out about that car."

Joss didn't want to wait anymore. The tension was getting to her. But Grant made sense.

Grant parked around the corner from the bank, near a kosher grocery store. Across the street Joss saw a bus stop. A bus pulled up, and a schoolgirl got off. She was wearing a blazer and a long skirt and led a small boy gently by the hand. They got a shopping cart in front of the store and went in.

Grant got out of the car and pulled up the hood of his jacket. Joss watched him walk down the street, then she kept an eye out the window. She had been so intent on watching for Grant's return that she didn't realize how tense she was, until she looked at her hands. Her knuckles were white, and her palms were wet. Joss shifted in her seat and realized she had been perspiring; her back was damp.

An old station wagon squealed up in front of the grocery store, blowing its horn, and Joss started. But it turned out to be a taxi, there to pick up an older woman who came out with grocery bags and got in.

Joss felt something on her arm.

"You have to stay down, Bailey," she said. "Under the blanket. Now."

He got back down, and Joss covered him again.

Although it seemed longer to Joss, Grant returned within ten minutes. He slid into the front seat of the car. "The two of them went into the bank and seemed to conduct some business. I don't know, Joss. They may be innocent, or they may not be. Or there may be some others we haven't even seen."

Joss took a deep breath. "That's it. I'm going in *now*," she said.

Grant drove to the corner and pulled into a spot. Joss heard the engine idle, felt Grant's hand on her arm.

"I'll be waiting for you, right here," he said. "Good luck."

Joss nodded and checked her wig in the mirror, then got carefully out of the car. She walked down the street slowly. From behind the thick, chin-length wig she glanced left and right. Besides a few pedestrians, the street was deserted.

88

When Joss reached the other side and began to walk up the steps to the bank, she felt dizzy and slightly queasy. She saw a bench and sank onto it and bent her head forward. Joss hadn't told Grant what else was in her safe deposit box, besides the money.

It was only when she stood up that she felt the wetness. She looked at the bench. It had rained the previous night, and a small hollow in one of the planks still contained water. No matter, she thought. It wasn't as if she were going to go home and change her clothes. There was no way she wasn't going in that bank.

Inside the bank, Joss noticed that she recognized no one from the last time she had been there, and none of the bank employees seemed to be from the Hasidic community. Hopefully, no one would challenge her. Joss went directly to the safe deposit box desk. The woman there was talking to another employee and didn't give Joss a second glance.

Joss leaned over the desk. "Can you help me, please? I'm in a hurry."

The woman looked annoyed as she glanced over at Joss and then past her. Joss turned to see a man behind one of the teller stations; he seemed to look pointedly at the woman and then at Joss. What did that mean? Joss wondered. Joss turned back to the woman, who handed her a card to sign.

"Follow me," the woman said.

Joss went to the back of the bank where the woman unlocked the metal gate, and they both stepped inside the vault. Then the woman closed the metal gate and went over to Joss's box. Joss felt her heartbeat increase as the gate swung closed. She had trouble breathing. Don't get claustrophobic, she told herself. The woman turned the keys in the locks and opened the small door.

Joss was afraid the box would be empty, that someone had cleaned it out. But it was reassuringly heavy. She held it in both arms as the woman took the keys out of the locks and handed one to Joss. With a twinge, Joss realized she wasn't going to need this box again.

The woman opened the metal gate and directed Joss to a small side room with a door. "You can open the box in here," she said.

When Joss opened the lid of the safe deposit box, she saw everything was there, just as she'd left it. Her heart was beating fast again; she was anxious to empty the box and leave. She quickly lifted flannel bags of jewelry and gold coins, and bound stacks of bills and bearer bonds out of the box, and dumped them in her purse. She was through a third of the box when she first noticed the whispers.

"Didn't you notice?" one voice said. "You were standing right next to her."

Joss paused, her hand with a package of bills suspended in midair. The answering voice was a low hiss, and she couldn't make it out.

"We can't let her leave here," the first voice said.

Joss heard that distinctly, and she froze. She listened for a response.

The second voice was slightly louder this time. "I'll talk to the manager and see what he wants to do."

Joss heard the sound of receding footsteps and squeezed her eyes shut. Were the bank people working for A.R. Labs? She opened her eyes and rapidly searched the small room. The only door led out onto the main floor of the bank. Should she leave now, the half-empty box on the table, and run for the front entrance? She looked down at the box; one of the most important things she'd come back for was at the bottom. She decided to gamble.

Grant kept an eye on the two men in the car he had checked out before Joss went in the bank. They got in and drove away. Before Grant could sigh with relief, another car pulled up. This one was also modern and contained three men. One stayed behind the wheel and seemed to give directions to the other two, who got out and walked toward the bank.

Grant saw the driver make a sign to the two men to split up. Oh, no, Grant thought. They're going to flank the entrance of the bank. This is it.

The driver picked up a cellular phone and spoke into it. He nodded his head. The two men reached the bank. Grant didn't see them pull out any guns, but he thought their menace was clear even from a distance. One of them spoke briefly to the other, who shook his head. They took up positions on either side of the entrance.

Grant's palms grew damp as he watched the scene. Apparently, the man in the car had talked with a third party. What should he do? Grant wondered. Stay in the car or warn Joss?

He hadn't counted on anyone being here, let alone three of them. If he tried to go in the front entrance to warn Joss, one of the two men from A.R. Labs might recognize him. And if he had to defend Joss, what would he do? They were armed; he had nothing.

Was there another entrance into the bank? Think, you idiot, he told himself. This is a bank. They don't want to make it too easy for people to get in. He glanced at his wristwatch. How long had she been inside? Maybe ten minutes. How much longer did she need?

Joss's heart was beating so hard she could feel blood thumping in her temples and her throat, but she thrust handful after handful of the contents of the box into her bag. She carefully upended the box, emptying the remaining contents into her purse. She dropped the lid of the box and closed her purse, picked it up and held it in both arms against her bulging stomach. She took a deep breath and moved closer to the door. For a moment she listened, her ear against the door. Nothing. Then she turned the knob slowly and opened the door.

The three of them were ranged in front of her. The woman who had opened the vault for her, the man who had looked at her and an older man who must be the manager. All of them were barring her way and looking uncomfortable. Joss knew she couldn't rush all three of them, but she had to get out. She looked beyond them to the door of the bank. There was no one there. Just these three in front of her. Just.

The manager spoke first. "We think you should wait here until they come."

Joss nearly dropped her bag with the shock. Oh my God, she thought. This is it. They're going to keep me here so the A.R. Labs people can kill me. I shouldn't have waited to empty the box. Her hands were like ice, but she held the bag tightly and tried to keep her voice calm.

"I can't stay here," she said. "I have to get home."

The three people exchanged anxious glances.

"They said you should wait," the manager said.

"Safer for you," the woman added.

What? Joss thought. Safer for whom? If they're going to kill me, nothing is safer for me. She took a step toward them and the front entrance.

Joss thought the second man had a threat in his voice when he said, "You should sit down and stay here. We don't want to be responsible." He pulled out a chair.

Joss felt dizzy. She swayed on her feet, and two sets of arms helped her as she fell into the chair. She hunched over her big stomach, the bag almost falling off her lap. She began to breathe heavily.

The woman looked alarmed. "What if they don't get here in time?"

"I called them as soon as you told me," the manager said.

Grant hunched behind the wheel. Every muscle in his body wanted him to leap out of the car, race across the street, tear Joss out of the bank and fight off anyone who stood in their way. But he knew he should stay where he was. There was just a chance that the man in the car—who seemed to be in charge—thought that Joss still hadn't shown up. If Grant got out now, they would recognize him and get both of them.

And what about when Joss came out? he asked himself. He didn't know. Grant's eyes were burning, and he realized he hadn't even allowed himself to blink. His chest ached from the tension. Joss, Joss. First he caused her to abandon her home and her career. Now she might abandon her life.

Grant started as he heard the wail of an approaching siren. He watched an ambulance tear down the street and screech to a stop in front of the bank. What had happened? Grant prayed it had nothing to do with Joss.

Two men leapt out of the ambulance and ran toward the entrance of the bank. Right behind them, the two A.R. Labs men moved closer to the entrance, too, their right hands in the pockets of their jackets.

As the ambulance siren got louder, Joss thought that all three of the people in front of her visibly relaxed. Something was wrong. What?

Joss finally asked the one question she could think of, "Who did you call?"

"The ambulance, of course," the manager said, surprised.

Joss was shocked into a rush of adrenaline that sent her staggering to her feet. "Why an ambulance?" she demanded.

They looked uncomfortable again.

"*Why?*" she nearly yelled.

The two men looked at the woman, and she answered. "Because of your condition...and what happened."

Joss caught herself just before she asked what condition. "What happened?"

The two men again looked at the woman for an answer.

The woman frowned as if she couldn't believe Joss didn't know. "You're pregnant, and the back of your dress is wet. We thought your water might have broken, so we called the ambulance to help you save the baby."

Joss stood swaying for a moment. Wet dress? Broken her water? And then it hit her. The little puddle of water she'd sat in had wet the seat of her dress.

She heard the ambulance siren grow louder. She had to get out of here. "It's all right. I have to leave." She took two more steps toward the door.

"I don't think you should do that." The two men reached toward her again.

Joss jerked herself away from the men. "You can't touch me. My religion doesn't allow any man but my husband to touch me. And I can't go in that ambulance. It is forbidden."

She held the bag close to her chest and swung her elbow to ward them off. "Out of my way," she said loudly. "Don't contaminate me. Don't violate me," she said more loudly, and other people in the bank looked up.

The three people in front of her broke up, looking confused and embarrassed.

Joss walked quickly on unsteady legs to the door. Through the glass doors she saw two ambulance attendants in uniform, nearly at the doors of the bank. Two other men with grim faces and their hands in their pockets were behind them. She had to move. Now.

The succeeding events took place in seconds, but to Joss it seemed frozen, molasses-sticking slow motion. She pushed the glass doors open and moved toward the ambulance attendants. She heard the manager behind her say, "That's the woman. Stop her." One of the attendants reached out to her and caught the edge of her sleeve. Joss was desperate and furious. Her arms felt like lead, but she swung the heavy bag at him, caught him on the chin and knocked him out cold. He flew backward and fell, taking down one of the grim-faced men who had been right behind him.

The other attendant, barely out of his teens, stopped in his tracks, legs apart and arms out. With a surprised look on his face, he stared first at Joss and then at his downed partner. The other grim-faced man screamed, "Get out of my way, you idiot!" But the young attendant was too dazed to move.

An explosion burst the air, and in terror Joss staggered, realizing he had fired his gun at her. Out of the corner of her eye she saw the young attendant swing around in shock in the direction of the gunshot and fling an open hand into the face of the man pursuing her with a gun. She heard metal clatter to cement and almost sobbed with relief at the reprieve. He must have knocked the man's gun out of his hands, she thought.

Joss ran now, into the street, not looking where she was going, heading straight for Grant and their car.

89

Joss tore open the door of the car, flung herself in. "Drive! Drive!"

But Grant already had his foot to the floorboard. Their car barreled down the street, Joss bracing her feet. They reached the corner, and Grant wrenched the wheel. Joss hung onto the door handle as the car skidded, making a wide right turn, half in the other lane.

Joss slumped in the seat, the heavy bag squashing her foam rubber pregnancy. She was so drained by the aftermath of the adrenaline rush, that she could hardly lift her head. But she made herself look back to see if they were being followed. She saw the man at the bank recover his gun. Then he was out of sight.

Joss started laughing hysterically.

"Joss, are you okay?"

"Why shouldn't...I be okay? I walked out...on my life...and the one place...I tried to...salvage something from...I nearly got shot...or hauled off in an ambulance. But," she said, patting her foam rubber stomach and sobering, "this saved me. This outfit and the fact that I sat in a puddle before I walked into the bank."

"Puddle?"

Joss wiped her eyes and briefly told him what had happened. "I sat on a wet bench. The back of my dress got wet. They thought my water had broken, and they called an ambulance. If those two ambulance attendants hadn't been there, everything would have been different."

She sighed and shuddered. "I would be dead and so would you."

As Grant swerved around another curve, Joss heard a thump in the back seat. She looked back to see that Bailey had slid to the floor. He got back up on the seat and lay down.

Joss looked out the window. They had found her and Grant twice; they could find them again, she thought.

"Where are we going?" she asked.

"Nyack. The river."

"The Hudson River! You're crazy. Why?"

Grant shot a look in the rear view mirror. "Because it's the only place we have a chance to go a long distance, fast, without being recognized or followed."

"Not being followed? We'll be right out in the open. In the middle of the river."

"We're right out in the open in a car, Joss. Whether it's this car or another one, we're in a glass box."

Joss tensed, wondering if she had gotten away from the bank, only to head into a dead end. "What if there are no boats?"

"There will be a boat," he said.

"How can you be so sure?"

"There has to be a boat. These towns are all along the river. There are marinas everywhere. We have to be able to get a boat."

Joss wasn't convinced.

Grant raced along Route 59. It was early in the day; there was plenty of light. Grant thought that if it made them more visible, it also made their enemies visible too. Except they didn't know who their enemies were.

Rain began to fall again, and Grant turned on the wipers. Soon the metronome of the wipers was the only sound he heard. As they got closer to the river, the rain let up, but a mist filled the air. Grant said a silent prayer of thanks. Maybe the fog would help hide them. When Grant got off the highway into Nyack, he just kept heading straight downhill toward the water.

He came to a restaurant near a marina. "I'll ask for the nearest rental. They have to know," he said. "It has to be close. The water is full of slips."

Grant was gone hardly two minutes, when he knew the truth. He returned to the car disheartened.

He had barely opened his door when Joss burst, "What's the matter?"

He shook his head. "They don't rent boats here."

"But what about nearby?"

"They don't rent boats anywhere. Something about safety and insurance. They only let people who have their own boats go out."

"What about charters?" Joss asked.

He hadn't been listening. "What?"

"What about charters, chartering a boat to take us somewhere?"

"That can't work, Joss. You can't charter a boat ten minutes before you want it. They must have reservations months in advance. We have to find something else."

Joss shook her head. "You brought us to the edge of the river. You convinced me that this is the best way to make some time. We're not leaving until we know if charters are a possibility."

"We can't afford to stay here long," Grant said, opening his door. "If this guy can't tell me anything, we'll have to leave."

Joss put her hand on his arm. "I'm going in. I can ask as well as you can. And I have to go to the bathroom."

Joss was gone nearly five minutes. Grant was getting edgy, watching all around them, expecting to have a car screech down on them as it had last night.

Finally Joss appeared at the door. Her mouth was set in a trembling, tentative smile. She got in.

"What?" he asked. "Tell me."

"A charter is going to pick us up at Stony Point."

Grant couldn't believe it. "How did you get a charter?"

"They had a cancellation, so he was free."

"How far is that from here?" Grant asked.

"About ten miles up the coast. The boat is anchored at Peekskill, but it's leaving now to meet us at Stony Point."

90

On their way to 9W, the road ran between a hospital on their right and a graveyard on their left. Grant fleetingly felt sorry for the sick people, looking out onto tombstones, until he thought of his own predicament.

Route 9W was a two-lane road that wound up the coast, following the river. Grant drove through one small seacoast town after another. Under any other circumstances, it would have been a wonderful drive. Instead, Grant's stomach was in knots as he drove at the speed limit.

Grant saw the fog start to roll in. He couldn't see far to either side of the road. On the right, the land dropped gently or precipitously to the river. On the left, there were tree-studded hillsides and bare stone cliffs. Scattered along the narrow strip along both sides of the road were businesses, houses and restaurants. Grant kept glancing in the rearview mirror.

He drove past Rockland State Park on his right, with a large lake and mist rising from it, and came to his first traffic light since Nyack. Grant was tempted to run it, but he didn't want to chance being pulled over by an unseen cop. He drove on, past another lake. The road rose and wound, running down again to a T and another light. He took the right arm.

Grant followed the road as it rose again and curved, and the right side of the road dropped off into an immense gravel pit—with mounds of gravel and sand, conveyor belts and equipment—the Haverstraw Plant. The light at the gravel pit was green, and he kept driving. Grant noticed that train tracks ran right next to the road and that the hillside rose up on their left. A bad place to be hemmed in, he thought.

That was when Grant first noticed the car.

"Joss. There's a grey Ford about seven cars behind us that's been moving up every chance he gets. Get down in your seat so they can't see you."

"What good will that do?" she said. "They saw us at the bank."

"If they don't see you and Bailey," Grant said, "they may think I dropped you off somewhere. Then at least they may wait to find out, rather than just shooting us from their car." Joss slid down until she was nearly completely nestled into the space between her seat and the dashboard. Grant put some newspapers over her. He glanced back at Bailey. "Stay on the floor, Bailey."

The car continued to gain on them. Finally, when there was a break in the traffic, it passed them. Out of the corner of his eye Grant could make out a man in the passenger seat, so there had to be at least two of them. It was all that Grant could do not to hit the gas pedal and speed away from them as fast as possible. But he couldn't. They would just catch up, shoot him on the run. He had to pretend that he'd done something that would make it harder—or impossible—for A.R. Labs to kill the three of them.

The car pursuing him slowed down a little, and Grant glanced again in his rearview mirror. Another car was moving up! How many of them were there? The car was just two lengths behind Grant. Then it was right behind him. They were boxing him in. Grant had to make a move. He couldn't let them lead him and Joss—and Bailey—like lambs to a slaughter.

He searched the road, looking for a place to turn off. But the road was abutted by a cliff on his left and by a string of stores and shops and eating places on the right, with small parking lots. No roads leading off to either side. Where would a side road go anyway? Grant wondered. Just down to the river or part of the way up the hill. Not far enough to get away.

Then, up ahead on the left, Grant saw it. Between the stone cliffs and the road, looking out to sea: A graveyard that ran along the road for as far as he could see from here. Grant didn't have time to think. Or to look for someplace else.

When he was parallel to the entrance to the graveyard, he wrenched the wheel, directly in the path of a car in the oncoming lane. Twelve wheels, at least, screeched as Grant swung the car off the road and up into the graveyard. He didn't look back. He had to find someplace to drive between the gravestones. He headed straight up the bumpy ground along the narrow road in.

Part of Grant's brain told him it was insane to turn off the road into an old graveyard. He didn't know what the ground was like; it could have been mud. He didn't know how the myriad of tombstones was arranged—they didn't necessarily have to be in straight rows, leaving room for a car.

The front of his car bounced up and down as he tore up the narrow lane, making the tombstones—old slabs of stone that must have been set there a hundred years ago for men who had died at sea—look to Grant as if they were riding on the crests of waves.

Joss had wriggled herself out when Grant turned off the road. She was hugging the back of her seat and watching out the rear window. "He's following us in, Grant. He turned around, and he's coming up the same road we took." She turned her head to the right. "There's another car, coming up further down. There must be a horseshoe-shaped road running through here. They're trying to pin us in the middle."

Grant had already reached the top of the horseshoe and was heading across toward the other leg and the second car. He scanned the sea of tombstones. And saw it. In the middle of the graveyard there was a clear strip running straight back to the road—not paved, but appearing to be wide enough for a car. Grant jerked the car off the graveyard road, out between the gravestones. He gunned the engine, praying that there were no slabs on the ground. But the way proved clear, and he was headed back to the main road when Joss called out.

"They're turning around, heading in this direction. There must be a second crossroad down there, perpendicular to this one. They're trying to head us off."

Grant could see the two cars, slipping on the wet macadam as they rushed to cut him off. Grant searched the ground straight ahead of him. The way still appeared to be clear, but it didn't lead to a road out. There was a railing atop a small concrete wall between his car and the road.

A wrenching bump told Grant his luck was running out. The ground was uneven and rocky. The car bounced heavily and the going was slower. Then the right front wheel hit a flat slab, and Grant's side swung around and lifted. Grant thought in a moment of horror that they might flip over. Then, almost in slow motion, the car fell back down. Grant hit the gas again and kept going. He'd rather take another chance with the gravestones than with his pursuers.

Joss must have seen what he anticipated. "You're heading straight for the railing," she said. "There's no exit here. We can't get past them. They've driven down the last row."

91

As they bumped along the ground, Grant's attention was caught by an immense monument ahead of them. To each side of the man-sized stone was a hovering angel, reaching with upstretched arms toward the figure over the stone: Christ, triumphant in his resurrection, his right hand raised in benediction.

For a split second it seemed to Grant that the three lifted hands were waving him on. But he knew he had no other choice. He slammed his foot to the floor, and the car leapt between the last two tombstones, straight for the metal railing.

Grant's mind raced, gauging his chances. He saw that the railing had been set in a concrete wall, four feet above the height of the road. But the graveyard was old, he thought, and the railing had been there, through rain and sun, snow and ice, for hundreds of years. Perhaps the concrete at the base of the railing had developed cracks. Perhaps water had seeped into those cracks, frozen and broken the concrete, loosening its hold on the railing. Maybe after hundreds of years, the railing had rusted in spots.

Grant's car hit the railing and crashed through, sailed over the trunk of a car that passed just under him, scraped it and landed with a crash and a grinding sound of metal. Grant hit the gas, scraping the tires against the fenders as he made a ninety-degree turn to the left. Out of the corner of his eye he saw Joss looking back. Her voice was tight, and it rose as she told him what had happened.

"The car you hit. It must have scared the hell out of him. He swerved the car across both lanes. And a bunch of other cars—from both directions—ran into him. It's bumper to bumper."

Even though Grant hadn't wanted to cause an accident, he was grateful that it would slow their pursuers down. As fast as he could drive, he continued up the coast road, past the graveyard. There was a light, but he ran it and hoped that he wasn't stopped by the police.

A commercial strip bordered the road, and Grant saw there was more space on each side of the road, now that he didn't need it. He tore along 9W, watching only to see that the road ahead of him was clear and that no one was following him. Within a couple of miles he reached Stony Point, but he saw no sign of the marina. He followed the road for another mile or so, his gaze glued to road signs, afraid he might already have passed it.

Finally, Joss called out, "Marina District. Low clearance—ten feet."

Grant turned down Tomkins Avenue, squealing down the winding street, skidding on the wet pavement and barely pausing at the stop sign at the bottom of the hill. When he went under the train track, he came to a T.

Grant took the right arm—which he soon found led him nowhere. He backtracked, watching for glimpses of the dock between the masses of boats.

"There it is," Joss said, "Willow Cove Marina."

"Where's the boat?" Grant asked. His chest was tight.

Joss pointed. "There!"

Grant saw it, docked on their left. He backed up.

'What are you doing?" she yelled. "We have to get on the boat."

"We can't leave the car here, Joss. I have to pull it off the road. If they see it, they'll know what we did. Get the bags ready."

He didn't intend to spend much time looking for a hiding spot. They needed to get out of here. There were a number of buildings for the storage and repair of boats. Grant picked one out and drove in, toward the back.

Grant was worried that Bailey might have to be carried, but he kept up with them as they raced down to the dock, to the waiting boat.

92

Grant and Joss ran clattering down the wood slats of the dock, to where the charter bobbed in the water. They jumped over the gap between the dock and boat, first Joss, then Bailey and Grant.

"Let's go!" Grant shouted to the captain.

Grant stood on the deck, his chest heaving, watching the dock recede. Too slowly, he thought. His heart was in his mouth as he watched the dock and the road leading down to it. Any second he expected to see racing cars and running men.

Finally, they were almost in the middle of the river. Briefly, as Grant surveyed the boat, he wondered why the captain hadn't seemed surprised at their frantic arrival and hurry to get away. Grant shrugged; charter captains probably got every conceivable kind of passenger and request.

The boat had to be about fifty feet long; it was solid, big. Grant felt better; it would be steady in the water. From where he stood, Grant looked all around him, trying to get his bearings and to see who else was on the boat. The captain took them directly into the main cabin, which had sofas and was enclosed by paneled wood and glass. Grant could see the front deck through the window over the captain's wheel. To the rear of the main deck was an aft deck, like a Florida room, with its zippered plastic windows open. Grant knew there was also a fly deck, because he had seen it from the dock. Stairs led down just to the right of the captain's wheel. Grant could see a booth in the galley.

And then they were enveloped in fog. As if it had come out of nowhere, it dropped down around the boat like a curtain, until the shore was only an indistinct line.

Grant's first concern was their own navigation, but the captain assured him that they were all right, this was one of the bigger boats on the river.

"Keep heading north," Grant told him. Why hadn't the captain asked him? "Are we going against the current?" he asked.

"It changes with the tides, but we'll be able to sail for about six hours."

The captain still hadn't asked where they were heading or made any comment about Bailey. Maybe that lack of curiosity was usual. Grant didn't know. He had never spent much time on a boat, outside of the Circle Liners that cruised around Manhattan.

But after his adrenaline-draining race, Grant didn't want to do anything but collapse. He took the stairs down to the galley. Grant sank into the booth; Joss and Bailey joined him.

"Thank goodness, Grant, at least we're on the boat," Joss said. "We could sail to Canada for all I care."

Grant nodded. "At least right now we're heading as fast as we can away from them." He leaned his head back and for long minutes he didn't budge.

"Maybe some good angels are watching over us," Joss said through closed eyes. "This boat, being here for us."

Joss's comment made Grant's heartbeat speed up again. Every time things seemed peaceful, something happened. He slowly opened his eyes, half-expecting some crazed murderer to burst into the galley. But everything was quiet. He could feel the boat under him moving strongly through the water, and the engines were almost soundless. He decided it would take him weeks of calm before he would unwind.

Finally Joss got up. "Where's the bathroom?" she asked him, putting the oversized purse over her shoulder.

"The *head*," Grant corrected with a smile and pointed down a small hall. Grant stayed with Bailey, stroking his head. "You give me more reassurance than I'm giving you, buddy," he said.

Grant suddenly realized he was starving. He got up and crossed to the refrigerator. There was a plate of wrapped sandwiches and cans of soda. "Are you hungry, Bailey?" he asked. "It looks like there's roast beef, ham and cheese and turkey sandwiches."

Bailey looked expectantly at the sandwiches. When Grant unwrapped one, Bailey leaned over to sniff it. Grant was about to take a bite, but Bailey pushed his nose in between Grant and the sandwich.

"I guess eating on the high seas in front of a hungry dog is a crime," Grant said. He opened one of the sandwiches and took out the roast beef. He tore it into pieces, put it on a paper plate and gave it to Bailey. He expected Bailey to wolf it down, as usual; he hadn't eaten since the night before. But Bailey sniffed at the meat and looked up at Grant. He whimpered slightly.

"It's all right, Bailey. The first one can be for you," Grant said.

Bailey put his nose near the food again and then backed off. He looked up at Grant, his ears slightly back.

"What's the matter boy?"

Grant was still shaking inside from the chase. He had begun to feel some respite from the constant tension of the past two days, but the unwinding had just touched the surface. His inner core was still tensed.

Grant didn't feel like coaxing Bailey to eat. But it was funny; Bailey was almost never picky about his food. The only time he hadn't eaten what Grant had given him was when he'd put in a vitamin that Bailey could never get used to. Or when the meat had been bad...

When Joss returned, Grant watched her eyes light up when she saw the sandwiches. She was heading for them when Grant said, "Bailey won't eat the meat. There must be something wrong with it."

Joss lifted one to her nose. "It smells fine to me, Grant." She paused. "Okay. Maybe there are crackers and cheese here."

She rummaged through the cupboards, but she didn't come up with anything. "I'm not really hungry."

"I'm going up on deck," Grant said.

"Shh."

"What?"

"SHHHHH."

Grant listened and mouthed, "What?"

"Can't you hear it?" Joss asked.

"Hear what?"

"The engine," Joss said. "A motor. Can't you hear it rumbling?"

"You mean like another boat?" Grant's heart rate immediately soared. His body was gearing for life-and-death defense at the first sign of danger. It was exhausting him.

"Maybe... no," she said. "It sounds more like a plane." Her eyes widened, and Grant saw fear in them. "No. It's a helicopter."

93

Grant climbed the stairs with Joss to the main salon, but he couldn't see anything from there. He went out of the cabin to the front deck, where the motor was very loud. Mist and air swirled violently around him, whipping his hair and clothes. Grant squinted his eyes as he craned his neck to see what was above.

And then something seemed to be swinging in the mist. Someone was suspended on a rope ladder that was being lowered from the helicopter. As Grant registered this, the man's feet came down to rest on the deck of the boat. Grant's heart sank and all his energy drained out.

The man was holding a gun.

Grant recognized him immediately. It was Robbins, Dell's p.r. man.

"A fine day for a cruise on the river." Robbins shouted to make himself heard above the thocking sound of the rotors.

Joss was silent. Grant shot a look at her. Her hair was whipping in the wind, but her face was as frozen as the figure on the prow of a ship.

Robbins pointed the gun toward the ladder. "You're expected above," he shouted with a sarcastic smile.

"We're not going!" Grant yelled.

"Not you," Robbins said. "Her. Dell knows how much she helped you."

The rotors had partly dispersed the mist, and Grant looked up to see the underside of the helicopter. The noise and the wind from the rotors buffeted him. The boat must be at anchor, he thought. Was the captain involved too?

Grant had been looking up; he hadn't been watching Joss. Suddenly he saw her at the ladder. "No, Joss! Don't go!"

But Robbins held the gun on him.

"What else can we do?" she shouted, swaying on the ladder, her hair blowing around her face. Her eyes were wide with fear.

"Maybe I can reason with Dell." With her long dress flapping around her body, Joss slowly ascended until she disappeared into a cloud of mist.

It was almost ludicrous. Grant couldn't believe that they were going to end like this—killed by an egomaniacal political hopeful who wouldn't stop at drugging, maiming or killing people to get the office he coveted.

Grant saw a slow, nasty smile spread over Robbins's plump face. "Dr. Granite Freezer," he said. "Alone at last."

Grant didn't care what Robbins had to say.

Robbins moved closer to Grant. "The brilliant Dr. Fraser wasn't smart enough to elude capture for a whole forty-eight hours," he taunted.

Grant ignored him.

"When you tore away from the bank, I told them you were heading for the river. Dell thought I was crazy, but I checked all the charters and found one reservation made just this morning. Bingo. Two for one."

So those had been *Dell's* men at the bank, Grant thought, not A.R. Labs. Grant looked at Robbins's gun and wondered grimly what difference it made who killed them.

Then he realized Robbins had said "two for one"—he didn't know about Bailey. Maybe the dog had a chance. The mist had breaks in it, and Grant caught a glimpse of the bank of the river. Could anyone see them?

"Was the doctored food your idea, too?" Grant asked, playing for time. To do what? he wondered. He had no plan.

Robbins smiled. He had a particularly repellent smile, Grant thought.

"Indeed it was. Pity that you didn't eat it. It would have made everything so much easier. We could have pushed you into the river without any trouble."

"The captain is yours?" Grant asked.

Robbins shook his head no. "But now he's nobody's." Robbins looked as if he were snickering; Grant couldn't hear him. Robbins's gaze dropped to the deck, and for the first time Grant saw the man's body lying there. It was the captain.

A scream tore through the mist, louder than the rotors. "NO!"

Grant's heard jerked up. What he saw made his hands spasm in pain, as if a high current were shooting through them. Joss was dangling by one side of the rope ladder that she had ascended. Dell had cut the other side. She rotated and swayed below the helicopter. Grant could see Dell above her, at the open door. The rotors were loud, but Grant could make out Dell's voice over the din.

"Now she's all yours," he screamed. "You can both go to hell."

Grant watched, frozen, as Joss swung from the rope. No. Not even Dell would... Then he saw Dell lean over the edge, something glinting in his hand. Dell was going to cut the rope and let Joss fall to her death in front of him on the deck.

"No!" Grant screamed. "No, you bastard, no!"

Grant saw the helicopter tilt slightly, trying to maintain its position above the boat's deck, and Dell had to grab the side of the helicopter. The helicopter steadied itself, and Dell reached down toward the rope. But Joss was swinging in a wide arc, a wider one than before. What was happening? Then he understood—she was trying to swing out over the water so she would miss the boat when she fell. She had guts. Help her, God, Grant prayed.

And then she fell.

It took just seconds, but every detail burned itself into Grant's senses so that it seemed to happen in slow motion. Joss screamed one long, continuous scream as she fell, gripping the rope, finally letting it go when she realized that it anchored her to nothing. Her hair streamed above her head like a red plume. Her eyes and mouth were wide open, fixed on the deck and sea rising fast to meet her. Her long dress flapped around her like a flag on a pole. She was so close, Grant couldn't tell if she would clear the boat. Oh, God, no, Grant thought in horror. Not like this. Not for Joss.

Grant felt, rather than heard, the second boat. It sped past them rapidly on their starboard side, its wake pushing Grant's boat slightly away from Joss. She dropped into the water with a loud, smacking splash. By the time Grant had run to the railing, the water had closed over her head

He was about to throw himself over the side when Robbins said, "No. He wants to be sure about you." He lifted the gun and pointed it at Grant.

This had to be it, Grant thought. No more reprieves. No Fred to come along and save him at the last minute. One bullet, and it would all be over. He wouldn't save Joss, but he wouldn't know what happened to her, either.

"One more thing that you might want to know," Robbins said. "Michael Horcroft died in the hospital today." Robbins smiled.

The life went out of Grant. He sagged to his knees. The little boy was gone. He *wanted* to die.

Grant hardly saw the blur behind Robbins, it moved so fast. Bailey had come out of the main salon and run onto the front deck. He hit Robbins from the back, knocking him down. Robbins's gun flew out of his hand as his head hit the railing with a sickening thud.

"Bailey. Good dog. Good dog." Bailey ran to Grant and jumped up on him, licking him and making soft growls. Tears were streaming down Grant's face. He didn't want to make any more effort to keep himself alive, but he had to help Joss. "Stay, Bailey. I have to get Joss."

Grant used the boat's railing to pull himself to his feet. He had to put thoughts of Michael out of his mind. If he didn't, he knew he would just let the water close over him and drown him. Then he leaned over and dropped like a rock into the middle of the Hudson River.

Bailey, obedient dog that he was, leaped over the side after him.

94

Grant hit the water and every part of his body contracted. It wasn't that cold yet—maybe high 50's or low 60's. But he wasn't used to it, and his shivering and the tension in his body made him use extra energy to keep his head above water. Bobbing in the diminishing wake of the speedboat, he spat water out of his mouth repeatedly. Surface, Joss, surface, he thought. I'll never find you if you don't.

He swam to where he thought Joss hit the water, but he saw nothing. He turned in the water, making a full circle, stretching out his arms and legs to feel for her. Nothing.

God, Joss, no, he thought. Jackknifing his body, he dove under the water, thrusting his arms out in the cold, wet darkness, trying to find her. Out of breath, he surfaced, gasping. Then he dove again. And again. Trying to cover as much area as he could.

Nothing.

The last time he surfaced, choking from water he had swallowed, he saw Bailey swimming away from him.

"Bailey, no!" he wheezed. But what difference did it make? he thought, hope seeping out of him along with his body heat. Soon he and Bailey would wear out and sink, too.

Then Grant saw that Bailey was swimming toward something.

His arms and legs feeling like lead, Grant followed the dog, who stopped and paddled in place next to something just below the surface. Shock and fear jolted Grant when he realized it was Joss.

When Grant pulled her head above the water, her eyes were closed, her face white. Grant was gasping and just barely able to tread water to keep his own head above water, and waves lifted him and made it nearly impossible to keep Joss's head above water, too. He put his mouth on hers, blowing into her lungs. Waves lifted him and nearly pulled her away. He blew into her lungs again. He forgot to tread water and nearly pulled both of them under. He blew into her lungs a third time. Her lips felt so cold and flaccid. Good God, Joss, breathe! he thought. It wasn't that long. It couldn't have been.

She choked, spitting water from her mouth and nose straight into his face.

Struggling to keep both of them afloat, Grant blinked and hugged her fiercely.

Spluttering, she wiped her eyes, trying to keep the water out of them so she could see. "He dropped me, Grant, he dropped me." Her voice rose, unbelieving. She was chattering in the cold water. "Out of a helicopter."

Joss bobbed in the water, looking to Grant like a half-drowned puppy: frightened, hurt and bewildered at what had happened to her. Grant wanted to save her, protect her. But he didn't even know how he was going to get them out of the water and onto the shore. They couldn't go back to the boat. As soon as Dell figured out that Joss had survived the fall and that Robbins was dead instead of Grant, he would come after them again. Another chase. More adrenaline.

"Bailey!' Grant suddenly remembered the dog.

Grant craned his head around and saw Bailey patiently dog-paddling near him. What had he gotten them into? Grant wondered. They were in the middle of the Hudson River at the end of October, already getting dangerously cold. How long before hypothermia set in? Certainly much less time than it would take to swim to shore, if that were possible under any conditions. Joss shivered violently in his arms. How many feet of sinking, cold water lay beneath them?

While he held her, treading water, the pleasure boat came back. Like a great white whale, he thought, it emerged from the mist, sliding smoothly to pull up next to the charter boat. It loomed over the three of them bobbing in the water like so much flotsam. Thank God for the mist, Grant thought—they can't see us.

On its first pass, Grant had thought the pleasure boat was a godsend. The wake it had created had saved Joss from hitting the deck. Now Grant realized that the presence of the boat hadn't been an accident.

So A.R. Labs had tracked them after all, he thought. After he'd raced to Stony Point, after he'd hidden the car. How they had done it, he didn't know. But there couldn't be any other explanation for four men with rifles in the bow of the pleasure boat.

This was it. A three-way tie for efforts to kill them: By freezing and drowning in the water. By Dell. Or by A.R. Labs.

One of the men on the pleasure craft called out to the charter boat, "Captain!" But no one came out. There must have been just the captain on our boat, the man Robbins killed, Grant thought.

Grant suddenly realized that the helicopter was above the boat. It had lifted up and swung away after Dell cut Joss loose, and Grant thought Dell would be heading far away. But instead, he'd come back—why? Of course, Grant thought. Dell had no way of knowing about A.R. Labs, or what they were after. All of his dealings had been with Smith, alias Walter. When Dell saw the pleasure craft, he must have wanted to make sure that Grant didn't survive.

The men on the pleasure craft looked up at the helicopter. They gestured to each other and to it. Virtually as soon as they had decided that the helicopter must be connected to the boat, they fired on it. The helicopter returned the fire.

"Are they both crazy?" Joss whispered through trembling lips.

Nearly too numb to keep moving so they could keep their heads above water, Grant vaguely wondered if Dell and A.R. Labs would kill each other. Then he and Joss could have one of the boats for themselves. He watched as a man on the pleasure boat, in one fluid movement, lifted a heavy rifle to his shoulder and fired at the helicopter. In the next moment the helicopter exploded into a fireball. Large, sharp, flaming metal and plastic fragments rained down on the river near Grant and Joss.

With the last of his energy, Grant swam away from the falling debris. His clothes were dragging him, his limbs felt like stone. Bailey followed them, looking tired. His fur was matted close to his body, and his tongue hung out, panting. Grant was almost grateful for the cold. At least they would be numb when the inevitable happened.

95

"About twenty feet more."

Grant heard the voice, hardly more than a whisper, and not far away. The shock of fear that ran through him—at the thought that A.R. Labs had come up behind them—made his heart beat painfully in a frozen chest. He swung his head in a panicked circle until he saw the source—a small fishing boat about twenty feet from them.

Half-sobbing with relief, Grant dragged Joss through the water to the fishing boat. Her skin was blue, and her eyes nearly closed. Her dress clung to her, making her look thin and helpless, but she was heavy, heavier than he remembered—even with the buoyancy in water.

There seemed to be only one man on the fishing boat. He reached over the side for Joss, pulling her up himself. He put her down on the deck and came back, pointing to Bailey. Grant nearly went under, pushing up Bailey's hindquarters, the wet fur dripping in his face. Lastly, the man reached out a hand to Grant. Bracing himself against the side of the boat, he pulled while Grant scrambled over the side.

Cold and wet as he was, Grant could have lain on the deck indefinitely, so grateful was he for not having to pump his legs and arms anymore. Even now the cold was retreating enough so that his muscles ached. Never mind, he was alive.

But, "Inside," the fisherman said. He kept shooting glances at the boats and the burning fragments on the water.

The four of them crowded together in the small cabin. The fisherman passed out blankets and handed them a thermos of hot coffee. Grant wrapped a blanket around Joss and then toweled Bailey dry. Fleetingly, he wondered at the man's lack of surprise at finding them in the water. The man went straight to the wheel, and, with the engine running as quietly as it could, he pulled away from the other boats, heading straight upriver.

Grant offered Joss a cup of coffee, but she refused it. She was crying, the tears running down her already wet cheeks, her body shaking softly with sobs. Grant thought he knew why she was crying. It wasn't just the emotional exhaustion following another narrow escape. He put his hand on her shoulder.

"We're all right, Joss. We're all alive. That's all that counts—even though you had to leave your purse behind. We'll find a way to get money."

She shrugged off his hand and burst out, "I *didn't* leave it behind!" She hit her midsection. "I put it in the waistpack. It damned near drowned me." She resumed crying.

Grant stared at her with open eyes and mouth, shaking his head in disbelief.

She looked at him through her tears and finally began to laugh. "You look like a fish," she said. She unwrapped the blanket and reached through the fabric of her dress to unhinge the waistpack. She stood up, and it fell with a thud on the wood planks. "After yesterday, I swore I would never again wait for a second chance to do anything. I transferred as much as I could as soon as we got on the charter. In plastic bags. When I went to the *head*."

She bent over to pick up the waistpack. Her face was streaked, her dress clung to her and her hair was matted to her head. But she stood there triumphantly, holding up the loaded waistpack with both hands like a trophy.

Grant felt something turn in his chest; he didn't know what it was.

Then she opened the waistpack and pulled something out. She tossed Grant a small plastic bag. He held it up, droplets of water still running off the bag. But the contents looked fine.

His Zip Disk. Grant stared at it. Then he stared at Joss. She'd risked her life to get the disk. That was why she had gone to her safe deposit box.

Suddenly a second explosion rocked the fishing boat. Grant looked out to see the charter boat in flames. Now only the pleasure boat was afloat. Grant wondered how many of the men aboard it were still alive. Would they see this small fishing boat and suspect anything of it?

"Come on, river police," the fisherman said in a low voice. Something in his voice caught Grant's attention. Grant watched the man and looked carefully into his face as he cast a glance back now and then to watch the pleasure boat.

At last, Grant knew. "Fred."

Fred didn't even look at him.

"Fred," Joss said.

Fred turned his head to look at her and smile. "It's getting to be a habit, pulling your chestnuts out of the fire," he said. "It's a lucky thing, A.R. Labs getting out here this fast."

"Lucky?" Grant couldn't believe it.

"Of course. If those bastards on the pleasure boat decide you were on the charter, you may have a chance. Otherwise, they won't stop looking for you."

"And if the pleasure boat hadn't been there…" Joss began.

Grant figured she meant she would likely have hit their boat's deck and been killed when she fell. He shuddered. It had been close.

Grant held his breath as he watched the pleasure boat. When it pulled away from the debris bobbing in the water, Grant tensed, expecting it to come after them. But it took off in the other direction. Grant's relief was profound, until he realized that every time he'd thought there was an end to it, someone else tried to kill him.

"What's next?" he asked Fred. "How much further?"

"This boat won't make the progress your charter did," Fred said. "But it will get us to where we need to go."

Grant wanted to press Fred, but he was too tired. His eyelids were heavy, and he wanted to sleep.

"You should get out of those wet clothes," Fred said. "There are dry clothes in the bench." He nodded toward it.

Grant and Joss peeled off their wet clothes and dumped them in a soggy heap. After they changed, Grant again offered Joss a cup of hot coffee. This time she accepted it.

Grant sat across from her, watching her face, waiting for her to drink some of the coffee before he told her.

"When Robbins was ready to shoot me, he told me something."

Joss looked expectant.

"He said that Michael died at the hospital today."

Joss's hands trembled, and she put down her cup. She lowered her head and cried.

Fred glanced at them. "Maybe Robbins doesn't know what he's talking about," he said.

Grant thought Fred was trying to make them feel better. But he was afraid it was the truth.

After a while, Joss wiped her eyes and asked Fred, "How did you know how to find us?"

Grant saw Fred look away. "Followed you," he said. And that was all he would say.

"Where are we going?" Grant asked.

"Well, this boat isn't very fast, and right now we're going against the current. Also, the man who owns this boat didn't have the foresight to fill the tank."

Fred smiled, and his larcenous personality inexplicably warmed Grant. Fred continued, "So I think we're going ashore in Cold Spring."

"And then?" Joss pressed him.

"You're going east in an eighteen-wheeler with a friend," he said. "He has a big cab. It won't be that comfortable, but one of you—and Bailey—can always stay out of sight. He drives practically twenty-four hours a day, so he can get you there in a day or so."

"Where is there?" Joss asked.

"Maine. A small town," Fred said. "They're desperate for anyone who does anything useful. Do you two do anything useful?"

Grant watched Joss's face. For a moment Joss's lip trembled. But she said, "Anything they need."

Grant turned to watch the river. His stomach stayed tight as his gaze swept the river; he was programmed to expect another ambush at any moment. But the boat arrived in Cold Spring harbor safely.

Grant began to relax. They were almost safe.

Grant discovered that their destination was a small, cozy house on a side street not far from the river. The woman who opened the door was a plump, motherly type who didn't ask any questions. As soon as they were inside, she led Grant and Bailey to a bedroom where the dog could rest. Then she took them to the dining room, where she had just set out dinner.

"Eat," she said and bustled off to the kitchen.

Grant sighed with gratitude as he sank into his chair at the table. He was so hungry he was weak. The woman, whom Fred called Mrs. Parker, had made veal cutlets, mashed potatoes and fresh green beans. No food had ever looked better to him, served on the woman's mixed patterns of china.

They ate in silence. In spite of his grief, Grant was somehow comforted by the homey sound of glasses clinking and the scraping of silverware against plates.

Grant's gaze strayed to Joss as they ate. Her eyes were still red. Joss did a double-take and asked him, "Do you want me to pass something?"

I must have been staring, Grant thought. "No, thanks."

He turned his attention briefly back to his plate, then lifted his head to watch Joss some more. And he saw Fred smile at Joss and say something. Fred was being kind and solicitous, handing her dishes, asking if she wanted anything. And yet Grant suddenly resented him. His heart began to sink when he saw Joss's face light up a little.

Grant wasn't paying any attention to what he was doing, and he dropped his steak knife on the floor. When he reached down to retrieve it, for a moment he had the childish urge to stay under the table. His head was still under the table when he heard the conversation and the silverware noises stop.

Grant heard a voice that made his blood turn to red ice. "I think you'll want to see this, Dr. Fraser."

Grant lifted his head. A man stood there. Grant had never seen him before, but he knew it was Smith. He had a gun in his hand and an ugly smile on his face. So he had managed to follow them, Grant thought. Grant felt tired, the way he had felt in the river when he was just about ready to stop treading water.

Grant noticed that Fred was holding the bowl of green beans with both hands.

"Put the bowl down," Smith said. "And keep both hands on the handles."

Fred lowered the bowl to the table. Grant couldn't read anything in Fred's eyes.

"You've been a great deal of trouble to me," Smith said to Fred.

"Just doing the job you sent me to do."

"After you figured things out, you should have left," Smith said.

Grant saw Fred shoot a glance at Joss, but he said nothing. So he was right, Grant thought. There was something between them. Even though he knew they were all about to be killed, that somehow made it worse.

"This was going to be very big," Smith said to Fred. "I could have retired on what Dell was going to pay me. Now my candidate is dead. A.R. Labs blew up his helicopter." Smith started to laugh in what Grant thought was a crazy way. "They'll be after me next. But not before I settle some scores."

Grant heard footsteps in the hall behind Smith, and Smith smiled slowly, without turning around. "Come in and meet my friends," he said.

"Ready for coffee?" Mrs. Parker appeared behind him with a pot and a smile.

Smith's face looked to Grant as if he'd heard the last sound he'd expected. He backed away from her, keeping the gun on her and the table. "Where did you come from?" he demanded.

"I live here," she said, advancing toward him. She put the pot on the table.

Grant stared at her, wide-eyed. Didn't she see the gun in his hand? Why was she acting as if there were just one more for coffee? How could she just waltz into the room and put the pot down without her hand shaking?

Mrs. Parker smoothed her apron. "Cream and sugar are on the table," she said. She turned to go back to the kitchen.

Grant thought Smith seemed to be taken unawares. He shook himself. "Wait!" he said to her.

Mrs. Parker turned.

"Are you the only other person in the house?" he asked.

She looked surprised. "Well, of course. Who else are you looking for?"

Grant's heart sank as he saw Smith's self-possession return. A cruel smile spread across Smith's face. He lifted the gun toward her. "Then we can start with you," he said.

Grant yelled.

He didn't know that he was going to move until he was lunging toward Smith's throat. Fury had been building up in Grant. He had done nothing to this man, nothing. But Smith had arranged for Grant and Joss to be killed. Smith had probably killed Nathan Horcroft. Because of Smith, A.R. Labs had hunted Grant and Joss—from the motel room to the bank to the boat. Now Smith had cornered them here. Smith's threat against the woman who had taken them in, who had given them sanctuary, had been the last straw.

Grant thrust himself over the table like a projectile, knocking his chair back to crash against the opposite wall, his legs kicking dishes against each other and onto the floor. His eyes were on Smith's face and his arm was stretched out, still clutching the steak knife, pointed end toward Smith's throat.

Smith swung back toward Grant as soon as he yelled. Grant thought Smith's face looked pleased.

Grant knew he wouldn't reach Smith before he shot him. But he knew he had to try. Maybe he could distract Smith long enough for Fred to do something. Maybe Joss and Fred would even be able to escape.

At the very least, a part of Grant's brain thought, if he were going to die, he was going to die first. He wouldn't have to watch Joss die.

Grant heard the gunshot and knew it was over. And then he saw Smith's head jerk, and blood splattered the dining room. Grant landed in a heap on the floor, holding his breath, unable to believe that he wasn't the one who was dead.

Grant saw Joss and Fred run toward him, but Joss reached him first.

"Are you all right?" she demanded. Her face was white.

Grant nodded, Smith's blood dripping down his face. Gently, Joss helped him to stand; his legs felt like rubber.

Who had shot Smith? Grant wondered. He looked at Mrs. Parker, then at Fred. Both of them were holding guns. Mrs. Parker was frowning down at Smith. "You get credit for this one," she told Fred.

"Thanks for the diversion," Fred said to Grant, and Mrs. Parker nodded.

Mrs. Parker crossed to the window and looked outside. "There were two with him," she said. "They're both taken care of."

Grant gaped at her. She looked like somebody's grandmother, and she must have just killed two men.

He watched Mrs. Parker put the gun away in her apron and reach for his face. As if Grant had done nothing more serious than spill gravy in his lap, the woman said gently, "Come with me. We'll clean you up, and you'll be fine in no time."

98

The four of them sat close together in the living room. Fred watched Joss warm her hands on a steaming cup of coffee.

Joss seemed fidgety, Fred thought. As if she had something to say. Finally she looked at Mrs. Parker. "How do you know some of Smith's other people won't come here?"

Mrs. Parker was looking in her coffee, as if she could read the future there, Fred thought.

"Because I persuaded one of the two men he brought with him to call in and say they were somewhere else."

Fred thought Joss wasn't finished. He knew what she wanted to say. So, apparently, did Mrs. Parker.

She smiled at Joss. "You're welcome," she said. "Both of you." She sighed and put her cup down. "And that's enough excitement for me for one day. Good night, all." She got up and left the room.

Fred was silent, thinking. He had a few more details to clear up before he took care of what was really important to him. "Edith has clothes and essentials for both of you," he said to Grant and Joss. "Between us, we got everything we could think of. But I'm still glad you salvaged some of your money." He smiled at Joss.

Joss's eyes teared, he noticed, and he took heart. He was in a good mood.

Bailey got up and licked Fred's face. Fred reached over and stroked his fur. "This is one special dog," he said. "I was watching him from the boat." Fred rubbed Bailey's back.

Fred leaned his head back against the sofa and closed his eyes. Was it time to give Joss a choice? Was the connection between them strong enough and recent enough for him to have a chance with her?

He looked up to find Joss watching him. Her eyes were unguarded, her face open. As if she were expectant. Fred shot a glance at Grant He still didn't have a clue. Too bad.

"I have to go away soon," Fred said.

Joss's face tightened, Fred thought.

"Where are you heading?" Joss asked. She didn't take her gaze from him.

"West."

"I've never lived out West," she said. "I've spent my entire life on the East coast."

"So far," Fred said.

She smiled. Her face lit up when she smiled. The room was quiet for a minute. As if something were gathering force.

"What will you do out there?" Joss asked.

The question surprised Fred. He hadn't thought of any occupation in particular. The prospect of an entirely new world had been so exciting that he hadn't wanted to narrow his choices yet. "Acceptance and commitment are the very opposite of the limitless potential of chaos." He'd read that once. He thought it fit.

"Anything. I can be anything," he said.

Joss smiled. "I'm sure you can," she said.

They all drank their coffee.

But then a small cloud passed over her face. "Won't you miss what you did for A.R. Labs?" she asked.

The question cut Fred like a knife. He suddenly felt apart from her. Defensive. He remembered Monday night, when he'd stood outside her library window and said, "I kill people. I kill people." Now the affinity he'd felt for her seemed an illusion. The connection between them seemed flimsy. It would never be enough to hold them together. Because, whether or not she intended it, her question would be a wedge between them. Joss was moving away from him as surely as if they had been in two separate boats without paddles in an infinite ocean, drifting away from each other.

His heart ached. He closed his eyes and tears slid from them. He felt someone brush his face. He opened his eyes.

"You must have been having a dream." It was Joss, her kind, smiling face close to his. She had mopped the tears with a tissue.

Fred wiped his eyes with the back of his hand. They were still wet. He must have dozed off, and it had just been a dream But it could have been real. It would be real. He struggled to get control of himself.

"Where were we?" he asked.

"We were asking about identification," Joss answered.

Fred felt a clutch in his heart, felt fate take a fork in the road. But he nodded and pulled two small packages out of his pocket. He handed one to Joss. With the slightest hesitation, he handed the other to Grant.

"Anne Swift," Joss said.

"Jack Cummings," Grant said.

Joss was absorbed in looking at her ID; but Fred watched Grant frown as he looked at the photo.

Fred said quickly, "I had to work fast, and I didn't have a good picture of you. So I used one of myself. We're not that different looking."

Joss was still studying her ID. But Grant looked at Fred, and Fred knew he understood. "Thank you," Grant said. "Thank you very much."

Fred glanced at Joss before he looked away. With his gaze on the hallway leading out of the living room, Fred said, "Get ready for another surprise."

Joss looked up, confused, Fred thought. How beautiful she was.

"Why?" Joss asked.

Fred didn't answer her. He got up and left the room.

He came back into the living room, leading a sleepy little boy by the hand.

"Michael!" Joss said.

99

Fred thought Grant looked as if he were having a heart attack. He didn't move, and he kept shaking his head.

Joss's eyes lit up and tears rolled down her cheeks. She got up from the sofa and ran over to the child, dropping to her knees to take him in her arms and kiss him and hold him tightly.

"Don't squash me, Aunt Joss," he said sleepily.

"Robbins told me he was dead. How can this be?" Grant asked.

"I said Robbins might not know what he was talking about," Fred said. Fred looked away from them. "I found out that Angie gave the black twin to Michael a couple of times. When they needed to distract Horcroft."

Fred glanced at Grant. His face was ashen, but his eyes said murder.

"I got through to Horcroft at the hospital yesterday morning," Fred said. "It was time for him to make a decision. He knew he wasn't able to protect Michael. Smith kidnapped Daniele and cut off her fingertip to force Horcroft to give him a toehold at Altimate. Horcroft was always afraid that Smith would go after Michael. And I don't think Daniele was very interested in the boy. Getting control of Altimate was more important to her than anything. Faking Michael's death was the only way to protect him."

Joss picked Michael up and carried him to the sofa where Grant was still sitting. Fred watched as Michael gradually recognized Grant. He hugged and kissed Grant, and curled up contentedly in his arms.

That broke the spell, Fred thought. Grant wrapped his arms around him. Joss stroked his head, dropping tears on him until he rubbed one off his ear. Bailey put his chin on Michael's leg, and Michael rubbed his head.

Something in Fred's chest tightened. He was jealous of them.

"He looks so much better," Grant marveled, tears in his eyes.

"All he needed was to get away from them," Fred said.

"But how did you do it?" Grant asked. "And why?"

Fred didn't know how much he wanted to tell them. If he told them everything, he might lose Joss forever.

"Horcroft and a doctor that he knew helped. Money smooths out everything," Fred said. "Horcroft knew what you were doing, what you suspected. He wanted you to find out. He said he encouraged you." He paused for a moment. "Why did I help?" He shook his head and smiled tightly. "Maybe just because he's a nice little boy." Like I was, Fred thought. Fred watched the frown on Grant's face.

"Nathan said he encouraged me?" Grant asked. Then light dawned in his face. "A few days ago, Nathan came into my lab," Grant said. "He told me to trust my intuition and to follow it, in spite of what anyone said. At the time, I thought it was just some kind of pep talk."

"Horcroft wanted you to find out," Fred repeated. "And he wanted you to have Michael."

"What are you saying?" Grant asked. "He's not mine. Why didn't you take him to Horcroft? He must be frantic." And then Grant whispered, "Horcroft is dead." Grant held Michael more tightly.

"Daniele and Horcroft are gone," Fred said. "And Anne, while she loves Michael, isn't as close to him as you are."

"But he isn't mine," Grant said. "This is kidnapping."

Fred watched Grant's face for a long moment. It's now or never, he decided. He said three words, emphasizing each one. "He is yours."

Grant frowned. "What do you mean?"

"Michael is your son," Fred said. Fred thought Grant looked stunned. Worse—as though Fred were insane.

"Stop thinking that I'm crazy," Fred said. "How could it never have crossed your mind? I noticed Sunday at the memorial service that he looked like you."

"But I never even touched Daniele..." Grant began.

Fred shook his head, a small smile twisting the corner of his mouth. "Oh, no, sir. You did more than touch her, I assure you. Just maybe not that you're aware of. Even today, Shakespeare's bait and switch can happen. There must have been some time—maybe she even drugged you, and you didn't know who you were with. After all, Dena and she were twins. It's not so hard to imagine."

Fred saw a change in Grant's face, and Fred said, "Tell me."

"One night I was staying at the Horcroft's, not long after Dena and I got engaged and moved in together," Grant said. "I had a lot of wine for dinner. When I went to bed, Dena came. It must have been Daniele."

Joss was holding Michael. She said softly, "That explains a lot of things. Daniele's envy of Dena. Why Daniele made a play for you after Dena died—and why she got angry when you rejected her."

"It couldn't be. The chances against it are too great," Grant said.

"The hell with chances," Fred said. "If it happens, it's possible. And it happened. Because I got a sample of your blood on Sunday. And I had it compared to Michael's blood when he was in the hospital. He's yours."

Grant shook his head, frowning. "How could you have gotten blood from me at the memorial service?"

Fred sighed. "When Michael fell. When you reached for him, you cut your hand on a tombstone. I could see it from ten feet away."

Grant was still shaking his head.

"It doesn't take much blood, Grant. And the technology is very advanced. Check it out for yourself," Fred smiled, "sometime in the future, of course. I *guarantee* you that he is your son."

Fred saw Grant's face start to light up and then fall.

"But what can I give him?" Grant asked. "I have nothing. And I'm on the run."

Joss had been bent over Michael, hugging him. Now Fred saw her lift her head, that beautiful head, he thought.

"*We're* on the run," she said quietly. "We can always give him love."

Grant was moving his mouth wordlessly. You look like an idiot, Fred thought. A lucky damned idiot. Spit it out, Grant.

"We?" Grant asked.

"He needs a mother and a father," Joss said. "He's gone through enough trauma as it is, without having more. What he needs is more important right now than what we're afraid of, or what we want."

Grant took her hand and squeezed it, and she reached over to brush the sleeping boy's hair back from his brow.

"It could be worse," Joss smiled. "I could have to work with you."

That was it. Fred couldn't take any more. "I think I'll leave this touching family scene to go to bed," he said. "I suggest you do the same. Soon. We'll be getting up very early."

Friday
October 31

100

Around 3:00 a.m., Grant felt someone shake him. He awakened to see Fred's grinning face above him.

"Rise and shine," Fred said. "Today is the first day of the rest of your life. Have a nice day."

Still feeling groggy, Grant said "Okay." Then he was hit by a thought that woke him up instantly: My son. I have a son. I have to help Michael get dressed.

He almost knocked Fred over in his eagerness to get to the other bedroom.

He found Joss there already, sitting on the bed with Michael, tugging on his socks. Grant felt the slightest bit cheated out of his first chance to dress his little boy. But it was more than compensated for by seeing Joss with Michael. He wondered if she meant it.

"Joss, did you mean it?"

He watched Joss glance at him out of the corner of her eye, but she kept her attention on Michael's socks.

"No 'good morning?' Is this what life with you is going to be like? No 'good morning,' and I have to figure out what you're talking about?"

Joss meant it, he thought. She meant it. And that made him feel like the luckiest man in the world.

Fred and Edith drove them in a van to a truck stop. They got out next to a large, shiny eighteen-wheeler, where they said goodbyes.

Grant watched as Edith gave Joss a large paper bag. "Breakfast and lunch," she said. "And I made cookies for Michael." Michael's face beamed.

Grant hugged her, still not able to believe that this sweet grandmother had wiped out two men to save their lives.

Grant stood outside the truck, reviewing the plan. Joss and Michael would ride in the cabin with Bailey. He would sit up front, his clothes, haircut and hat making him a near twin for the man who drove.

Fred came over to Grant.

"I hope this is goodbye," Fred said.

"I..." Grant began. He had so much to say.

"Don't say it," Fred said.

Grant had to say it. He had suspected, and last night he knew, that Fred had wanted Joss. He took a deep breath. "I know how you feel about Joss," he began.

Fred shook his head and waved his hand.

"Thank you," Grant said. "For both of them."

Fred smiled, and Grant was glad of that.

"You'll know where we are?" Grant asked.

"Yes, unless you get antsy and decide to strike out for yourselves. But that still doesn't mean we'll see each other again."

Grant offered him his hand. Fred took it.

"Look out for Joss," Fred said. "I mean it. And Michael. Bailey will be fine. He probably has more sense than you do, anyway."

Grant laughed, the first real laugh in a long time. It felt good. "Thank you—for everything."

Fred nodded. "Get going."

Grant had his foot on the step to get into the cab of the truck when Fred's voice stopped him.

"One more thing," he said.

Grant took his foot down and turned to Fred.

"Your Zip Disk," Fred began.

Grant nodded. "Maybe someday there will be something for me to salvage from three years of work."

Fred shook his head. "More than to salvage," he said.

Grant looked at him. Knowing Fred—no, not knowing Fred—he didn't know what to expect.

"When I took a sample of the black twin from your lab, I took a sample of the white twin, too," Fred said. "I had them both tested. You were right; the white twin has potential. A lot of it."

So the preliminary results animal testing had told him about on Wednesday had been right, Grant thought. The white twin wasn't a failure. It might still be the great drug he'd always believed it would be...Then, in spite of himself, Grant glanced up with fear at the cab of the truck. So much that was precious to him had been taken away. He was afraid that if he got back the white twin, he would lose something else. Like Joss or Michael.

"Don't worry so much," Fred said. "It's going to be all right."

Grant thought that Fred looked as if he had something else to say and was deciding whether or not to say it. Grant didn't want any more surprises. "Whatever it is," Grant said, "let me have it."

Fred nodded his head. "Last night I told you that Horcroft knew what you were doing. He also knew if you succeeded in finding out about Smith's little business, there would be fallout. He knew you would have to run. He wanted to help you."

Grant nodded. But he still didn't know where Fred was going.

"There's money for you in a Swiss bank account," Fred said. "And a research director at a small Swiss drug company is waiting to talk to you. If you decide to go there."

Grant took the card Fred offered. He was dumbstruck. He stared at the card. And then something hit him. Joss just might end up working with him.

Barreling along in the cab of the truck became hypnotic several hours into their journey. By the time first light broke, Grant was nodding. When his head hit the side window, he sat up and opened his eyes. They were on a six-lane highway somewhere in Connecticut, the leaves in various stages of turning colors and falling. The sun was out. The day was clear. And Grant was feeling good just to be alive.

Hank, the driver, offered Grant a donut.

Grant looked at it and remembered what Fred had told him about the sugar. Even if he couldn't stop them, Grant thought, he wasn't going to help them, either. "No thanks."

Then he heard the droning of engines, and his insides became ice. Engines meant pursuit. He searched the road to the left and right of the truck. It sounded like a swarm of bees.

Then he saw the source. Twenty or so men on motorcycles were riding, two abreast. They were in every kind of outfit. Some looked very clean-cut, with short hair and clothes that were as straight as denim jeans and jackets could be. Others looked like young or aging hippies, with long hair, ponytails, bandanas and patches covering their jackets. But all had something in common: The emblazoned "Blue Knights" on the backs of their jackets.

"Blue Knights—what are they, a motorcycle gang?" Grant asked Hank.

Hank laughed. "Of sorts. They're all law-enforcement people, active or retired. They formed an organization because they like to ride. They go on trips all over the country. Even send their cycles over to Europe on a plane and ride there."

Grant watched with curiosity as the parade of men rode past.

Near the end, one of the riders looked up at him. He had long hair in a ponytail, a mustache and small, dark glasses. But the wave and the smile were unmistakable.

Fred. Grant thought they might not have seen the last of him after all.

ACKNOWLEDGMENTS

For their help, encouragement and good wishes, I
am very grateful:
Andrew Spewock, Stephanie Wilson,
Anke Gray, and M.F.

And In Memoriam: Penelope Adelmann.
Friend, I will always remember you.

Correspondence to the author should be addressed to:

Sandra Feder
P.O. Box 1442
New York, NY 10156-0606